Just One FAVOR

STEPHANIE ROSE

To Avery,

Thank you for all your help w/ this book & for your amazing friendship

♡

Stephanie Rose

JUST ONE FAVOR

STEPHANIE ROSE

That's What She Said Publishing, Inc.

Just One Favor

Cover Design: Najla Qamber Designs

Cover Art: Lindee Robinson Photography

Editing: Jessica Snyder Edits

Proofreading: Inky Pen

ISBN: 978-1-945631-86-3 (ebook)

ISBN: 978-1-945631-85-6 (paperback)

020622

For Lisa—
always my sister,
always my hero

ONE
TYLER

I love my family.

I love my family.

I recited this in my head like a litany, my body going rigid with a fight-or-flight reaction that tensed every muscle in my body. It was as if I were getting ready to march into battle, not my grandmother's house for her birthday. I was exhausted and annoyed before I even shut off the engine of my truck.

At thirty-five years old, one would think I could show up at a family function without being so goddamn keyed up. It had just been too many instances of the same thing. The flippant questions about my business were often followed by a *tsk* when they'd inquire if I was seeing anyone. The nosy questions about my ex-fiancée's brand-new husband, who happened to be my former best friend. I tried to keep the answers short and deflect until I simply had to walk away when none of that worked.

It had been a very long year, and it was about to be a very long fucking day.

Sucking in a deep breath, I pulled the screen door open and walked inside. I caught my grandmother's gaze first as she sat on the couch, guilt poking at my gut when a slow smile spread across her face.

"Happy birthday." I smiled as I made my way over to her, planting a kiss on her cheek.

"There's that smile." She pinched my cheek between her bony fingers.

"What? I smile."

I had to laugh when she tilted her head and cocked a brow.

"Not as much as you should. Such a beautiful smile," she said, cupping my cheek.

"For you, I'll smile today. A little."

"Tyler, honey, did you remember the bread?"

"Hello to you too, Mom." I turned around and pulled her into a quick hug before handing her the paper bags under my arm.

She kissed my cheek quickly, then scurried to the kitchen.

I'd worked as a pastry chef in several places, both restaurants and bakeries, before I'd saved enough money for a shop of my own last year. Business was going so well that I was able to add more staff this week, but whenever I'd bring up how great the bakery was doing at a family function, no one had any interest.

"Tyler!" My cousin Alan slapped me on the back. "Still keeping baker's hours?" He snickered, taking a pull from his beer bottle.

"I guess I am." I felt my grandmother's gaze on me and forced a tight smile for her sake. Family or not, I could never stand the condescending prick, but I attempted to hold on to my cool. "When you own a business, the days are long."

"A bakery isn't like what I do. What's the most stress you have, making sure you have enough flour?"

"Now, Alan," my uncle Ken said, clutching my shoulder as

if he were offering me sympathy, "baking is a noble profession."

My cousins Ross and Alan were both stockbrokers, so no matter how well I was doing or what awesome plans I had for the future of my business, I'd never measure up to success in their eyes. What my uncle meant by "noble" was that I was probably able to support myself without any public assistance.

"Thanks," I replied, even though my uncle's defense of my livelihood was a lukewarm sentiment.

"Thanks for the discount on the cookies," Ross chimed in. "The family ate them up. And I agree with my father. Why take a stressful job if you don't have to? Make it how you can, right?"

I nodded without a word. Last week, he'd come into the bakery with his wife and kids, telling the cashier to give them the family discount. When the staff behind the counter asked me what the family discount was, I had to make something up because as much as I wanted to tell my cousin to fuck off I couldn't with customers around.

I checked my watch and held in a groan. I had at least two hours of this to suffer through.

But in the end, it was my fault. Why did I expect anything different? I always left more pissed off at myself than anyone else.

"Carla and Olivia are here!" Mom rushed up to me with a smile as if this was good news.

"What? Why?"

Her smile faded, and she exhaled an already frustrated sigh.

"Carla has known our family since we were five years old and wanted to see your grandmother. You and Olivia are adults, not kids anymore. Can't you two find a way to get along?"

My jaw went slack as her gaze traveled over my shoulder.

"Ah, the rest of the food arrived." She tapped my shoulder and pointed her finger. "Go in the kitchen and say hello. Be nice, please. For me."

"It doesn't matter if I'm nice or not. You know how she is."

Mom stilled, her chin dropping to her chest with a groan.

"I know that you should be able to greet her without starting an argument."

"*I* can, Mom. She can't."

"Are you sure about that?"

Why did I even come here today? I could have made up an emergency and saved myself from this needless aggravation.

"Carla is your best friend, but I'm your son. It would be nice if you were on my side, just once, when it comes to her evil daughter."

Her shoulders drooped as she exhaled a long sigh. She came toward me, and I looked away, meeting her gaze only when she cupped my cheek.

"I'm *always* on your side. Carla and I decided when you were kids to leave you both alone to resolve it yourselves as long as there was no bloodshed. Did we think it would take thirty years?" She shrugged. "No, but I think you're both old enough now to say a polite hello and deal with it when you have to be in the same space. Just try." When she kissed my cheek and rushed off, all I could do was groan in defeat.

I'd anticipated dealing with my family. The antichrist in heels lurking in my grandmother's kitchen... That I wasn't prepared for. My mother and her best friend were *so* sure their kids would be just as inseparable, Olivia and I had been thrown together all the damn time.

I'd avoided her presence for as long as I could remember, but she'd always found me. Everyone else saw the sweet little girl in pigtails who used to say *please* with an adorable lisp. Fake lisp—because she was calculating as fuck even then.

I straightened and made my way into the kitchen to get the pleasantries over with.

"Tyler!" Carla rushed toward me and wrapped her arms around me. "You look great." She pushed me back by the biceps. "Building your own business has bulked you up, kiddo."

A smile snuck across my lips. I liked Carla, treacherous daughter aside.

"How about a hello over here?" Olivia let out a throaty chuckle behind me.

They said the devil took on the most pleasing forms, but the dark prince sliding into Olivia Sanchez's voluptuous body was just showing off. The fact that she was more gorgeous every single time I saw her irritated the shit out of me. I hated that I'd always noticed, and I'd loathed that the more we'd argue, the harder my teenage dick would get.

My eyes did a quick sweep down her body before I could help myself. She was all soft and full curves, the sinful contours of her body torturing me still. Long dark waves of hair cascaded down her shoulders, swaying as her perfect lips curved into a grin. Those hips were both my ultimate fantasy and worst nightmare at the same time. All the old and confusing feelings clouded my already frazzled brain.

"Are you going to come give me a hello hug, or what? I don't have all day." A playful, almost genuine, smile crossed her lips as she looped her arms around my neck, pressing her body into mine and goading me like usual. I pulled away before she felt me stiffen below the belt.

"Mom is right. You look great. And now that I'm back, I need to make a stop in your bakery."

"Back?"

A grin pulled at her lips as I squinted at her.

"Your mom didn't tell you? I moved back last week. I'm remote so I can work anywhere, and I felt like I should be closer to home." Her smile faded for a quick second. "No excuse to be strangers anymore, right?"

She wanted to come into my bakery and, what, hang out? We were not doing this again. I was too old for this shit. I rubbed at my neck, wondering where the cooler we usually kept full of liquor was, and I almost cheered when I spotted it by the back door.

"No, I'm fine with being strangers," I whispered with a tight smile.

Instead of being insulted, she lit up. Crimson lips pursing, eyebrows lifting, ready for the same game we'd played over and over as kids.

A montage of our shared childhood rushed through my brain. This woman had known how to press every single one of my buttons from the time we were toddlers. And because she was my mother's best friend's daughter I couldn't tell her to fuck off.

I might've been a grumpy asshole, but I liked to believe that I was a decent man. Though, with Olivia, that was always more of a liability than an attribute.

"Excuse me." I cleared my throat. "Nice to see you, Carla. Olivia."

I stalked toward the cooler and fished out a bottle. I didn't even care what it was as I twisted the cap off and took a swig, welcoming the numbing tang down my throat.

"Tyler!" my cousin Donnie called out and grabbed my arm. "I was just about to ask Aunt Helen where you were. Good to see you, man."

I shook his hand, exhaling with a little relief at finding a friendly and nonjudgmental face and noticed the beautiful redhead on his arm.

"This must be Cassandra." The corners of my mouth lifted in a real smile, and I extended my hand. "Nice to finally meet you."

"Nice to meet you too." She took my hand, peering up at my cousin with hearts in her eyes. Donnie was a coder by day and gamer by night—and the nicest guy I'd ever known. I was thrilled he'd found a girl to moon over him like he deserved.

"I'd meant to introduce you sooner, but Tyler is busy with his bakery. Which brings me to my next question." He flashed her a grin and turned back to me. "You make wedding cakes, right?"

"I do. I don't take too many orders for them, but I've made quite a few in my time. Why do you ask..."

I trailed off when I noticed the fat diamond on Cassandra's finger as her hand drifted across Donnie's chest.

"Congratulations, man. I'd be honored to make you a cake." I pulled him into a quick hug. "If that's what you were asking me."

"It was. Also, I wanted to talk to you about something else." His beaming smile faded into a hard line.

"Sure," I said, nodding to the back door with my chin and not liking the ominous twist in my gut.

"A couple of things," Donnie started as he slid the screen door shut behind him. "The wedding is next month. My job is moving me to Seattle for a few months to set up their new office, and Cassie is coming with me. One of my hotel clients was willing to close their restaurant for a night to accommodate a small wedding. We didn't want anything big anyway. Friends, family, eat, drink—in and out."

"Sounds like a good plan." I nodded, bristling at the memories of planning my wedding to Amy. We had been at *full speed ahead* until everything had come to a halt. She'd said she was too busy to worry about planning at the moment and we had plenty of time. *Busy* was her code for fucking my best friend, and I'd never been able to fully forgive my stupid ass for misreading every single sign.

"A wedding cake is a special order, but a month is plenty of time if you give me a headcount the week before. Don't worry about that." I slapped his arm. "Happy to do it for the one cousin I actually like."

I flashed him a grin, but something about the way his mouth turned down made my stomach drop.

"Well, I'm not sure I can keep that title after what I'm about to tell you. Turns out Amy is a cousin of Cassandra's. Small world, huh?"

He coughed out a humorless laugh.

"You're kidding me."

He shook his head. "Second, but close enough to be invited to a wedding. I'd never seen her at any family functions so I had no idea they were related until I saw the guest list."

Fuck. I hadn't seen Amy in a year. Donnie's wedding would be the first time I'd have to face her since she'd pushed her engagement ring into my palm and left our apartment. I winced at the thought of seeing her again—the pity thrown in my direction as my heart and my pride were beaten to a pulp all damn night.

The timing of Donnie's cake was the least of my problems.

"Look, I totally get it if you want to skip the wedding and just have the cake delivered. I wish I could disinvite her, but apparently Cassandra's father and Amy's father are friendly."

I'd never met anyone in Amy's family other than her parents. In the year that we were together, there were no family functions to meet her extended family—or at least any that she'd asked me to attend with her. The more I looked back on our life together, the more I realized we didn't have one.

"No, it's fine. I was going to run into her somewhere eventually." This would be the worst possible place, but my shitty love life was no excuse to bail on Donnie's wedding. I'd be a man and say a cordial hello before I camped out at the open bar.

Donnie let out a long breath, his shoulders relaxing in relief.

"I've had a knot in my stomach since I found out. Thanks for being so cool about it."

"Of course," I said, hoping I sounded genuine. My issues shouldn't ruin the best day of his life, and I'd make sure they didn't.

"Hey, Donnie! I think the last time I saw you was at Helen and Sam's anniversary party. Nice to see you."

I found Olivia standing behind me, looking between us with enough scrutiny to make me wonder how much she'd heard.

Family parties mostly consisted of my two uncles and their families, sometimes a few neighbors, but we had more extended relatives in attendance today. They knew Carla and her family but didn't have any real insight into the strife Olivia inflicted upon my life.

Donnie, however, knew and had witnessed most of it. He looked between Olivia and me with a quick grimace.

"I think so. Nice to see you, Olivia. If you'll excuse me, I better go rescue Cassandra," he said, motioning behind him. "Uncle John has her ear and is probably asking her why she'd marry a computer nerd."

"A computer nerd who can afford to close a restaurant for a night." I slapped his chest.

"And you own a successful business." He shrugged. "Why do we pay them any mind? Fuck them, right?" He tipped his chin toward the smug bastards in the back of the yard as they laughed at something—most likely us.

A laugh slipped out despite the sour feeling in the pit of my stomach.

"Yeah, fuck them."

Donnie went back to his fiancée while I tried to forget about Olivia standing behind me.

"What do you think about trying to get along like our mothers always begged us to? Could we learn to be nice to each other—or civil at least?" Olivia asked before she had the audacity to sigh.

I turned, eyes wide.

"We could if we were two different people. Do you really want to be nice now? Sorry for not buying it."

"Let's talk, just for a few minutes." She waved a hand for me to follow her.

"Fine," I sighed and nodded toward a couple of empty chairs in the yard, an annoyed gust of air leaving my lungs as I waited for her to go, following her even if it was the last thing I'd wanted to do.

I'd expected a long and irritating afternoon, but there wasn't an open bar or cooler big enough for the mess I'd walked into today.

TWO
TYLER

"Okay, I'll admit it," she said, chuckling as she settled into one of the lawn chairs, "maybe I did have a little fun aggravating you growing up." She shrugged with a tiny smile. "Arguing was our thing, but maybe I pushed too far sometimes."

Her seemingly genuine remorse made me stumble for a moment. I recalled our elementary school days when the two minutes we'd play without fighting came to an abrupt halt when I wasn't doing things her way. She'd run to our mothers in tears, and I could only shrug.

As we got older, the fights only got worse.

"Hey, Bennett, isn't that your cousin or something?"

My friend Louis motioned to where Olivia stood next to the field exit. Poor Micah had no clue that he was being used in one of her little ploys to get to me. He was too busy drooling over her. She leaned in close to whisper something in his ear, throwing her head back and sneaking a glance back at me, a devious side smile playing on the side of her mouth.

Why the hell did she have to come to every single game? Her school wasn't even playing us today, but she and her entourage were almost always here.

The one good thing about her presence was that it made it easier to get a hit sometimes. I'd channel the rage she'd set off into a line drive and watch it sail.

"She's not my cousin, she's not something. Olivia is the daughter of a family friend, who I can't seem to get away from."

"You want to get away from her?" He snickered before an odd recognition flashed in his eyes. "Oh, I get it. You hooked up with her, and she comes here to piss you off."

"No, she likes to piss me off for sport," I spat out. "She's good like that. Come on, let's go put Micah out of his misery."

"He doesn't look miserable to me."

I didn't look back as I strode to the exit. She was gorgeous, but after sparring with her for my entire life, I knew that behind those doe eyes and sinful lips beat a black heart. Her mission was to antagonize me as much as possible, and she'd had a perfect score so far.

"Tyler," Olivia said, folding her arms over her chest, knowing full well it pushed the swells of her breasts over the neckline of her tank top. "I was just telling Micah how long we've known each other." She cut me a look and turned to Micah and saying in a loud whisper, "He doesn't like me very much."

"And she knows why. Come on, guys. Early practice tomorrow." I leveled them with a glare, hoping they'd follow.

"Do you ever smile? You're like an eighteen-year-old miserable old man," she said.

I spun around. "Do you have to be at every game? Can't you and your minions find somewhere else to go?"

"Free country. Last time I checked it was anyway." She inched closer to me until we were chest to chest. Ready for battle, just like always.

My dick was ready for something else. It didn't care how

heinous she was. It just wanted inside her. My mouth and my hands had the same traitorous impulses. The girl made me crazy on so many levels I couldn't see straight.

"Leave me alone, Olivia," I growled, my eyes so glued to hers I barely blinked. "Why are you always everywhere? I can't even have a fucking break without you lurking around."

"Why do you care? If you hate me so much, why do you care what I do?" She sighed, her dark eyes narrowed to slits at me. "I don't have time for this tonight. I'll wait for my minions outside."

Her boots ground against the dirt as she stormed away. Everyone, including me, tracked each sway of her hips until she was out of sight.

"Why do you hate her so much?" Micah asked. "She seemed nice. If I take her out, is there going to be an issue?"

"Nope. If you want to date the antichrist in heels," I said as I walked ahead to the parking lot, "don't let me stop you."

She was a constant thorn in my side whenever she was in my proximity, but now she wanted to be friends?

I guessed, looking back, there were times that I gave as good as I got. I was too exhausted at the moment to attempt to keep score. If she wanted to call a truce, genuine or not, my inclination was to just take it.

I nodded, scrubbing a hand down my face. I couldn't not go to Donnie's wedding, and even if I decided to be an immature dick and sit it out, I was responsible for his wedding cake. I needed to nut up and figure out how to get through the day.

"What Amy did to you sucked," Olivia said. "And to have to go to your cousin's wedding and see her is awful."

"I figured you heard enough." I groaned, rubbing the back of my neck. "And my mother told your mother about what happened with Amy. Not much is sacred, I suppose."

She leaned forward in the chair. "Did you really think I

would make fun of you for any of that? I'm not that bad, Tyler. Give me some credit."

I glanced at her, quirking a brow.

"Family functions aren't exactly fun for me to begin with," I said. "Not like your family."

She let out a throaty laugh that, even in the throes of my pity party of one, ran right through me. Nice, evil—Olivia was ridiculously attractive in all forms. As a boy and as a man, I never knew how to respond to it.

"My family is loud and insane."

"But nice. They treat you like the princess with the keys to the kingdom, not the loser with a job they look down upon."

"They don't think you're a loser. They're all jealous. You own your own business and make your own rules." She motioned to the cluster of cousins next to the grill. "They're just suits. Boring. Go to Donnie's wedding with your head held high, and don't give them a second thought."

"Easier said than done." I scoffed, but not because of my cousins. Seeing the woman I'd once thought of as the love of my life with the real love of her life was what took the wind out of my sails today.

"Take a hot date, throw them all for a loop." Her lips curved in a devious smile.

Dating or even meeting women hadn't been a priority for me for a long time—my work schedule didn't exactly allow hot nights out, at least not right now. I had to be up at three, at the shop by five, and in bed before most middle schoolers.

"I don't know of anyone I hate enough to subject to that shit show." I leaned my elbow against my knee, rubbing at my eyes.

"Then take me with you."

My jaw dropped, as I was sure I'd heard wrong.

"Oh my God, would it be *that* terrible to take me to a wedding with you?"

"Well, judging how this is the longest we've gone without an argument, a whole wedding is reaching a little, don't you think?"

She scowled when a laugh escaped me.

"I'm the perfect solution. You don't have to work on impressing me or shielding me from any asshole cousins because I've met them already. Think of the shock." Her lush mouth curved into a devious grin. "My whole purpose for being there is to hang all over you and look good doing it. Take it as a peace offering for more amiable times ahead. Come on, Tyler." She jabbed my arm. "Loosen up. For once. Could be fun."

Fun. Of all the things I expected from Donnie's wedding, fun—no matter who I was with—was not one of them.

"Oh, there you are."

I turned at Carla's voice. She looked between us with that hopeful gaze one of our mothers would have when they noticed a lull in our constant battles. I honestly hoped Olivia meant it when she said she wanted to get along, even if life experience told me that she was full of shit. But again, I didn't have the energy for Olivia today, or the crazy offer she'd just made me, or to ponder why for a split second I almost said yes.

"I'm sorry I haven't been to the bakery. Your mom has been telling me all the wonderful things you've been doing, and I love the name!"

"Thank you," I said, surprised when my lips curved up. "People seem to like it"—I shrugged—"especially when baseball season starts."

In high school and part of college, I was more focused on baseball than baking. A blown-out knee from sliding into second in my sophomore year of college put a damper on any kind of professional future. I wasn't devastated but I still missed playing, and since the old bakery space I'd leased out wasn't too far from the local minor-league field, I decided on renaming the bakery *Hey, Batter*. Everyone was surprised that I picked such a cheeky name, but my homage to my old life got us into local newspapers and the attention of some food bloggers.

"I'll be in there soon for a box of cookies. Your mom raves over the chocolate chip—"

"Because that's just what a diabetic needs, Mom." Olivia's back went rigid on the chair. "A box of cookies."

Carla's shoulders fell with a tiny sigh. I looked between them, surprised to see the sudden tension radiating from Olivia toward her mother.

"I take insulin, so I can eat sugar. All things in moderation are fine." Carla's smile was tight as her eyes bore into her daughter's.

"We have some sugar-free stuff. Not much, but one of my assistant bakers is always trying out sugar-free and gluten-free options. Tell me when you're coming, and I'll make sure I have enough for a box."

"Thank you, Tyler. My daughter likes to worry." She heaved out an audible sigh. "Just like her father."

After Carla went back inside the house, I caught a huff from Olivia. She glared into the distance, her chest rising and falling slowly.

Carla's husband had passed away two years ago. Both of Olivia's parents pulled out all the stops for their only child: huge birthday parties, a new car when the rest of us were begging to use our parents' used ones. She was spoiled often for most of her life. After his sudden death, my mother had told me that Carla and Olivia were devastated and still weren't the same. I hadn't seen her since the funeral, but that annoying fight Olivia had within her, while very much there, seemed muted now. She still owned every room but didn't shout it like she had before.

Maybe that had something to do with the truce she'd offered?

I wanted to ask Olivia what was wrong, but it was none of my business. The same as she didn't have to get involved in my pointless and futile quest to gain a tiny bit of validation from my family.

Yet the sad gloss to her eyes wouldn't let me drop it. Swallowing another groan, I leaned forward, shifting toward where Olivia now sat with her arms crossed.

"Is… anything wrong?"

"Nope," she answered quickly. "I'm just, well, I'm glad I'm home again. Let's leave it at that."

"Yeah, you said you're remote. What do you do?"

"Digital advertising. All I need is Wi-Fi."

"Must be nice having a job you don't need to leave the house for."

The side of her mouth quirked up, drawing my attention to her lips—again.

"I leave the house. Just not in a nine-to-five kinda way." She winked. "So are you going to let me do this favor for you, or what?"

"Favor?" I snickered. "Just because I haven't dated in a while doesn't mean I need a pity date."

"That's not what I meant." Olivia swung her long, toned legs around and sat on the edge of the chair. "It's not a date. It's just one favor. As I said, no first-date awkward moments, no tension meeting family—I'm just a pretty ornament for the night, nothing more. I'll even help carry the cake in."

"Wow." I coughed out a laugh. "You heard it all, huh?"

"Yes or no? Come on." She cocked her head to the side. "I know fun isn't your usual thing, but think about it."

"Tyler!" My father bellowed from the garage, a metal table folded under his arm. "We need an extra table for the food. Come help me set this up."

My dad and I were the grumpy ones, or so we were told, but my father was a retired fire captain who preferred to be left alone at these things. He never minded appearing unapproachable and excelled at it. I wished he'd share his secret with me on how he pulled that off.

I nodded and jogged toward where Dad stood.

"Grandma still has this old thing? Didn't she used to play cards on it or something?" I helped him open the table and push the legs out.

"Don't knock it because it's old. Nothing is made this well anymore." He nodded with his chin toward the end of the yard. "I guess I saved you from Olivia." He glanced in her direction. "You could never handle that spitfire."

"I can handle her," I grumbled as we lifted the table to place it next to the rest of the food, not turning to where I still felt her eyes on me.

Her offer was more than I could handle though. That's why I had to say no. I'd take the humiliation on the chin and move on, just like I did the last time I saw Amy. It would be easier if only I had something—or someone—to move on to.

THREE
OLIVIA

"I still can't believe you moved back," my best friend, Morgan, said, her chuckle reverberating in my ear. "You had the sweetest apartment in the best location, all to come back to this sleepy town on Long Island and move back in with your mother."

"First of all, Morg," I started while trying to pay attention to the last few numbers in my expense sheet before I fired it off to my accountant, "like I've said, I am living in the lower-level apartment in her house, not technically living with her. I have my own side entrance, and this apartment has a laundry room, patio, and can fit two of my East Village apartments inside."

Once I saved the file and emailed it away, I fell back in my chair and prepped for what seemed like the hundredth iteration of the same exact conversation. Was my old place in a great neighborhood with the best restaurants? Sure. But even before my father passed away, I'd started to outgrow it. I wished it hadn't taken a family tragedy to make me realize I wasn't where I belonged.

"I know," she grumbled. "I'm just upset we can't have any

more nights in the city. We still could, but now we have to take the LIRR home or get a hotel, neither of which sound fun."

I laughed at her exaggerated tsk.

"I *am* glad you're back, although I don't know how you're managing a living out here."

"It's not that bad." I shut my laptop and pushed off my seat, my stiff back and legs telling me in a loud voice I'd been working too long without a break. "I still have my freelance job, and as for the other one, it's actually more convenient. I'm driving to restaurants and not chancing the train or a late-night cab. I can't indulge in too many cocktails, but I can sip enough to form an opinion. There are lots of hidden gems to be found out here."

I tried to sound chipper about it, but it had been a little too easy to pick up and move. I had nothing—and no one—to regret leaving behind.

"But I'm sure it put a damper on your social life. Unless... you met someone already..."

"And how would I do that? When I'm not working, I'm unpacking and assembling. That can wait."

"Men always seem to find you though."

"They do." I sighed. Admitting how exhausting it was, even to my best friend, would make me sound full of myself. But it had been a long time since anyone had garnered my interest for more than a drink or two. Men were always a fun pastime, but fun didn't interest me much these days. When I was working, I'd politely but firmly stop anyone's attempt at flirting. That was the old, selfish me. And as much as my new therapist reiterated how I needed to allow myself some good times, I was still too pissed at myself for too many things to comply.

"Liv? Honey, do you have a second?"

I bit back a smile at my mother's tentative tapping on my door.

"Hold on, Morgan." I pressed my phone to my chest. "Sure, come in."

She creaked open my apartment door—my apartment on the lower floor of *her* house. She was so thrilled when I asked to rent the now vacant lower-level apartment and swore she'd never invade my privacy. And she didn't, she just enjoyed visiting—a lot. But that was why I was here.

"I better go," I whispered into the phone. "I'll text you later."

"Yes, maybe I'll go on one of your foodie excursions with you someday. How's she doing?"

I hated the concerned dip of my best friend's tone.

"Good. So far." I smiled at Mom, masking my own concern the best I could, as I'd done since I'd moved back.

"We're all glad you're back. Go talk to your mom, we can talk about your lack of *D* and what to do about it later. Love you."

"Love you back. And I look forward to it." I exhaled a long breath and ended the call.

"Sorry to interrupt." Mom's nose crinkled.

"You didn't. What's up?"

"If you have no appointments today, would you like to take a walk into town with me? Do a little shopping? Only if you can."

"I don't have anything scheduled until later on in Seaford. I'm free as a bird to take a walk with you."

My heart cracked a little when she beamed at me. "I'll grab my purse, and we can go in a few minutes. Unless you're in the middle of something."

"Nope," I said, heading over to my still-cluttered kitchen table to stuff my phone into my purse.

My mother was beautiful. Tall with deep chestnut hair that only had a few sparkles of gray and light hazel eyes. We resembled each other except my skin was a richer olive tone and my hair was thick and curly, courtesy of my Puerto Rican father. The wide curve of my hips and love of all things cheese and wine came both from my dad and my mother's Italian side.

After I locked my side door, I followed Mom upstairs.

"Are your pills up to date?" I asked, glancing at the counter where her pill box for the week usually was.

"Yes, *boss.* Filled in for the week with another week's worth up in the cabinet." She squeezed my shoulder. "You don't need to worry about me."

A pang nudged at my stomach as my eyes lifted over the dry-erase board. Mom's latest dosage of insulin was listed in a red box, originally drawn by my father, along with the name and dosage of her blood pressure medicine in his handwriting. She'd never erased it, claiming it served as a good reminder even if it was a little painful to see. When I was a teenager, she was diagnosed with type 1 diabetes. My father immersed himself in everything he could find about the condition and usually set up her daily medication. It was his love language to look after her—and us—in little ways like that.

Now, Mom was on her own. Or was until I moved back. Other than being a little sad, nothing about her seemed overly concerning, but I had the need to be close to her anyway. I told myself it was to watch over her, but living in my parents' house brought me the comfort I'd needed, even when one was missing,

Helping Mom navigate her new world without her larger-than-life husband soothed some of my grief, but nothing would ever help the guilt.

"Anything you have in mind?" I asked after I followed her out the front door.

"Cookies," she replied with a sly grin. "Helen told me that Tyler had a nice assortment of sugar-free cookies this week—before you give me crap about eating sweets." She raised a brow at me as we strolled down the block. "It's a bit of a walk to his bakery, but it's a nice day." She bunched her shoulders in an exaggerated shrug, and I couldn't help the roll of my eyes. "And you haven't seen it yet. I know you're curious."

She lifted a brow before we continued on.

"I did say I wanted to see it. I'm glad he's doing well," I told her honestly while I kept my gaze straight ahead.

When I saw Tyler a couple of weeks ago, I welcomed the familiar rush that ran through me. Whenever I stepped into a room, his proverbial hackles would shoot right up, and I admittedly took an inappropriate amount of joy in pushing him. He'd cut me a scowl, those dark-and-stormy eyes searing into me, and a shiver would roll up my spine.

When I finally put in some effort to get along at his grandmother's party, he regarded me as if I was about to stab him in the throat.

Looking at it from the outside, especially through Tyler's perspective, I was a spoiled only child with an overbearing personality and a constant need for attention. I couldn't argue with some of that, but the truth was that I needed *Tyler's* attention, regardless of how I'd get it.

I wanted to be the only thing he noticed. If he was playing with a toy when we were little, I was jealous of the toy. A *toy*. I'd knock it out of his hands, and it was game on. Inevitable fights gave way to constant bickering.

I didn't yearn for confrontation and seek out fights with others like I did with Tyler. So if he rejected my peace offering, I had no one to blame but myself.

I didn't always have to be in the spotlight, but for some reason I had a lifelong obsession with being in *his* spotlight.

And I was, but for all the wrong reasons.

"Here it is," Mom chirped as she pointed to the large, blue awning. *Hey, Batter* was printed in large, white letters next to a baseball diamond with cupcakes for the bases. Despite all the fights I'd had with Tyler at his games, the memory of him in his uniform was a favorite. We'd gone to different schools since we didn't live in the same district, but I always made an excuse to go to his games despite—but really because of—him making it clear how much he didn't want me there.

His strong legs and tight ass filled out those fitted white pants to perfection. I loved watching him run the bases almost as much as when he swung at home plate, his broad torso twisting as he swung, a crack echoing when he made contact.

He was poetry in motion, and my eyes would be glued to him every at bat. Morgan caught me once or twice but never uttered a peep about it.

I followed Mom inside, a couple of girls at the counter looking in our direction when the door chimed. The shop wasn't huge, but every inch of space was filled with something. Cookies lined the front display, cakes and loaves of bread were stacked on shelves against the wall. We headed to the end of the short midday line as I drooled over everything.

"This place is great. He's done so well," Mom told me in a loud whisper.

My chest filled with an odd sense of pride as I scanned the space. I'd been to the old bakery that occupied this building years ago, but Tyler's hard work to make the place his own was evident everywhere.

"What do you want to get?" Mom asked, startling me for a moment. "I'll get a few sugar-free cookies if you look the other way with those chocolate-covered ones."

I laughed at her quirked brow.

"I'll share whatever you get. Sugar and I have a complicated relationship." I shrugged, a nervous laugh escaping me.

Tyler and I had a complicated relationship too, but not from his end. He simply couldn't stand me while I could never get over my fixation on him.

You wouldn't think you could sabotage your adult love life while you still had baby teeth, but as my dad used to say, I was always in a class by myself.

He'd kept me in line yet also praised me all the same. But it was hard to stay my ball-busting self after I'd lost my biggest fan.

"I'm really sorry," a squeaky female voice said behind me.

I turned and spotted Tyler making his way out of the back with his cousin Donnie and his fiancée. Tyler kept nodding while the poor girl's face crumpled as if she was on the verge of tears.

"You're making us this amazing cake, and we're making you see my horrible cousin. Please know I would absolutely disinvite her if I could."

Tyler wore a blue T-shirt the same shade as the outside awning, the sleeves freckled with flour and straining against his biceps. I clenched my eyes shut and forced my gaze straight ahead.

"Amy was at my parents' house over the weekend and drilling me about what food we were serving at the wedding. Because one person is pregnant, I have to change my whole damn menu."

Before I could help it, my head whipped back around to Tyler. He was stoic for a long minute, his eyes fluttering a moment as if he was absorbing the fumes from the bomb that Tyler's fiancée had just dropped at his feet.

How miserable would that be? He had to attend a family wedding knowing he'd see his pregnant ex-fiancée, now married to his former best friend. Mom had filled me in when it happened, and I'd overheard most of his conversation with Donnie at his grandmother's house.

I didn't mean to be rude and eavesdrop, but my eyes and ears always seemed to track Tyler wherever he was. Even though I was aware, lifelong habits were tough to break.

Donnie winced behind her as Tyler replied with a slow side-to-side shake of his head.

"It's fine. It's not about her, it's about you guys. Please don't give it another thought." He reached out to squeeze her arm, his rasp giving away the defeat in his voice.

I was tempted to march over and reiterate my offer, but he didn't want to go on a date with me no matter what the circumstances were. I'd only humiliate myself by asking again, and while I was still working on a truce, I wasn't going to be pathetic about it. Even if the inclination was so strong I had to sink my teeth into my bottom lip to halt the words from falling out of my mouth once he noticed us.

Mom was so into the cookie display that she hadn't heard a word. After Donnie and his fiancée said their goodbyes and left, my eyes were still glued on Tyler when he noticed me. My stomach sank when his eyes closed, as if the blow he'd just gotten hit that much harder because I was there to witness it.

"Tyler, there you are!" Mom rushed off the line to greet Tyler with a hug. "This place looks amazing. I can't decide what to get—it all looks so good!"

"Thanks, Carla," he whispered, his deep timbre still weak. "Come with me." He led Mom around the line and up to the counter. "Give this lady a pound of whatever cookies she'd like, no charge."

Mom's eyes widened in protest before he held up a hand. "Pick whatever you want. I promise we're working on different sugar-free kinds. There's a demand I didn't anticipate." He turned to me, his brows pinched.

I was surprised when he left Mom and strutted up to me. "Olivia, can I talk to you for a minute?" He nodded to the swinging door behind the counter.

"Talk... oh, sure," I stammered, holding back a grimace at how flustered I was. Tyler never initiated conversation. If he spoke to me, it was because of our mothers and the forced proximity we were always trapped into.

I straightened, trying to regain a little composure as I followed him.

"Look," he began and let out a long, frustrated sigh. "You don't need to pretend that you didn't hear all of that. And I can't believe I'm asking this, but does your offer to come with me to Donnie's wedding still stand?"

My head jerked back, Tyler's question rendering me speechless for a moment.

"It does. But, if I don't have to pretend I didn't overhear, is this because Amy is pregnant?"

"Yes—well, yes and no." He scrubbed his hand down his face. "I don't hate my life. I don't even hate her. We both moved on, but I think being there with all that pity thrown my way, I'm afraid I won't handle it very well and ruin my cousin's night. I need a buffer, and I can't think of a better distraction than you."

My cheeks heated as his lips curled into a smirk. There wasn't a hint of malice or exasperation in his gaze. Familiarity and gratitude shone back at me instead. My silly heart swelled as I realized how long I'd been waiting for this moment.

If I hadn't been such a brat toward Tyler since we were toddlers, maybe this moment wouldn't have taken thirty years to come to fruition, but I'd dwell on that later. Right now, I had a role to play and a plan to make. Every cell in my body hummed in anticipation.

"Do you have plans tonight? You close mid-afternoon, right?"

He squinted at me, the typical suspicion creasing his forehead.

"We close at three. I leave by four usually."

"Great—give me your number. I have a work thing in Seaford tonight. Why don't you meet me?"

"Um…" He studied me, his brows pulling together. "You're my date to my cousin's wedding. I'm not looking for a relationship or anything."

"Right." I held in a groan. This was like pulling teeth but nothing I shouldn't have expected. "But maybe we should get used to being nice to each other before we pretend to be a couple."

I bit back a laugh when his eyes widened at the same time his jaw dropped.

"Again, I'm taking you as a *date for the night*. A lot of the people there who know us know our history of not getting along—why pretend we're something they'll know we're not?"

"A lot, but not all. Imagine the looks and the whispers. All the years of being at each other's throats, and now we're together. You'd stun everyone." I stepped closer. "How fucking fun would that be?" I asked in a loud whisper.

His full lips pursed, and I had to will my eyes away from his mouth. I always wondered if Tyler was a gentle kisser or an angry one. With me, I'd hazard angry, but my heart rate kicked up at the possibility of finally testing that fact.

"Either way, regarding me all night as if you expect me to poison your dinner won't be a good look." I held out my phone, raising a brow until he took it.

We were practically extended family, so we should have

had each other's cell phone numbers years ago, just in case of emergency with our mothers. That spoke to our history more than anything else, but the tides were turning—I hoped. I was just learning to acknowledge my low-key obsession with the guy, but I sincerely wanted to be friends, not enemies. Was it too late? I guessed we'd see.

His phone chirped in his jeans pocket as he handed mine back.

"I'm not a work-party kind of guy." He stuffed his hands into his pockets, creating another bulge in his biceps. This proposition would never work if I kept eye-fucking my pretend date before it was time. "I can meet you before Saturday somewhere else if you think it's necessary."

"No party, just me. I'll text you the address and explain when you get there. I promise, I'm the only one you'll be making uncomfortable conversation with." I winked and turned to join my mother in the front, giving my hips an extra sway, knowing that Tyler was watching me the entire time.

The rush when Tyler looked at me, however he looked at me, was something that never wavered, no matter how unhealthy I knew it was.

"What was that about?" Mom asked with a deep crease in her brow.

"Donnie is marrying Amy's cousin, so since he doesn't want to go solo, we're going to pretend we're together for a night. I could do him this one favor after being a jerk to him since we were kids, right?" I grabbed the bag and headed for the door, keeping my resolve even as my perfect plan sounded completely ridiculous when I tried to explain it. I held the door open for my mother, but when I looked back, she hadn't followed. Her feet were rooted to the floor as her wide eyes studied me.

"Come on, those cookies won't eat themselves." I tilted my

chin toward the exit, praying she'd stop gaping at me and leave Tyler's bakery.

She nodded slowly and finally padded out the door.

"I thought you'd be happy at us not being at each other's throats for once." I laughed until I saw the crease in her forehead. "It's not a big deal—"

"Not a big deal?" She grabbed my arm to pull me back. "I was happy to see you amicable at Lucy's party, but it's a big leap to be his date at a family wedding."

Her words made all the confidence I'd had with Tyler only moments ago dissipate into the ether.

"You were too into the cookies to overhear that Amy is pregnant. Her husband is Tyler's old best friend, who she left Tyler for. He shouldn't be there alone, and we didn't get along because of *me.* I can admit that. If I could do him just one favor, maybe it won't make up for it all, but it's a start."

I swiveled around, hoping Mom's jaw would close before we made it home. Nothing about this offer was normal—most of all the fact that he actually took me up on it.

I couldn't admit that it was a big fucking deal and wouldn't allow myself to consider all the reasons why.

FOUR
OLIVIA

I didn't say much on the walk home. My mother's words poked at me the entire way back to the house, but why? I knew it was a stretch. Dinner tonight was probably going to consist of me working for every word I pulled out of Tyler, so how were we going to be fake lovers for a night? I'd thought of it as a game, but hearing how impossible it would be didn't entice me to rise to the challenge like normal. Defeat and confusing disappointment weighed on me as I trudged up our outside steps and unlocked the inside door of my apartment.

I eyed my closet and changed my solo reservations to two, which felt pointless as I wasn't sure if Tyler would even show up. What the hell was I doing? Mom was right—we never could occupy the same space without arguing. There were times I'd actually started out trying to be nice, and then I'd spot his disdain for my presence and couldn't help egging it on.

Tyler and I were in our mid-thirties, yet when we saw each other, we turned into petulant kids. I did want to make his cousin's wedding better for him, but the more I'd thought about it—or obsessed since we left the bakery—the more I thought I should just text Tyler and call the whole damn thing off.

I plopped onto my bed, falling back and covering my face with my hands. I was Olivia fucking Sanchez. I never backed down from anything. When I wanted to start my own freelance business because my company wouldn't promote me like I deserved, I found a way. I was never intimidated by new clients or being the only woman in a room full of men at a business meeting at my old job.

Maybe that was because, during all of that, I knew I wouldn't lose. Or if I did, I didn't care. There were always more clients, more opportunities. Why waste my time if one didn't work out?

This was a no-win situation, and the worst part about it: now it did bother me to lose. But what other outcome could there be?

"Hey," Mom called before cracking open my door. "You left me to eat all these cookies by myself," she teased, peering at me from the doorway. "Come sit with me." She motioned toward my small dining room table. The space could fit a much bigger one, but it just fit in my old apartment. I'd considered getting a bigger table, but I never had more than three people over at a time.

I slid into a chair across from her as she pulled the string off the box, the sight of Tyler's bakery logo souring my already terrible mood. Mom gingerly shook the box until she plucked out the chocolate chip cookie I knew she was searching for.

"Did I ever tell you how your father and I got together?"

I rolled my eyes, grabbing a half-chocolate-covered cookie despite myself.

"Of course. He was Uncle Frankie's friend. Classic *older brother's best friend* syndrome."

"No," Mom scoffed. "That's how I *knew* your father, not how we got together. That happened much, much later."

I sat back, squinting at her. "Okay, then I guess you didn't. How did you get together?"

She grabbed a napkin and placed the cookie down after swallowing a bite.

"Javier and Frankie were inseparable from the time they met. He was over at the house all the damn time." I laughed at her heavy, annoyed sigh. "All my friends were like, 'Javier Sanchez was at your house—you're *sooo* lucky.'" She pressed a hand to her chest. "'He's gorgeous.'" She rolled her eyes, breaking off another tiny piece of cookie. "But they didn't know that he was a gorgeous *asshole*."

"What?" I shrieked. My father was the best person I ever knew. When I got into trouble, which when I was little was often, he was stern yet loving. I couldn't see my dad ever being an asshole even when he was young. "I can't believe that."

"Believe it. I dreaded when I'd hear him in the backyard with your uncle when I came home. He always had something to say about my friends, the guy I liked, the clubs I was in at school, *everything*. It was like his day wasn't complete unless I stalked away from him with steam billowing out of my ears like those cartoons."

"Uncle Frankie let him do that?"

I cracked up at her pursed lips.

"Your uncle was a different kind of asshole, and that's a different conversation."

"Okay," I said, another laugh escaping and surprising me. Talking about Dad was still painful, but this was one of the only recent times I was able to enjoy a memory of him. "So how did he go from *asshole* to *the love of your life*?"

Her smile faded a minute before she sucked in a breath and continued.

"Frankie worked late and your grandparents were out, so when Javier showed up at our house, I had to let him in as I was getting ready for a date. But this time, he didn't try to agitate me, just grumbled. I asked him what his damn problem was, and he said he hated seeing me go out with guys who didn't deserve me. I asked him who I should date instead, and he said him." Mom's eyes were glossy as she chuckled to herself. "His hair was longer then, so he kept running his hands through his curls, all flustered and strung out."

"Is that when you fell in love?" I asked, my own eyes getting wet.

"No, I told him he had some nerve being a jerk all this time and now all of a sudden saying he wanted to be with me. I stormed out the door, met my date, and was miserable as hell the whole time. I came home early, and your father was still waiting for me on our stoop with an entirely different attitude. He confessed that he liked me too much and thought if I hated him, then he wouldn't be so tempted to love me."

I swallowed the lump growing in the back of my throat. The memory of how much my father adored her and what he said all those years ago pierced my gut with unexpected resonance.

"Then he started to show me who he really was. I wasn't the easiest sell. After years of him being a jerk to me, one night of sweet words didn't cut it, but when I got to know him, the *real* him, he was the best." Her voice cracked as she took the last bite of the cookie, not bothering to wipe the tear streaking down her cheek.

"Some people embrace the love they feel for someone else, some get spooked and fight it. And then just keep fighting until they make everyone involved miserable."

"Mom," I breathed out, running a hand down my face,

"that's a sweet story, but I don't know why you're telling me this."

"I think you're smart enough to know why." She leaned in and squeezed my arm. "I've watched the two of you fight since you learned how to talk, and as much as we told you to just leave Tyler alone, you never could. Poor guy."

I had to laugh at that. I never gave Tyler a moment's peace when we were kids and did nothing but go out of my way to annoy him as we got older.

"Sometimes, as backward as it sounds, it's easier to have someone dislike you than reject you. You'd fight and storm away, but you never veered very far out of his orbit." She bit back a laugh. "Your father and I used to crack up at the dumb excuses you'd make for going to his baseball games."

I spied her shoulders shaking in my periphery but wouldn't look up.

"My friends went to baseball games—I just tagged along." That sounded defensive and pathetic to my own ears.

Mom exhaled a long breath.

"*Morgan* went because you dragged her. And you never refused an invitation to attend a party or dinner Helen invited you to. If you couldn't stand her son, you certainly never attempted to avoid him."

"No, he always avoided *me*." I dragged my fingers through my tangled-up curls. "Which is totally my fault." I rubbed at my temples. "He thinks I'm a spoiled brat, and I don't blame him—"

"Then show him who you are. Without the games, without the fighting." She cupped my chin. "Take off the mask, Olivia. You may find it easier to breathe."

FIVE
TYLER

I pulled into the restaurant parking lot, lingering in my truck before shutting off the engine. As Olivia had noted, the GPS had the exact location slightly off, and I had to drive around a few times to figure out where the hell the entrance was. I loved hole-in-the-wall restaurants that took effort to find. It usually meant the food was worth it, but I couldn't shake the urge to bolt.

This was a bad idea. After she witnessed me at my lowest point, I took Olivia up on her ridiculous offer before I realized it and had nothing but regret over it all damn day. But I wouldn't stand her up, no matter how fucked up my head was today.

I was never the most talkative at work, but I was so mute for the rest of the day that the staff all watched me with concern. Amy wasn't the issue. I let go not long after she did, but she was full steam ahead in her new life while I remained stagnant. Sure, my business was doing okay, but as much as I'd always been a loner, the actual loneliness hit me hard sometimes. There was no one to share the small successes with other than a couple of close friends or my parents. I'd get a *That's great, Tyler.* It was a genuine but hollow sentiment.

Before I climbed out of the cab, I pulled out my phone to text Olivia that I was here. It felt so odd to have her number after knowing her for most of my life, but that was never our dynamic. Spite was how we rolled, so this new venture into being a fake couple was going to be quite the uphill fucking battle.

I noticed a text from Eli—one of my assistant bakers who'd become a good, if ball-breaking, friend—as I unlocked the screen. I'd told him about Amy after Donnie and Cassandra left the bakery and now wished I hadn't. Not that I didn't trust him, but I hated that I was so upset in the moment that I had to tell someone—right after I'd agreed to a pretend date with the bane of my childhood existence.

Eli: *I think you need a spite fuck. A few of them actually. Get you right back on your feet.*

Tyler: *Please don't suggest one of those stupid apps again.*

Eli: *You need to get over yourself with that. That's how busy people find other busy people that are on the same page as they are. And there are places to find the spite fuck you need. Where are you? I figured we could meet for a drink.*

Tyler: *I'm meeting someone for dinner. Maybe tomorrow night.*

Eli: *Hey, that's great. Good for you. I look forward to hearing you're back on track in the morning.*

I was about to say *not so great* because the someone was Olivia. But I didn't want to explain what I was doing since I had no clue myself.

The place was small inside, very few tables facing a large wall-size window overlooking the water. I spotted Olivia right away, sitting at the bar with a snug black top over jeans that hugged every curve to perfection. She smiled at the bartender and rose from the stool, dropping a bill onto the counter while my eyes tracked her the whole time. Without the usual irritation holding me back, I drank in every gorgeous inch of her. It was unfair how one woman could be that damn beautiful. She smoothed her thick, black waves of hair over her shoulder and smiled with full, blood-red lips.

She was a woman who could lure anyone under her spell like a siren, and now that I didn't actively hate her as in years past, the sudden pull to her was dangerous.

I raked a hand through my hair and groaned. My head was all over the place, and I needed to reel myself in.

"Glad you made it," Olivia said, grinning as she approached.

"I said I would," was all I could say, holding in a cringe at how rude I knew it sounded. Olivia only nodded, and I felt even worse. Battle mode was my default with her, but she seemed to be trying, and she was doing a big favor for me so I needed to readjust my bad attitude.

"Now that you're here, they'll seat us. Come." She turned toward the hostess's desk and waved a hand for me to follow.

"I know it seems empty now, but from what I hear this place fills up quickly since there aren't many tables," Olivia told me when we were seated.

"I can imagine." I picked up a menu but studied her instead.

She smirked as she scanned the laminated specials card inside.

"Still watching to see if I'm going to poison you?"

There was the Olivia I'd grown up with.

"Maybe," I said, half kidding. "So you said this was a work thing?"

She nodded a thank-you to the waitress who placed our water glasses on the table.

"You know that I work remotely. I have for a long time

since I quit my old agency. I have two different jobs," she began, resting her elbows on the table. "For most of the day, I'm a social media consultant. I create and monitor social media accounts for different clients—mostly small businesses now, although I did freelance for a few large companies for a bit."

"As someone who is mostly clueless on social media and gets by on luck, I'd call that an important job."

"Well, thank you." Her eyes were wide, the curl of one side of her mouth in a teasing smirk reminiscent of our lifelong arguing. But if I wasn't mistaken, there was a tiny blush creeping up her cheeks, almost as if she was preening from my compliment. "If you ever need help, I'd be happy to meet with you. You can have your staff search me for weapons when I come to the bakery if that makes you feel more at ease."

"If it came to that, I don't think that would be necessary. I'm still buying into the truce you said we came to." The notion of patting down her body unnerved me enough to make my cock twitch inside my jeans.

"I'm good at knowing what will make customers react and want more of, whatever you're selling. There's more to it than a pretty Instagram grid and snappy posts."

"I'm not surprised that you're good at making people react. You've had lifelong practice." She laughed when I cocked a brow, and I felt a smile pulling across my lips. Was I actually enjoying a conversation with Olivia?

"We're here for my other job, and I keep this a secret. I'm a food blogger. I find obscure places that not many know of with great food. I post a photo of whatever I ate, give it a nice description and the right hashtags, and I can usually make it go viral. Since I started a website, a lot of restaurants find me now and offer to pay for features, which I do sometimes. Mostly I'm just the mystery diner."

"Why is that such a secret? You get paid to take a nice picture of your food. That's pretty smart."

"It's more than that," she started but held up a finger when the waitress took our order.

"I don't show my face."

My brow furrowed at Olivia. "Why don't you show your face?"

"For a few reasons. I like when I come to a place, no one knows it's me. I'm just a regular customer so I could really tell the experience one of my followers would have if they came to the restaurant on my recommendation. And when you show your face on social media, trolls come out of the woodwork sometimes. I'm confident in how I look, but I don't need the aggravation of being scrutinized about it."

"Why would they scrutinize you?" An odd sense of protection for her washed over me. Why would people say anything bad about her face?

"I knew of a food blogger who would get comments about her weight all the time. Again, I have a pretty decent self-image, but I'm human. That kind of stuff weighs on you no matter how thick your skin is. I can come to any restaurant, order whatever I want, and not have some keyboard warrior telling me I should start skipping dessert."

"What's the name of your account?"

She tapped at her phone screen and slid it over. "I'm trusting you with this. Mom and a few friends are the only ones who know."

I burst out laughing at the name at the top of the page. "Cleopatra, Her Royal Foodie. You still have a Cleopatra obsession?"

"What do you mean 'still'?" She squinted at me while my shoulders shook.

"I forget what birthday party it was. I think we were seven

or eight. You wore a wig and crown and called us your subjects. Congrats on living the dream."

I expected her to laugh with me, but she fell silent.

Not wanting to ruin the unusual good rapport between us tonight, I scrolled through her posts, impressed at the interaction she had on each one. Then I noticed the number of followers at the top of the page and almost swallowed my tongue.

"You have eight hundred thousand followers? Holy shit," I breathed before handing her the phone. "And you managed to keep your identity under the radar all this time?"

"So far." She shrugged, grabbing her phone off the table. "Maybe one day I'll change my mind. Even the sponsors haven't seen me since I deal with them via email. I'm sure eventually I'll have to show my face. Anyway, tonight dinner will be on me as it's a business expense." She winked and leaned forward, deepening the tempting slope of her cleavage. "Now that that's out in the open, let's talk about Saturday. If you're still interested, that is."

The sick part of it was how interested I actually was. Not only to not feel like a loser around Amy but shocking my family would be worth it. I'd have to get my parents on board with this charade, but I thought they'd go along with it. Mom would be over the moon that Olivia and I were getting along enough to join forces for something like this.

The years of ice between us seemed to be melting a bit, at least so far. Maybe this wacky plan would end up doing us all some good.

"I still am, as insane as it is. Maybe we should start by getting our stories straight. Like when we started dating and whatever." I was distracted by a bread basket the busboy dropped onto our table. The baker in me itched to sample all the different rolls and toasted breadsticks, but I kept my focus on the task at hand. "The last time they saw us, I was running away from you." Another grin crept across my lips, surprising me. "Like usual."

"Good point," she noted, tapping her chin. "Maybe say it was all new, and after a lifetime of being childhood enemies we didn't know how to act just yet. I don't think that's too far of a stretch," she whispered, and my grin grew wider.

This was getting too comfortable and freaking me out.

"No, I don't think so. Always a good idea to weave in a little truth."

"And honestly, after that, we don't need many details. We have to show a little PDA, but I can take one for the team if you can."

I flinched before I could help it. "What kind of PDA?"

She rolled her eyes and heaved a loud sigh. "I don't bite, Tyler. I mean, I could if you think it would help us look believable." She quirked a brow. "Is the idea of kissing me *that* repulsive?"

No. No, it wasn't. Despite spending most of my life wishing she'd just leave me the hell alone, once I hit puberty the urge to kiss her was always present, even when she'd sent me into a rage and I had to force it away, which only half worked.

But I wouldn't have to this time. I could actually consider it now and do it without wondering if she would lure me into some kind of trap later on.

I was walking into this trap with my eyes open, and the scariest part was that I wasn't even trying to look for a way out.

SIX
TYLER

"I'm not surprised that you became a baker," Olivia told me after swallowing a bite of her dinner. I'd followed her lead and ordered the double cheeseburger on a fresh-baked roll with truffle fries and had to fight a moan with every bite.

"Why is that?" I asked, keeping my eyes on her as I took a pull from my beer bottle.

"Remember how we used to fight over my Easy-Bake Oven?"

"We fought over *everything*." I narrowed my eyes at her. "You let me mix the batter once and then knocked it out of my hands before I could put it into the oven. *But it was an accident.*" I mimicked her evil little girl voice. "And they all believed you, like always."

"Not all." Olivia put her napkin down. "After you left that day, my dad hid the oven for a week as my punishment. Our mothers never wanted to get involved when we'd fight, but he'd seen me knock it out of your hands and said that I wasn't being kind and he didn't like it. But he kept it between us."

Once when my mother left me with Olivia to go shopping

with Carla when we were little, Olivia's father stood by and watched us play. Our mothers held out the dumb hope we'd naturally start getting along if they just let us be and never totally got over that denial. Or at least my mother hadn't.

It was the first time I'd seen someone notice that Olivia was picking on me. When she left the room for a minute, he whispered that if I wanted to knock over the block tower she was building, he'd pretend he didn't see. Javier Sanchez was good people and died too young.

"I'm sorry about your father. He was awesome."

"He was," she replied, focusing on her glass of water as she poked at what was left of the ice with her straw. "He was gone so fast, it almost feels like it didn't happen, you know? Almost."

I reached across the table and covered her hand with mine before I knew what I was doing. Once I saw her eyes water, comforting her was a confusing reflex that I couldn't control, along with the jolt down my forearm when my skin touched hers.

She stiffened for a moment, staring at my hand on hers with a pinched brow. I didn't understand my reflex either, but I couldn't take it back. I tried to slide my hand off her wrist rather than jerk it away.

"Thank you," she whispered. "Wow, look at us tonight. Getting along, getting personal." She snickered. "It's almost as if… Never mind."

"No, go on," I pressed. "I don't remember you ever holding back, so no need to start now."

"Good point." She nodded, moving her empty glass away. "I've known you my whole life. I knew how to piss you off early on, or how to make you bristle at my very presence." She crossed her arms, her eyes meeting mine with a playful glare.

"All true." I nodded slowly, taking a sip of water as my

mouth was parched from the sudden tension between us. Not the usual *will this woman just go away* tension, but heavy air between us since I'd met her at the entrance that I couldn't explain.

"Sitting here, having a meal with you, it's like—"

"We're meeting each other for the first time? Sort of."

She stilled, and also for the first time, I witnessed Olivia speechless.

"Hm, maybe." She scooted her chair closer to the table, jerking her shoulder in a quick shrug. "So weird. Plus, since we graduated college and I moved, I've only seen you sporadically anyway. The occasional family function or funeral..."

"I've seen you enough." My scowl drew a chuckle out of her. "Maybe we were so fixated on being enemies from the beginning we never gave each other a chance to be friends. It's nice to know this non-sinister side of you, Cleopatra."

"Shh." She brought her finger to her lips, the side of her mouth curving up. "Don't blow my cover."

"Your cover?" I scoffed. "Sorry, Batman."

"It's nice to know you too." When Olivia smiled, *really* smiled without appearing to have some kind of nefarious agenda, she was stunning. Her dark eyes twinkled at me, stealing a little air from my lungs. "Other than being a grumpy baker with a baseball fixation."

"You've seen me in situations that make me grumpy. That doesn't mean I'm grumpy by nature."

"Every time I've seen you, you've been grumpy. But"—she paused with a slow nod— "that was probably because of me."

"Not always. When you saw me last it was mostly my family and the news that the only cousin I like was going to be related to my ex. You didn't help, no." Another smile pulled at my lips. "But I don't think I've been grumpy since we sat down, have I?"

"No, you haven't." She looked away for a moment before she returned my wide grin.

"Did you get the money shot?" I nodded at her empty plate. I'd tried not to stare when she made such a big effort to position her phone perfectly earlier. I usually rolled my eyes when I noticed someone do that before they ate, but Olivia had an actual purpose other than documenting every second of her life on social media.

"I did. That was a pretty damn good burger. They should get some awesome traffic after my post tomorrow."

"I'm sure they will, your highness."

"Now, if you had just started calling me that all along, we would have been friends a long time ago." She smirked at me, her red lipstick faded but still beckoning my eyes to her mouth.

Olivia paid the bill, then I followed her out to the parking lot.

"I have to be at the venue early to drop the cake off. Can you be ready by four?" I asked as I walked with her to her car. The parking lot was packed compared to how empty it had been when we'd arrived.

"That's not a problem." She tossed her purse onto the passenger seat and turned back to me. "What color is your suit?"

"What is this, prom?" I scoffed. "It's black."

"Good. My dress is red, so we won't clash."

My brows shot up. "Why doesn't that surprise me?" I sighed, trying to ignore the possible images parading through my brain of her body covered in what I was sure would be a tight red dress. She'd turn every head in the place—most of all mine.

"Well, that's kind of the point of this endeavor, right?" She shrugged. "Tyler showing up to a family wedding with the girl he always hated. People eat up a good enemies-to-lovers tale. If we do it right." She shut the door behind her and crossed her arms, squinting at me as she leaned back against her car. She looked like she was about to issue a challenge.

"I guess. Good point. Thank you for dinner." I shifted toward my truck. "This wasn't so terrible."

"'Wasn't so terrible'?" She held her torso as she burst out laughing. "Your game is *stellar*, Bennett."

"My game is on a long hiatus, and I don't think game is necessary for what we're doing. Good night," I said before she grabbed my arm.

"I have an idea. This was good practice for friendly conversation, but if we kiss for the first time in front of everyone, it's going to look forced, no?"

"I still don't see why we'd have to, but probably if we did, it would look awkward as fuck."

"Well, why don't we get it out of the way now?"

My brows jumped. This woman was full of surprises.

"You want to kiss? Now? In a parking lot?"

"No one is really out here, and if we fumble now it's not like anyone will notice or care. Come on," she purred, inching closer to me. My eyes fell to her mouth as it curved into a slow, wicked grin. "You know what they say about that line between love and hate."

"What's that?" I rasped, my mouth dry and my palms damp like I was a thirty-five-year-old teenager. She got a rise out of me in more ways than one when we were young, but I could never see past the lifelong animosity. Tonight, we'd managed to take that out of the equation, and nothing was stopping me from tasting the lips I'd wanted for longer than I cared to remember.

"It's thin. *Really* thin," she whispered, sliding her hand to the back of my neck and pulling my mouth toward hers. She brushed my lips with a feather-light kiss and leaned in for another when I didn't pull away. Her mouth was warm, her lips pillow-soft. If we were on a bad-decision streak anyway, I wasn't settling for a cheap little kiss after all this time.

I speared a hand into her hair and hauled her to me, gliding my tongue along her bottom lip until she opened her mouth on a surprised moan. Her arms looped around my neck as I pulled her closer, her full breasts pressing against me as the kiss went from tentative to desperate. I licked inside her mouth with long strokes, drinking it all in to quench the thirst I'd never wanted to acknowledge.

A few weeks ago, if anyone told me I'd be making out with Olivia in a restaurant parking lot, I would have sworn they were delusional. Not because I never wanted to, because even when I couldn't stand her I wanted her. Part of me hoped this was a trick, that she'd stop the kiss and say "Gotcha" with a wink.

Because if Olivia wanted me too—*really* wanted me—then I was powerless. There would be no way I'd be able to resist.

Tension spilled out into mindless passion as my hand traveled down her hips while Olivia grabbed my ass. Her nails scraped against my denim-covered skin and coaxed a tortured groan to rise from my throat. I was hard to the point of pain and two seconds away from opening her car door and pushing her into the back seat.

Every time one of us would back away, the other would go in faster and harder. The push and pull were familiar—both of us had always wanted the last word, but this game of dominance was a new one that I liked. Hell, I fucking loved it. Instead of winning whatever stupid argument we'd fallen into, I wanted to claim her in another way, make her scream and writhe beneath me until she was nothing but a little puddle of

Olivia. The thought made my blood run a little cold, but not enough to douse the scorching heat between us.

If we were supposed to act like lovers who couldn't keep their hands off each other, we'd have no problem convincing everyone on Saturday since I wasn't sure how I'd stop touching her now.

The blaring of a horn made us break apart. I wasn't sure if it was at us or not, but it was enough of a shock to bring us panting back to reality.

Olivia clutched my biceps, gulping while she caught her breath. Her lips were swollen and the rest of her lipstick was smeared across her mouth. While it was mostly dark other than a few street lamps, I spied the soft vulnerability in her hooded eyes. It was as unmistakable as it was breathtaking.

"What was that about my *game*?" For once, I'd managed to shut her up, and my chest swelled with pride.

"I think," she began, running a hand through her hair, "I think we'll be fine on Saturday. You focus on the cake, I'll focus on the show. Got it?" She grinned, but her words came out stunted and shaky. Pride pumped through my veins as my head spun with lust. My teenage fantasy had come true, and the reality was a thousand times better than anything I'd conjured in my silly brain back then.

"Goodnight, Tyler." She turned before I could reply, almost jumping into the driver's seat and peeling out of the parking lot.

I rubbed the back of my neck, unable to stop the wide grin causing my cheeks to ache. When I stepped into the cab and started the engine, reality set in.

This game of pretend already felt too real.

SEVEN
OLIVIA

"Well, this is a surprise," Morgan mused, regarding me with a suspicious crease in her forehead as she leaned against her doorway.

"Can't someone stop in to see their best friend if they're in the neighborhood?" I clutched my chest in mock offense.

"They absolutely can, but you usually don't just show up without texting or calling. Not that I mind at all, but when you just show up, it's usually for a reason." She crossed her arms. "What's wrong?"

"Nothing's wrong. Mom had some cookies leftover from Tyler's bakery, and I thought I'd surprise you and Leah."

"And you stole sugar-free, leftover cookies from your mother as a cover." Her brows lifted as she adjusted the messy chestnut bun on top of her head. "Oh boy, this must be serious." She stepped aside and nodded behind her. "Get in and spill."

I stalked past her and down the hallway. I'd been climbing the walls since last night and had to tell someone what happened before I exploded.

Tyler had beat me at my own game for the very first time,

and I had no clue what to do about it. How was I supposed to pretend to be fake lovers at his cousin's wedding when all I could think about was not pretending? I'd painted myself into a corner and couldn't find a way out. Unable to stand myself anymore, I'd swiped the box off Mom's kitchen counter while she was out and raced over here.

Men did not rattle me—ever. The few long-term boyfriends I had never affected me like this, even after we parted ways. I'd maybe feel a little sad for a day or two and then brush myself off and move on without giving any of them much thought. Other guys didn't worm their way under my skin enough for me to obsess over a silly little thing like a kiss.

But other guys weren't Tyler. He was always my unhealthy focus. Now that I'd kissed him, I didn't have to wonder how it would be because it annihilated every single one of my expectations. I'd planned on putting on a good show at Donnie's wedding—hanging on his arm and nuzzling against him to make it look believable. While it wouldn't have been a hardship to have to be close to him all night before, now it was all I could think about.

"Where's Leah?" I asked.

"She had teacher conferences after school but should be home soon. Why? Can't she know whatever you're about to tell me?" Her brows knit in concern.

"No, I wouldn't make you keep something from your wife, and it's not like it's a big deal. I'm just probably being dramatic like usual." I took the frayed string from the cookie box between my fingers and sifted it back and forth.

"Well," she prodded, tapping her finger on the table.

"It's about last night," I started, rubbing my temple.

"I thought you had dinner with Tyler to make peace and clear the air before this ridiculous fake wedding date on Saturday."

"We did." I sighed. "It backfired on me, let's put it that way."

She reared back. "Backfired on you? Like how?"

"We actually got along. It was nice. Odd but nice. Then I suggested we kiss to get over the awkwardness of when we kissed on Saturday."

"Why would you have to kiss?" The crease in her brow deepened. "You aren't the bride and groom. Just maybe hang on him a little if you want people to think you're dating, but kissing isn't completely necessary, right?"

I clenched my eyes shut. She needed to stop with the logic.

"I thought PDA would make it more believable, and maybe part of me still wanted to get a rise out of him, to see if he'd back down. He didn't."

Her hand flew to her gaping mouth.

"So all those years of blistering sexual tension finally came to a head!"

"Morgan, please stop," I pleaded as she folded in laughter.

"I can't believe you finally kissed Tyler. So now this little game you offered to play got a bit too real. Do I follow?"

"Yes." I sighed, draping my hand over my eyes. The smooth glide of Tyler's tongue against mine as he moaned into my mouth played on a continuous and torturous loop, my imagination adding parts at the end with every repeat. Extra footage included me palming his cock through his jeans or him turning me around after growling at me to put both hands against my car door as he plunged his hand down my pants.

Pissing him off to the point of distraction had been a euphoric high for years now, but kissing him, tasting his lips and the memory of his body pressed into mine? That was bliss on a level I never thought existed. What could come of this though?

A bruising kiss didn't mean anything other than that he could rise to the challenge and put me in my place for once, no matter how much I'd loved every second of it.

"I remember when you guys were, like, this teenage inferno of hormones and lust," Morgan said. "You'd argue, and we'd all stare to see if you would finally make out and get it over with."

"Well, we're thirty-five, and he hates me. You know this. He only agreed to this fake date because his ex is pregnant and he didn't want to lose face in front of her or his family."

"What did he say when he agreed? Like, did he even say why he'd take you?"

"He said I was the perfect distraction." I shrugged.

Morgan snickered.

"I'm sure he just meant that I pissed him off that much." I groaned. "I'm a shitty person, I can admit that." I dragged a hand down my face.

"Did he recoil when you kissed him or something?"

"Oh, no, he didn't recoil. He *went* for it. For a second, I thought he was inching me toward the back door of my car." I covered my eyes, rubbing my lids as Morgan laughed. I'd come home freaked out, my nerves shot and my panties ruined.

"Sex is going to be epic and may ruin the both of you." Her shoulders rolled with an exaggerated shiver.

"Sex?" I gaped at her. "Are you kidding me? This was a freak thing. I'll do this favor for him, and we can be sort of friendly, distant acquaintances."

"I bet he looks good in a suit."

"You're not helping," I said as my head fell against the table with a thud. There wasn't much that didn't look good on Tyler. I'd seen him in a suit a few times and almost gave myself a migraine trying to tear my eyes away, and that was when we were young. With his baker's biceps and broad chest now, I'd have to fight just as hard not to ogle him all night.

"All kidding aside, I'm worried about you." Morgan reached out to squeeze my hand. "You need to stop blaming and punishing yourself for everything."

"I'm not punishing myself." I let out a long gust of frustrated air. "I've been selfish and spoiled, and in my mid-thirties it's finally time to snap out of it."

"I know that part of the reason why you moved back was to atone for all this guilt you torture yourself with but..." She paused, grabbing my hand. "A shitty person wouldn't have fought anyone who looked in my direction the wrong way when I came out in school after all my other friends acted like I had the plague."

"I didn't fight *everyone*—just the assholes. And you'd do the same for me."

"I think it takes a special kind of person to break someone's nose for upsetting their best friend, even if you freaked out after that a nose could bleed that much."

A real laugh fell from my lips for the first time all day.

"Or," Morgan added on a long sigh, "when you asked your parents if they could adopt me in case my mother got mad when I told her I was bisexual and threw me out. You even offered to give up half your room. I wouldn't have fit with all the clothes and makeup, but I was touched by the gesture."

I flinched. "You heard that?"

"I did. It was easier to tell my mom that night knowing I had a sort of plan to fall back on." Her eyes glossed over. "That's the Olivia I always knew. Ride or die, didn't give a shit about what anyone thought because she was always herself. You deserve to be happy, whether it's with Tyler or someone else. Or even start celebrating your birthday again someday instead of—"

She held up a hand when I opened my mouth to argue.

"But one thing at a time. If I know you, what flashy dress are you planning to wear?"

"The red one with the deep neckline and sequins and super-high slit."

I cracked up when her jaw dropped.

"Poor Tyler is going to drop the cake."

My heart was lighter yet heavy at the same time. Happy wasn't something I'd let myself consider for a while—two years, to be exact. Being on Tyler's arm, even if it was fake, was something I looked forward to. Maybe if I started being honest with myself about that, being friends wouldn't be so hard. Anything more than that wasn't possible, despite how nice the potential picture was.

"Too much?"

"Nope." She looped an arm around my shoulder. "For you, it's just enough."

EIGHT
TYLER

"Your cousin is going to love this cake!" Tegan, my new baker and cake decorator, gushed as she stepped back to eyeball the cake after we pulled it out of the refrigerator. Tegan was twenty-five and fresh out of pastry school. She had great technique and liked to make different varieties of vegan and sugar-free desserts. I'd never done a wedding cake with chocolate icing and white roses, but with her flower piping expertise and assistance from the rest of the staff, we'd pulled off a true team effort.

"I hope so," I breathed out as I eyed the final product. It did look pretty fucking awesome. I was glad to do this for Donnie. As long as I delivered it intact, this would be one thing I could count on going right tonight.

"That cake almost makes me want to get married."

Tegan and I whipped around to stare at Eli, who was snickering under his baseball cap.

"I said almost." He held his hands up and tossed a towel over his shoulder. "Go up the block and pretty up. Leave me the keys, and we'll get this masterpiece into the truck so you can prep for your hot date."

I groaned, shaking my head. "It's my cousin's wedding, not a hot date."

"Well, you're *bringing* a hot date, so that counts in my book."

"A hot *fake* date," I grumbled as I hung up my apron.

"Ah! But you admit she's hot." He snapped the towel against my arm, but I wouldn't turn around. Yes, Olivia was hot, and this hot fake date was an impending disaster on more levels than I'd originally anticipated, but I wasn't going into that with the people who worked for me or anyone else.

"I don't like going to weddings on a first date," Tegan noted, her pierced brow furrowed as she leaned back on the counter. "I usually get so caught up in the love and promise of happily ever afters that I end up hooking up with the guy and wind up with an *un*happily ever after the following morning."

"The boss doesn't need happily ever after, just a happy ending for the night," Eli said, smirking at me before sliding the two-tiered cake onto the bottom of the box we'd made.

"My date is an old acquaintance, so romance or happy endings won't be involved," I told Tegan, digging the keys to the truck out of my pocket and handing them to Eli. "I'll be back in a half hour—if you wouldn't mind starting it and cranking up the AC once you guys have the cake back there, I'd appreciate it."

"No problem," Eli replied with a mock salute.

I'd found an apartment a short distance from the bakery right after I'd leased the space, which helped with the ungodly morning hours I kept. All I had to do was shower, shave, and pull on my suit before heading to Olivia's. There'd been a stir-ring in my chest all day long as we worked on the cake, but I reasoned it away as nerves about delivery and having to be in the same space with Amy and Jayden for the first time in a year—but that was bullshit even to my own ears.

Olivia always triggered things in me. She annoyed me on a good day; infuriated me when I let her get under my skin; and, fuck me, captivated me more than I ever wanted to face. And then, I had to go and kiss her and make this fucked-up night potentially even worse. The woman could *kiss*. It had been nearly impossible to tear myself away from her in the parking lot, and I kept imagining what it would be like to finish what we'd started. It was as if everything up until this point was foreplay, and now I was all but panting for her every time I remembered how good she'd tasted.

I thought for sure I'd spend last night tossing and turning, but when I crawled into bed and shut my eyes, Olivia was there. My sex-deprived mind conjured the skimpiest and tightest red dress painted on her gorgeous curves with red lips to match. I could feel the silk of her almost-black hair as I pictured weaving my hand around a fistful to bring her sweet mouth back to mine. That needy whimper of hers had been reverberating in my head since our lips broke apart, and it had me wondering how she'd sound if I tasted her in other places.

Before I knew it, my hand was around my swollen cock, pumping hard as I imagined dropping to my knees and really shutting her up. When I thought of lifting her dress and snaking my tongue inside her, I came all over my stomach. After I'd cleaned myself up, I fell into a dreamless and almost restful sleep until I had to wake up to the reality of this very long day.

That wasn't the first time I'd come with her name on my lips and her beautiful body burned into my brain.

Or the second.

Or the tenth.

Being that attracted to a woman you couldn't stand was a years-long mindfuck. I'd become angry at myself every time for letting her have that power over me, but the notion that maybe she wanted me too messed with my resolve more than anything else. I didn't think she was luring me in to humiliate me with a rejection. Her hooded eyes and swollen lips begging me to keep kissing her, to touch her wasn't Olivia goading me like when we were kids. It seemed real.

And if it was, I was so fucked.

I got ready on autopilot and texted Olivia that I was on my way. I hadn't even gotten to her apartment yet and this was the most stressful date—fake or not—I'd ever been on. Although the air conditioning in the car was turned up to arctic level, I had to wipe my damp palm on my suit pants at each red light. Damn this woman and what she always did to me.

I pulled my truck up to the front of Carla's house, making sure to roll into the spot slowly. The cake was more than secure thanks to Eli, but I'd still ride the short distance to the hotel in the right lane at the low end of the speed limit. This wasn't my first delivery, but it was an important one. I wanted to do something nice for my cousin and not allow my screwed-up life to screw up their big day—at least with this.

"Don't you clean up nice!" Carla called from the driveway where she had just parked. "Is the cake secure?"

"Couldn't be more secure if I had an armored truck."

Her shoulders jerked with a chuckle. "Must be nice to have a baker in the family. I know you'd be my favorite relative."

I barked out a laugh. "My family mostly thinks my business is a joke until they want something at a discount. Only a few think owning a bakery is a mark of success."

"As I've known your family for years and the good few you're referring to, I can attest that they're the only ones that count." She nudged my shoulder. "You make and measure your own success. So enjoy tonight and don't pay them any mind."

"Oh, they'll be talking about me for a whole different

reason tonight, I'm sure." I stuffed my hands into my pockets, glancing over her shoulder in search of Olivia.

"Maybe you can even enjoy that part too." She crossed her arms, peering up at the sky. "Javier would have gotten the *biggest* kick out of this."

"Yes, I think he would." A smile, despite all the tension surrounding tonight, stretched across my mouth. "He was the only one who didn't hope we'd just naturally stop fighting like you and my mother did." I lifted a brow, leaning back on the passenger's side of my truck. "He was our referee all through middle school."

I stopped laughing when I met her watery gaze.

"I think if both of you could let go a little bit, you may have a better night together than you'd expect." She shrugged. "Wouldn't hurt to try, right?"

"Sorry I'm late!"

We both turned toward Olivia's voice as she fumbled with the lock on her front door. A rush of air left my lungs when she turned to make her way toward us. That dress was painted on, all right. And low. Her perfect breasts filled out the deep neckline, taunting me already. Red sequins lined the bottom and brushed against her ankles. As she came closer, the high slit opened and stole the rest of my breath. She was stunning, and there was no way I'd be able to take my eyes off her tonight.

And to think I was worried about us looking forced. If I had to appear that I was into her, zero acting would be necessary.

Olivia's face softened when her eyes locked with mine. She eased closer and skated her hand down the lapel of my suit.

"You look hot, Tyler. Or maybe I just haven't seen you in anything not dotted with flour recently." Her lips stretched into a smile, red lips that I wanted to taste again—along with the rest of her.

"Thanks. I thought I'd leave the apron at the bakery tonight, even if I'm bringing the cake." My eyes canvassed every inch of her before I could help myself as my fingers itched to touch her. "You don't look too bad either."

The corner of my mouth ticked up when her brows raised.

"Wow, that game gets better and better."

"Do you really need to hear how gorgeous you look right now or how the bride may get pissed that no one will notice anything or anyone once you walk in? If your ego is that delicate, I guess I can tell you." I shrugged. "I just didn't think you were the type to fish for compliments, Sanchez."

Her lips pursed before they twitched into smile.

"I'm not, Bennett. Let's get that cake delivered and shock some people." She slid her hand into the crook of my elbow. "Lead the way."

Carla beamed as she looked between us.

"Glad to see after all these years, the both of you figured out how to get along. Have a good time and be careful. A bad storm is supposed to hit later tonight."

"My truck could handle anything. I just need to get this cake out of the car. Have a good night, Carla."

"Same to you both," she said, stopping to give us one last glance and shifting toward the house.

"I've had this dress for a while. I had a gala to attend for a company I freelanced for a few years ago, but it still fits." Olivia took her hand off my arm and twirled around. "I think this says *trophy date*."

"Trophy?" A chuckle slipped out of me. "What crazy contest did I win?"

"The one where you get to tell everyone to fuck off." She

adjusted her purse on her arm, and I followed the way her body moved under that dress. I couldn't tell where the zipper was, but if given the chance I'd happily search for it.

The minute the thought barreled into my head, I clenched my eyes shut. I couldn't go there tonight, no matter how blinding the temptation.

Olivia climbed into the cab, giving me one more tease of her thigh when the slit opened. She shut the door before I could close it for her, and for a reason I couldn't explain, it bothered me.

I jogged back to the driver's seat and started the car, stilling before I put it in Drive.

"What?" she asked, her brows knit together. "You're not getting cold feet, are you?"

"No," I replied, shifting in my seat to face her. "I have a suggestion for tonight."

"Okay," she said, scrutinizing me through her long lashes. "What's that?"

"Could we just be two people on a date at a wedding and not the two kids who were at each other's throats for most of their lives?" I took in a deep breath and continued. "No arguments, no dwelling on the past, just be Tyler and Olivia. A guy bringing a beautiful woman to a wedding to spite half the guests."

"So I *am* beautiful?" Her eyes lit up, and the strain of not kissing her almost popped a vein in my forehead.

"So you *are* fishing?"

"I thought you said no arguments?" Her dark eyes narrowed.

"That's not arguing, it's bickering. Different. That we probably wouldn't be able to stop."

"True," she said with a slow nod. "Sounds good to me.

Ready?" She jutted her chin toward the road. "We have precious cargo in the back."

I nodded and pulled out of the spot, unable to shake the feeling that whatever happened tonight, I was sure as hell *not* ready for any of it.

NINE
OLIVIA

Morgan was right—the fucker looked great in a suit. The jacket had stretched across his torso while he unloaded the cake from the cargo area. Watching the simple act of lifting something and putting it down shouldn't have soaked my panties, but my reactions to Tyler were never normal. When he picked me up and I caught his gaze raking up and down my body when we first saw each other, I flushed hot all over and welcomed the relief from his ice-cold car.

"Sorry we're here so early," Tyler said after handing off the cake to the restaurant manager. He flicked his wrist to glance at his watch, and the gesture shouldn't have sent a shiver up my spine.

Yes, I was a fake date only here to distract Tyler from seeing Amy and maybe create a barrier from his asshole cousins, but it seemed like more. Or maybe that was just my silly hope. I'd waited a long time for Tyler to not act like he hated me, even though that was mostly my doing. He had been chiding me a little when he said I was gorgeous, but warmth had flooded through my chest anyway.

I guessed swooning like a jackass over him all night could be key to this mission we were trying to pull off.

"I have nowhere to be but here with you," I said in the breathiest tone I could manage and threw him a wink.

"You don't have to lay it on so thick without witnesses." His mouth curved into a wry grin, his hazel eyes twinkling just a bit if I wasn't mistaken. "But that sounded good. Believable."

If he'd only known how believable it was.

"I wouldn't mind a drink at the bar. It's still empty." I slid my palm against his, tugging him to follow me, but he wouldn't move.

He'd said he just wanted to be Tyler and Olivia, but other than the panty-melting kiss we shared or an uncomfortable hug to appease our parents, we didn't touch. And that was not going to work tonight. I shook off the sting of his slight rejection and leaned in to whisper in his ear.

"It's okay to hold hands since we've already had our tongues down each other's throats. This night could be fun or awkward as hell, and that's up to you." I pulled back to meet his eyes. "So relax and play ball, Bennett."

The tension spearing across my shoulder blades lifted when I spied his crooked smile.

"I will, and I am. I think now that we're here and I don't have the cake to focus on, it's all hitting me a little. I shouldn't be this damn uptight. I just need to shake it off. A drink would be good." He inched closer, and a zap of electricity ran down my arm when he brushed my hair off my shoulder. "I can play ball, Sanchez." I swallowed a moan when he nuzzled my neck, his breath fanning hot against my skin. "See?"

"Yeah," I replied with a raspy, needy voice. God, he smelled good. I looked at his mouth and the dark dusting of stubble around his soft lips. I had a reputation for being pushy, usually asking for forgiveness, not permission when I wanted something. But could I ever really kiss Tyler? Not because I issued a challenge, just because I wanted to?

"Just making sure." I cleared my throat. "Come on, I'll even buy if the open bar didn't start yet."

A few people had trickled into the bar when we found our seats.

"Anyone you recognize?" I asked and took a sip of pinot grigio. Usually I enjoyed red more, but despite the bravado I was hoping to pull off, my insides were a little shaky. The last thing I needed was a giant stain on my dress.

Tyler took a long pull from his beer bottle and scanned the space. I was transfixed by the roll of his throat as he gulped down a mouthful.

"No. Maybe Cassandra's family or just guests at the hotel. I think only the restaurant is closed to the general public tonight." He set down the bottle with a groan. "I shouldn't be this rattled."

"Why shouldn't you? You're human. After all that happened before you broke up, you have to face her here, with her husband, under the eyes of people like Alan and the rest of your cousins." I wrinkled my nose in disgust. "I'm glad I'm here for you tonight, even if you still hate me a little." I smirked as I twisted the stem of my wine glass between my index finger and thumb.

Tyler leaned back in his chair. "Despite it all, I never really hated you."

"So 'antichrist in heels' is a term you give to the girls you like?"

He blinked before his eyes grew wide. "Christ, do you have ears everywhere?"

"Sometimes." I lifted a shoulder. "You called me that to a guy on your baseball team back in senior year of high school. I was by the exit, and you didn't see me standing there."

"That's because you were flirting with him to get a rise out of me, and I didn't want him to get his hopes up."

"How do you know that was the reason? He was cute, whatever his name was." I shrugged.

"If he was *so* cute, why did you keep looking back at me while you were talking to him?"

My glass stilled in my hand as I met his narrowed eyes.

"Your memory is fuzzy. It was a long time ago."

"When it comes to you, I remember it all. Trust me." He pointed the beer bottle at me and took another sip, not breaking his gaze from mine.

"What did you care that I flirted with some guy on your baseball team? Or the bigger question, why did you watch?"

This was too much of a routine with us. The jabs back and forth, egging each other on, always having to have the last word. I had fought a confusing attraction to Tyler for most of my life that caused me to act out. But now that I was wondering if the attraction was mutual, I wasn't as free to be as brazen as before.

"You knew I watched," he growled in a low, sex-soaked voice. "That was your whole point. How about a little honesty for once?"

"Okay, then," I set the glass down and rested my elbows on the table, clasping my hands. "Yes, I did it to bother you, like I did everything else. But why did you watch if I was the antichrist in heels? What did you care if I flirted with anyone?"

"Because I didn't like it," he spat out. "For reasons that I never wanted to see but that had nothing to do with hate. And I'd bet you always knew that."

Air rushed out of my lungs along with any words to form a coherent reply.

The games I played with Tyler were the equivalent of a

dog chasing its tail. If he caught it, he probably had no clue what to do with it.

With Tyler's golden eyes growing dark as he bore his eyes into mine, I'd finally caught what I was chasing. Now, what the hell did I do about it?

"Okay, so you don't hate me." I swallowed a large gulp of wine, downing the rest of the glass in hopes it would cool me off. "Now that we talked about the usual tension between us, how are you feeling about the rest of tonight? About seeing Amy again?"

I wasn't sure he'd heard me until I spied his small shrug.

I sucked in a breath and scooted my chair closer, hating his vacant stare. I was almost tempted to start a little argument with him to get that fire back in his eyes from only a moment ago. "Before you see them both, maybe getting something off your chest would help. I'll try to be a good listener and not a demon."

He chuckled before sucking in a long breath.

"Like I said, it's been a long time. But I guess I'm more embarrassed than anything else. I was so into building up the bakery, talking to lenders, hiring staff that I didn't see it coming. Amy was never that on board with the bakery to begin with and I guessed she resented me for even opening it in the first place, but why couldn't she just tell me?" He scratched at the beer bottle label. "I even asked Jayden if I should take Amy somewhere for a weekend to talk it out, and he told me the best thing was to leave her alone."

"Because he was taking her out behind your back?"

He laughed to himself while slowly nodding.

"I think I hate him more than I hate her," I said, crossing my arms as I leaned back in the chair. "Best friends are supposed to *have* your back, not stab you in it."

His lips curved up for a moment.

"I've gone back and forth myself a few times, but I think it's a tie. Anyway, she said she was going on a girls' weekend trip the same weekend of the bakery opening. After I got home that first day, the friend that she was supposed to be on vacation with called me to tell me everything. She said she felt guilty being a pawn."

"So you couldn't even enjoy the first day of your brand-new business?"

My blood boiled as my hand clenched into a fist. Yes, I made it a hobby to torture him but I'd never hurt Tyler like that, and I found myself wanting to slug a pregnant woman for the very first time.

"So I waited until she got home to confront her, and she told me everything. She handed me my engagement ring and packed a bag. Jayden was there to get her in less than an hour without so much as an 'I'm sorry.' I think the only thing he said was, 'I guess I'll see you.'"

"Wow. I am so sorry." I reached over and draped my hand over his and gave it a quick squeeze, the same way he did when he'd noticed me tearing up over my father. Maybe deep down, we were sort of friends all along and the sexual tension blinded us too much to be nice to each other. Well, it at least blinded me. Whatever the case, he needed a friend tonight, and whatever happened later, I'd make sure he had one.

"Thanks." He nodded. "It's fine. I guess I just didn't want to face it all alone, as pathetic as it sounds."

"It doesn't. And that's why I'm here." I nudged his ankle under the table. "I think I can make you feel better. Remember when your cousin Alan broke his nose senior year?"

His brow pinched as he nodded. "I forgot you guys went to the same school. Yeah, some field hockey fight he said."

"Well, he lied," I said in a loud whisper. "Morgan was

dating one of his friends. She had just come out as bisexual the year before, and all Alan did was give her a hard time. Now that she was dating a guy, he had a field day with it. He'd scream 'pick a side' every time he'd spot them together." I draped my hand over my eyes for a minute. "Alan was relentless until her boyfriend broke up with her. I don't know if it was because of Alan, but I was certain that he didn't help. She was pretty devastated. I caught him snickering behind her back one day as we were walking home, and he said something stupid like, 'I guess it's back to the other team for you,' and before I knew what I was doing, I ran over and punched him."

"I'm sorry, what?" Tyler asked, gaping at me.

"Blood was *everywhere*. I almost threw up. And I never knew punching anyone would hurt that much." I shook out my hand, the memory of my knuckles cracking against his nose sending pain down my fingers even now.

"Holy shit. I had no idea." Tyler's eyes lit up. "He was always such a dick."

"Yep. But no one was around except him, Morgan, and me. He begged me not to say anything and promised he'd back off Morgan if I kept quiet." I extended my fingers, pretending to admire my manicure. "I did, but every time I saw him, I fiddled with my hand just to screw with him. Or commented in a really loud voice about how sore my hand was from a *past injury*." I lifted my shoulder in an innocent shrug. "What I'm saying is that your homophobic, probably small-dicked cousin is nothing to worry about, and neither is Amy. I have your back tonight. Does that help?"

"Yes, it does." Tyler's smile was wide, easy, and beautiful. "In fact, that's the new greatest story ever told." Childish little flutters took off in my belly in celebration. "And I'm grateful to be on your good side tonight."

I'd gladly slay anyone to make him keep looking at me like that. I grinned back, despite the panic churning my insides.

I was so fucked.

TEN
TYLER

"So explain this to me again," my father said as we found our assigned table. "This... tonight, you and Olivia. It's fake?"

He looked me over with a pinched brow. Dad usually went with the flow and didn't say much, so for him to notice enough to comment on it meant we were getting the attention Olivia swore we would.

"Olivia offered to come with me as a favor and thought it would be fun to get a rise out of people. Not a big deal," I told him as I found her across the room. She chatted with my mother, laughing at something. I couldn't tear my eyes away no matter how hard I tried. That dress, that body, and that fucking slit that was draining all the blood out of my head and into my cock every time it opened. I let myself look because we were supposed to be lovers. I could explain it away as acting in the moment, even if allowing my eyes to caress her body was instinct and the complete opposite of pretend.

I was dragged out of my trance by my father's snicker.

"What? We look ridiculous? Tell me something I don't

know, Dad." I scooted my chair closer to the table and took a sip from my water glass.

"If by *ridiculous* you mean *your tongue hanging out whenever you look in her direction*, then yes." His chest rumbled with a laugh. "It doesn't look that fake to me, son. Not that I'm surprised." He shrugged, still laughing. "I figured with how the two of you always fought it was just a matter of time."

I squinted at my father. "What was a matter of time?"

"Thank God we got here when we did."

My mother's voice interrupted us as she took a seat next to my father. "And thankfully this isn't an outdoor wedding. It looks like a monsoon out there."

"Seriously," Olivia said, sliding into the chair next to mine. "And good thing we got here early and secured that beautiful cake." She slid her hand across my back, sending a current down my body and right to my dick. Every move Olivia made tonight was a turn on, and I needed to snap out of it. Maybe I'd ask Eli about those dating apps I wouldn't touch. I'd told him I didn't want the distraction, but going so long without anyone's hand on my dick except mine wasn't helping me focus either.

It had to be that. I wasn't ready to handle the alternative.

"It is gorgeous, sweetheart," my mother gushed. "You are so talented, and I don't think we've told you enough. Right?" She smacked my father's arm, who was now back to his disconnected self and annoyed that she jostled the spread of butter on his dinner roll.

"Right," he mumbled, chewing without looking up.

I cut a look at Olivia, smiling when I caught her smirk. A month ago, I couldn't stand her, and now having her next to me was my only bright spot tonight. I'd enjoy having her beneath me too. And on top of me.

For fuck's sake, Tyler. Stop it.

I hadn't seen Amy yet, and I'd managed a wave to Alan and Ross when they'd snuck into the ceremony. I knew the empty seats on the other end of the table were for them and was pretty sure Olivia would dial it up between us for their benefit.

"Hey, everyone!"

I cringed at the sound of Alan's voice. Even when we were kids, it had a slimy edge to it. I swore he was born with his hair slicked back, a douchebag salesman from birth. He looked between Olivia and me and rolled his eyes. I promised myself I wouldn't let him get to me tonight, and with this new piece of history Olivia gifted to me earlier, I almost welcomed sharing a table with him. I had experience with Olivia's ability to torture someone without chipping a fingernail, and I looked forward to seeing her make Alan squirm.

"Hi, Alan, Simone," my mother said, greeting them both with a smile.

Simone had been Alan's girlfriend for about a year. He never settled down, but the girls became younger and younger. My theory was that once they matured enough to see past the fancy suits and watches and realized that he was just your typical self-absorbed prick, they moved on.

"I'm Olivia," Olivia said as she rose from her seat and extended a hand to Simone. "I don't think we've met."

"Nice to meet you," Simone chirped before settling into the seat next to my cousin.

"We were just talking about the cake Tyler made for Donnie and Cassandra," Mom said. My chest pinched at how her back straightened against the chair as if she were bragging. I guessed every kid chases praise from their parents, no matter how old they are. Maybe I let what others said color what everyone thought of me as a whole and I was the root cause of my sour attitude after all.

"Wow, you made that?" Simone's blue eyes widened. "It's so beautiful and different."

"He's *really* talented," Olivia added, looping her arm around my shoulders.

"I bet he stuffed the bread baskets too." Alan snickered. "So when did this start?" He moved his finger back and forth between Olivia and me. "I only saw both of you last month and you were hiding from her like usual."

"It was new," Olivia replied before I could answer. "Well, being together is new, but not wanting to be." She glanced over at me and scooted closer. Damn, she was good at this.

"Right," he scoffed. "Tell it to someone who didn't watch the two of you have to be separated at all of Tyler's birthday parties."

"Well, sometimes passion disguises itself as aggression." She turned to me, her chocolate-brown eyes pinning me in my seat. "Sometimes, someone makes you feel so much that you just don't know what to do with yourself until it all spills over." She ran her hand down my chest. "You know how it is when you affect each other like that... Oh, right, probably not." She snickered, cuddling into my side.

Alan's eyes narrowed for a second.

"Olivia's right." I put my hand on her thigh and inched it up slowly, a wide grin splitting my lips when I caught her gasp. "Come on, look at her." The mirth in her expression faded, her dark eyes wide as they bored into mine. "Who wouldn't want a woman this gorgeous?" I took her hand and laced our fingers together, the air between us thick and hot as the words fell from my mouth with the utmost sincerity because I'd meant every word.

Her lips pressed together in a hard line for a moment before that devious smile came back to play on that sexy mouth.

"Tyler likes to make me blush," she said on a giggle and slipped her hand away from mine. "Ouch!" she hissed, pressing her thumb into the palm of her hand.

"Are you okay, Olivia?" Mom asked with a concerned crease in her brow.

"Oh yeah, Helen. I'm fine." She glanced at me before aiming her sly grin at Alan. "I hurt my hand back in high school, and every once in a while, I feel it. The weather must be bringing it out."

Alan's jaw ticked as he glared at her across the table.

"Amazing how the past follows you," she said.

He cleared his throat and popped off his chair. "Come on, Simone. Let's get a real drink, not the cheap house wine on the tables."

Alan stalked away with his girlfriend, and I let out the laugh I was holding in once they were out of earshot.

"I probably shouldn't still bring it up, but he made that crack about the breadbasket and I couldn't resist. See?" she whispered, patting my knee. "I told you that I had your back."

I stretched my arm across the back of her chair and kissed her cheek. "Just this once, I'm going to admit you're right. Bringing you with me tonight was the best idea ever."

A blush filled her cheeks, and goose bumps prickled down her neck. I seemed to be good at this game too.

Even if it wasn't much of a game.

"Yeah, you're not a terrible date either, so far." She worried her bottom lip between her teeth. I remembered that mouth. And by *remembered*, I meant I was borderline obsessed. I'd always been attracted to her, but my constant irritation toward her kept me from ever wanting to make a move. What she said about aggression spilling over into passion was true because we were going to explode if we didn't stop acclimating so well into role play.

It was a little too easy to touch each other tonight. So natural that I couldn't stop doing it. My hand was back on her thigh, giving it a little squeeze before I sobered. I didn't need to drink tonight because I was already intoxicated by my childhood enemy turned fake date and real object of lust.

I glanced over at my parents and noticed they were watching our every move, as a lot of the people here tonight probably were. Maybe I was high on the crazy alliance we'd made or how good she felt next to me or the burning need to finish what our kiss started, but instead of dreading the hours we had to spend together, I didn't want the night to end.

My problem was what to do about it when it did.

ELEVEN
OLIVIA

"Is this a new thing now?" Tyler asked me as he swished around the pink liquid in his cocktail glass.

"Custom wedding cocktails? I've seen a few," I replied as I took another sip. The Mr. and Mrs. Bennett cocktail they conjured for Donnie and Cassandra was potent. I tasted rum, maybe a little coconut, and something else I couldn't pinpoint. I was no lightweight, but whatever this was shot straight to my head, and I was already loose enough in judgment tonight.

Tyler wasn't feeling much pain himself, loosening up after a few beers. It was good to see him laughing with Donnie at the bar earlier. Maybe he really wasn't that cranky and it was just some of the people in this room that made him that way. Usually that included me, but he seemed happy to have me with him. As much as I tried not to read into that, it was a struggle.

Pride swelled in my chest whenever I glanced at the cake he'd made. He blew off every compliment, saying it was a group effort by his staff, but the way he designed it was beautiful. The dark chocolate with the white roses cascading down the side was simple, different, and gorgeous.

"I've seen birthday parties with cocktails named after the guest of honor too. I have no idea how they come up with what to put into it."

"I could see you having your own cocktail at your next birthday party," Tyler teased, the corner of his mouth lifting. "You had everything else at your parties."

I gulped the last of the drink and set it onto the bar.

"I don't celebrate my birthday anymore."

His brows knit together as he placed his glass next to mine. "Right. You? I half expect the next May eleventh to be a bank holiday every year." He laughed until he caught my gaze, most likely noting the tension in my jaw that appeared whenever someone mentioned my birthday.

"I don't. And I don't want to discuss it," I snapped, regretting it when he flinched. The last thing I wanted was to go back to old Tyler and Olivia, the ones who sniped at each other all the time.

I darted my eyes away, exhaling a slow breath through my nostrils. "I'm sorry. It's a long story that I don't want to ruin tonight with. Okay?"

He nodded and seemed to let it go. I understood his confusion. I always lived for my birthday. My parents put on huge parties for their only child, and I reveled in every single one. Even after I'd turned thirty, I planned big dinners and trips with friends, treated myself to things weeks in advance. Then the universe showed me the price of being that selfish, and the past couple of birthdays all I'd wanted to do was forget. I spent them alone, hoping they'd pass as quickly as possible.

"Well, I know what I'd put in an Olivia cocktail," he rasped, leaning his elbow onto the bar. Grouchy Tyler was hot enough—playful-and-sexy Tyler was irresistible.

"What's that?" I asked, my words breathy as I tried to match his tone.

He tapped his chin. "I'd have to play with the mixers, but I know I'd start with Fireball."

"Whiskey?" I squinted back. "I'm not sure if that's a compliment or an insult."

He laughed, warm and low enough to make my toes clench in my high heels before he eased closer to whisper in my ear.

"Sweet at first, runs fire through you as it goes down, and ends up knocking you on your ass if you aren't careful. I think that's more or less accurate."

He pulled back, his eyes falling to my lips as they had countless times tonight. I'd thought he was about to kiss me every time, and the heat in his golden eyes left me breathless. Soon, the spell would be broken, and Tyler and I would be back to acquaintances, although the nasty bickering would hopefully not be our style anymore. The notion of going back to reality gave me a bone-deep sadness that I should have expected, but it plagued me all the same.

"There she is!"

Donnie's booming voice broke us out of the trance we'd fallen into. His smile was wide as he held his new wife's hand.

"Look, I need to shake your hand." Donnie extended his hand to me. "I always knew that field hockey story was bullshit."

My eyes widened as I whipped around to face Tyler.

"I know you were sworn to secrecy, but it's been, like, fifteen years and there was no way I couldn't tell Donnie. We've waited too long for someone to beat up that jerk. And since by family obligations we couldn't, well, tonight you became our new hero."

I laughed until Tyler's smile faded as he glanced over my shoulder.

"Sorry, we're so late. The weather is so awful, a ton of roads are closed. We almost didn't make it at all." A tall redhead fluttered by in my periphery and gave Cassandra a lukewarm hug. I remembered Amy from a few parties Helen had over the years. She always had a forced, saccharine smile with anyone she spoke to, and I had to hold back an eye roll each time I saw her. Of course, I set out to dislike anyone Tyler dated, but she truly rubbed me the wrong way.

They were the main reason I'd offered this favor in the first place, but we were having so much fun that I'd forgotten all about them. Now was the real showtime.

Amy rested her hand under the empire waist of her black dress as Jayden's gaze traveled around the room, looking everywhere but at us. I almost wanted to make a joke about him noting all the exits.

"Hi, Tyler," Amy said as Jayden wrapped an arm around her shoulder. All Jayden gave Tyler was a chin nod. The least you could do after stealing your best friend's fiancée was give him a decent greeting, but nothing about these two was decent.

"Hi, Amy. Jayden. I think you remember Olivia." Tyler snaked an arm around my waist. I didn't know how much he wanted to play us up now that we were in front of them, and I planned on just following his lead. When he shot me a crooked grin, I melted into his side and turned back to Amy and Jayden.

"Nice to see you again."

Amy's expression was all forced pleasantries and boredom when she first came in, but now as she looked between Tyler and me, her eyes narrowed to slits.

"You're here with Olivia?" Jayden barked out a laugh.

"You weren't the only one surprised," I shot back, letting my hand drift down the lapel of Tyler's jacket.

"Well, since you both always hated each other, I think you could understand that."

"You know what they say," I began, rubbing circles on Tyler's back, more for comfort than a show. "That line between love and hate is paper thin, right, babe?"

I worried I'd gone too far until Tyler's lips twitched.

"Very thin, sugar," he whispered and pressed a kiss to my temple.

I breathed him in, enjoying this charade for all it was worth.

"Dinner is still being served. Once you sit down we'll tell the wait staff to bring you something," Cassandra chimed in, breaking the tension.

"Thanks—we're starving. These two need to eat," Jayden crooned, sliding his hand over his wife's tiny belly, but Amy stiffened against him. As they walked away, the bitch in me hoped they were both always this miserable and karma served them well and quickly.

"It couldn't rain just a little harder so they couldn't come at all," Cassandra whined. "I'm sorry again, Tyler. I really can't stand her. I guess we have awful cousins in common."

Tyler smiled and waved a hand. "All good, really." His arm tightened around my waist even though Amy and Jayden were already out of sight.

"We're on our way to see the DJ. If we don't ask him to play the classics for at least an hour, the old people are about to riot." Donnie slapped Tyler on the arm. "See you guys later."

"*Sugar*?" I asked, raising a brow. "Not *honey*, not *sweetheart*. *Sugar* is what you came up with?"

He shrugged. "I'm a baker. It just came out. Take it as a compliment."

"Okay, I will." I squeezed his shoulder, unsure if we were still in the moment, but I couldn't not touch him. "Are you okay?"

He clicked his tongue against his teeth, leaning back. "You know what, I am. If they didn't think twice about fucking me over, they aren't worth having around or thinking about. Thanks for..." He dropped his chin to his chest before looking up at me. "Thanks for everything, Olivia. I mean that."

"My pleasure," I croaked out, unsure what to do with all that affection and gratitude in his eyes. I knew what I *wanted* to do—kiss him senseless and ask him if he wanted to keep pretending for maybe the next few years or so. But I couldn't do that. This was a favor for an old adversary who'd now become a new friend. That was enough of a gift, and I'd do well to leave it at that.

My gaze traveled to all the couples on the dance floor. At every party with a DJ, my father would request a salsa just to show off and always danced it with me. It was our thing at weddings. My dad and I had a lot of things like that together.

Things that didn't exist anymore because he didn't.

"Feel like dancing?" Tyler held out a hand.

"Seriously?" I crinkled my nose at him.

"Well, how could we call this a wedding date if we don't dance at least a little?" He stood and led me away from the bar by the hand, but by the time we arrived on the dance floor, the music had slowed. I stilled, unsure what he wanted to do or what we should do at that point. He tugged me to him by the arm, wrapping one hand around my waist while he took the other and pulled it to his chest.

I couldn't make out the song we danced to, too focused on

how close we were, how natural it was to sway back and forth like a real couple. Maybe it was the drinks, maybe it was the act we were putting on, but all I felt was real happiness tinged with despair when I thought of Tyler dropping me off later tonight.

"Are you okay?" Tyler asked when we left the dance floor.

"Of course." I forced a wide grin. The game was almost over, and I had to keep reminding myself that all of this was still just that, a game. It didn't matter how real it felt while I was in Tyler's arms or how natural it was when he took my hand or pulled me closer. It was for effect. A show. The absence of our animosity wasn't magically replaced with affection. The hope of this game of pretend bleeding into real life was something that had crept up on me—and it was time to start pushing it away.

Before I knew it, it was the dessert hour. We clapped for Donnie and Cassandra as they cut the cake despite the loud cracks of thunder outside. My cheeks ached from hours of laughing. In all the years I'd known Tyler—which was my entire life—I'd never seen him seem this happy. I thought it was the act at first, but he was never good at being phony.

That was my expertise.

I always faked it well. I pretended with friends and family that I was fine, that my heart wasn't broken, that it wasn't all my fault. Mom told me if I dropped the mask I'd find it easier to breathe. Tonight I'd let it slip and was gasping for air already.

I escaped to the ladies' room to get some air, the end of this awesome night looming like the rain pounding against the floor-to-ceiling windows. After I touched up my lipstick, I headed back toward the restaurant, almost falling back when a hand clutched my bicep in the dark hallway.

"I always knew, you know."

I turned to find an infuriated Amy glaring at me as if she was about to lunge.

"Always knew what?' I asked slowly.

She coughed out a humorless laugh. "I always knew something was going on between the two of you. He'd say over and over again how he couldn't stand you, but his eyes would track you at every damn party. I'd catch those little side conversations. Did you both think I was some kind of idiot? Between you and all his time with his stupid bakery. Thank God I got out like I did."

She scowled at me, seething as her nostrils flared.

"Got out like you did? Is that what you just said?" I stepped closer, the rage bubbling in my gut most likely evident on my face as she moved back. "Despite what you think, I can assure you that when you knew us, we were enemies, not lovers. Trying to explain away what you did is almost more despicable than doing it in the first place. That 'stupid bakery' is beautiful. He worked so hard for it, and you couldn't even let him enjoy his first day. Did you see how amazing that wedding cake was or how talented he is?"

My fists clenched at my sides as I continued, advancing as she retreated, a little fear in her eyes now replacing the audacity she came at me with.

"He deserved better than you. Than both of you. He's an amazing man who needed someone to support him, not whine like a baby that she wasn't getting enough attention and then use it to justify fucking his best friend."

I smiled as she squirmed against the wall. "Maybe you realized that you made a mistake. Good. Garbage like you deserves to be miserable, and Tyler only deserves good things. The best. Because that's what he is. Now, if you'll excuse me."

I turned on my heel, almost teetering on the stilettos I'd picked for tonight before I was pulled back again.

"Are you kidding me?" I yelled before I met Tyler's gaze.

"Easy, tiger," he whispered, folding me into his chest. The adrenaline from my outburst and the feel of him this close made me stumble for a moment.

"I guess Amy noticed us. She just—"

"I know. I heard." He cupped my face. Now I was full-on shaking, my jaw quivering as he swiped it with his thumb.

"You heard." I swallowed, my mouth gone dry as my heart pounded in my ears. "Everything?"

"I did." He nodded, his eyes hooded and dark. "And she's right. I *did* track you. Even when you drove me insane, I could never stop looking at you. That line you keep talking about *is* thin." He inched closer, so close our lips brushed. "So fucking thin."

Tyler pressed his mouth to mine, but unlike the kiss in the parking lot, our experiment to see if we could pull off affection, this was different. This was slow, deep, and soul-searing. His tongue glided against mine as I whimpered into his mouth, my body falling against him with each stroke as I raked my hands through his hair. Nothing about this kiss was an act. When he cupped my chin, dragging a finger down my throat to the top of my collarbone, my insides liquified along with my knees.

His mouth slanted over mine, deepening the kiss as he backed me against the wall. The show we'd set out to put on faded away, and I didn't care who was around or who saw us. All that mattered was the scratch of his stubble against my skin; the soft, warm glide of his tongue across my bottom lip before he sucked it into his mouth; and the growl escaping his throat as he glided his hand up my thigh, under the slit of my dress.

I had no idea who we became at that moment, but I had no interest in going back.

This was too much to hope for. I didn't want this to end or to ever stop kissing Tyler. And until I was forced to, I'd savor it for all it was worth.

TWELVE
TYLER

It was official.

I'd lost my goddamn mind.

Going into this tonight, I'd intended to be careful, but it was too easy between us. The flirting back and forth wasn't awkward or forced like I figured it would be when I'd first agreed to this crazy scheme. It felt natural, right.

Real.

In true reality, the whole thing was batshit crazy, but I was in too deep to bring myself out of it.

Whether I brought a date tonight or not hadn't mattered. It seemed ridiculous now to be worried about how I looked in front of cousins like Alan, who was nothing but a past-his-prime bully. Surprisingly, seeing Amy and Jayden wasn't the gut punch I'd expected it to be, even when he caressed her pregnant belly for effect. I'd felt indifference, not satisfaction at her discomfort.

Amy being jealous of Olivia was laughable when I'd first heard her come at Olivia. But the more I thought about it, the more sense it made. We'd attend whatever summer barbecue or family function that Mom had invited Carla and her family to, and I'd complain to Amy the entire way home about why they all needed to be included every damn time, reiterating over and over that Olivia was a viper and how I dreaded any event where I had to see her. Most times after I'd seen Olivia, I'd bitch about her afterward to whoever would listen.

Amy connected dots I never realized were there—or maybe never wanted to acknowledge—when she saw us together tonight. After what she did, she had a lot of nerve being pissed about anything when it came to us, but there was no denying that Olivia got under my skin. There were too many witnesses to the drawn-out arguments sparked by ridiculous things. A dirty look or under-the-breath comment, and we were off. We'd gotten more than a few raised brows when people saw us together tonight, but no one looked all that surprised.

Everything between us—the fighting, the tension, the denial of what we were really feeling all that time—finally boiled over. In this moment, despite the inappropriate display I knew we were putting on, nothing short of death would've torn my mouth or hands away from Olivia's body.

"You taste good," she croaked out as I ran my lips down her neck. She jumped in my arms when I nibbled her earlobe.

"So do you," I rasped. I wove my hand into her waves and took a pull, just like I had in a thousand fantasies where, despite our animosity, she held a starring role.

"Sweet as sugar," I whispered, smiling at her shaky chuckle vibrating against my lips as I dropped kisses down her throat to her shoulder.

"Such a dork," she chided. Her hands ran up and down my chest, stopping at one of the buttons under my tie. I sucked in a breath when she wiggled her red fingernail inside my shirt. My body jolted at the scratch. The thought of Olivia's naked body against mine almost made me blow in my suit pants.

Besides being sexier than I could handle, I'd seen Olivia in a new light tonight. I'd written her off as a spoiled brat a long time ago, but when she was on your side, she was fierce. A warrior. When I came out of the restaurant to look for her and heard her tirade against Amy, that wasn't acting. After all I'd said about her and to her over the years, she didn't have to defend me like that and shouldn't have wanted to. That was when the tiny bit of control I was grasping slipped, and I couldn't not have her.

A throat clearing behind me made us freeze.

I turned to find Donnie with his hand fisted against his mouth as if he were holding in a laugh.

"Sorry to be the one to interrupt, but the manager told me it's pretty bad out there. There's a ton of flooding, and a lot of the highway entrances are closed. They gave us a block of rooms that we didn't think we needed to use, but I wanted to offer it to you instead of trying to go home in this." He smirked, slapping my shoulder. "Up to you—let me know. I think your parents are taking a room and some of Cassandra's family, but I'll hold one for you."

"Thanks, Donnie." I steadied my hand against the wall, already hating breaking contact with Olivia. For the past hour, I'd been rehearsing what I'd say when I dropped her off tonight. I'd start with *Thank you* and *Maybe we can see each other sometimes as friends now that we learned how not to be at each other's throats*, but I wanted more than that. I just didn't know how that would work or if she would even consider it.

"It does look pretty bad out there." Olivia nodded at the windows at the front entrance, pounded so hard with sheets of rain that the parking lot was nothing but a blur. It would be a bitch to drive in, for sure, but a hotel room together held a different kind of danger.

It all depended on the risk we wanted to take.

"I'm not sure if you planned on an overnight stay when you agreed to this favor." I hovered over her, her body an inch away from mine, but we didn't touch. Her eyes were glassy, lipstick smeared across her swollen mouth. My hand went to my own mouth when I realized I probably looked the same, wiping away the evidence from our heated kiss that I couldn't see.

"I wouldn't mind. They'd probably give us double beds." Her gaze flicked to the floor, then back to me, expectant. The one thing Olivia didn't do was pull punches, but we'd never been here before, and I'd bet she was just as surprised as I was.

An ominous streak of lightning flashed outside and thunder boomed. This storm had been going on since the wedding started and wasn't supposed to let up until the morning. Staying in a hotel made the most sense, but if we spent the night together, I knew what it would mean. A couple of kisses had already fucked with our resolve enough. A whole night alone thrilled me as much as it scared the shit out of me.

"Olivia, you know as well as I do that it doesn't matter how many beds are in that room. I want you in *my* bed the whole fucking night. I want my mouth all over you until I'm so deep inside you, we'll feel each other for days."

I held her eyes, dark and pleading as she gasped, showing a weakness I'd never seen in her gaze. Her breaths were slow and steady, and neither of us blinked.

"If that's not what you want, you need to tell me now—"

"It's what I want." She grabbed the back of my neck and yanked my mouth to hers, kissing us both breathless. "Go tell Donnie yes, and let's get the hell out of here."

THIRTEEN
OLIVIA

"What room did they give us?" I asked, trying to keep the quiver out of my voice as Tyler and I made our way down the long hallway connecting the restaurant to the hotel elevators. Considering how we attacked each other against a wall only moments ago, it was laughable that we couldn't make eye contact now. The best thing for both of us was probably to cool off.

But that wasn't going to happen. The minute we slipped the key card into the lock, nothing would be the same. Everything had already changed.

"Three twenty-six," he answered, wholly focused on the elevator call button. He fiddled the white key card back and forth between his fingers until the loud ding startled us. He gestured for me to walk in, and I kept my gaze straight ahead as I turned to lean against the elevator wall.

Tyler seemed to be back to his old self with his rigid shoulders, impatience evident in every huff he made until we stopped on the third floor. I missed the carefree guy he was only minutes ago. We'd both become versions of ourselves that we didn't recognize tonight. The evening went exactly as it should have, and there was nothing else in it for either of us.

Or there shouldn't have been.

When the elevator opened on our floor, he stepped out, his hand hovering over the door for it to stay open as I made my way out of the elevator. I swallowed, my mouth suddenly dry, as I followed him to our room.

I knew what I wanted tonight, but as my gaze lingered on the hallway's ugly carpet pattern, I vowed to go with the flow and not force anything. Sure, Tyler said he wanted me during a heated moment, but maybe he'd gotten his senses back as the wedding came to a close. I'd take the nice memory, try to get some sleep even though Tyler would be only feet away from me, and move along with life.

When the lock beeped open, the first things I noticed were the two queen-sized beds. Relief and disappointment swirled through me as Tyler double-locked the door behind us.

"I told you they'd give us two beds." I laid my purse on the chair next to the desk. "This dress will be interesting to sleep in—"

Tyler cut me off with a kiss as he backed me against the wall.

"You aren't sleeping in this dress or by yourself." His hand drifted down my cheek, coasting down my neck, over my breast. "I don't think either of us is sleeping much at all tonight. Sure you're all right with that?"

His gaze was pinched, his eyes raking over me as if I were his last meal and he was dying to take a bite. To keep Tyler looking at me like that, just for a little while longer, I was so fucking sure.

Our mouths crashed together as I nodded, tearing at the buttons on his jacket until I yanked it off his shoulders.

"Where's the zipper?" He grunted out as his hand skated

up my thigh, spreading the already high slit wide enough to hear a tear.

"On the side," I breathed out, breaking from his embrace to feel around for the top. He swatted my hand away, holding my eyes as he tugged it down, the whir of the zipper and our ragged breathing the only sounds in the room.

He smoothed the dress off my shoulders until it fell, pooling at my feet.

"*Jesus Christ*. Look at you." He exhaled a long breath as his eyes roamed over my body. Chills and fire broke out on my skin along the path of his gaze. My bra and panties were still on, but I never felt more bare and exposed.

"Like what you see, Bennett?" I teased as I reached back to unhook my bra, but Tyler caught my hands.

"All me tonight, sugar." He shot me a lopsided grin and pulled me flush against his body, sliding his hands to my back. My breath caught in my throat as he unfastened one hook at a time, then tossed it on the floor next to my dress.

"So beautiful," he rasped, framing my face. "It was always so goddamn unfair how beautiful you are."

I gulped down the sudden lump scratching at the back of my throat. His mouth came back to mine as I slid his tie off and opened the buttons on his shirt.

"Wow," was all I could say. Tyler was all hard muscle, his skin smooth and hot under my fingertips. I feathered my hand down his chest, over the dusting of soft dark hair and down the V tempting me into his pants. He was so beautiful it almost hurt to touch him. I'd leave this room ruined, but I'd worry about that later. Right now, I wanted him every single way I could have him before the reality of who we really were came up with the sun tomorrow.

Tyler picked me up by the waist, dragging me over to the bed until we both fell back onto the mattress. For our entire lives, we'd had this constant competition. Each of us needed to have the last word and be in control during whatever dumb squabble we'd gotten into, mostly started by me over the years. One would go to walk away, the other would say something, and we'd be right back at it. From age five until adulthood, that was how we rolled. It exhausted us and everyone nearby.

Tyler wasn't one-upping me by holding my hands over my head as he ran his mouth all over my body, taking a nipple between his teeth and grazing his hard cock against my core. And when his lips came back to mine as he groaned into my mouth, our tongues tangling not in battle but in hunger, for the first time ever I submitted. And gladly.

This was the high I'd been chasing all my life.

I shut my eyes, savoring every single sensation so I'd remember it later. The scrape of his stubble against my stomach as his lips traveled over my body, the way he muttered a tortured curse when I hooked my leg around his hip, rocking against him and teasing us both. A shiver rolled down my spine from the dark desire in his eyes. I'd let him take whatever he wanted for as long as he wanted, as long as he wanted me.

"I want to touch you," I pleaded on a moan as he writhed on top of me. When he let go of my hands, I flipped us over, my mouth heading straight for his glorious chest, dragging open-mouthed kisses and bites down his torso until I got to his belt buckle. Locking eyes with Tyler, I slowly undid his belt, running my mouth over the bulge in his pants until I slid them down his thighs.

"Fuck, Olivia," he groaned, his head sinking into the pillow. I sucked him through his boxers, smiling wide when his hips lifted off the bed and his cock grew harder and bigger against my lips.

"If you keep doing that with your mouth, it's all over. Get up here," he growled.

"You don't want my mouth on you?" I asked, raking my nails over his abs as I trailed my lips up and down his length. I wanted him undone in every single way. His face was crumpled in a tortured grimace, sweat beading at his temple, and I loved it. *I* made him this crazy with need, and the pure joy of affecting him this way was more intoxicating than any drink we'd had tonight. I wanted him to explode in my mouth, across my breasts, and fill me up until he had nothing left.

"You're serious?" He squinted at me, sitting up on his elbows. "I've dreamed of my cock in your mouth for most of my life. But there's more I want first."

Tyler grabbed me under my arms and pulled me up, attacking my mouth with a scorching, bruising kiss. He hooked his thumb into the lacy waistband of my panties and dragged them down my legs. I chuckled until his hand grazed over my core, stroking back and forth at a slow pace.

"Feels like you're torturing the both of us, right? How long have you been this wet for me?"

"Always," I admitted, my legs flailing back and forth as his finger circled my clit.

"Get on top, now."

For once, I said nothing as I climbed on top of Tyler and straddled his waist.

"Do you have something? Please say you do."

"I do," he said, his eyes dark and full of heat. "But not yet."

He grabbed my hips and pulled me up to his chest.

"Hold on to the headboard, and keep your hands there." He scooted down the bed, spreading my thighs and settling them on his shoulders.

"Ride my face, Sanchez."

"What— Holy shit, Tyler!" I cried out as his tongue swiped

against my clit. He sucked on it hard enough to make my vision cloud up before kissing me deep, owning and torturing me with every glide of his tongue. I needed more friction, but I didn't move, afraid my thick thighs would somehow suffocate him in my lust-crazed haze.

"I said ride, Olivia," he growled, slapping my ass and bringing me closer to his mouth and snaking his tongue inside me. I banged my hand against the wall, not knowing what to do with myself and all this paralyzing sensation. The entire lower half of my body convulsed as Tyler tongue-fucked me without mercy, the beginnings of an orgasm coiling so tight I began to fear my own release.

One night with the man of my dreams was about to break me into nothing but shards of the tough girl I fought so hard to be.

"I'll kill you if I move," I croaked out, screaming when he went deeper and pressed his thumb against my clit.

"No better way to die," he murmured.

A guttural moan dragged out of his throat when, finally, I couldn't take it anymore and gripped the headboard, rocking against his face until my legs shook so hard I couldn't feel them.

"Just like that. Right there, please," I begged as Tyler dug his fingers into my thighs, moaning as his tongue curled inside me. My climax hit me fast and hard as I folded, resting my hand against the wall for purchase.

My eyes were still clenched shut when he moved me down on the bed. When I fluttered my lids open, his grin was wide and his mouth and chin were soaked with me. I raked a hand through his damp hair, brushing it off his sweaty forehead as his hazy eyes fixed on me.

"You *are* as sweet as sugar. Stay right there."

Tyler leaned over the bed and grabbed his wallet, sifting through it quickly before pulling out a foil packet.

I held out my hand, flashing a smile when he laid it on my palm.

"Make it quick, Sanchez. I need inside you before I lose my mind."

I tore it open at the corner and inched the condom down his length. He scowled, hauling me to him by the nape of my neck and plundering my mouth as he crawled on top of me. He slid right in with one thrust as I was still drenched, then moving slowly as he buried his head in the crook of my shoulder.

"Tyler," I breathed out, bucking my hips off the bed.

His handsome face flushed, wincing every time he slid in and out.

"Faster, harder," I begged. "Just take it all."

His forehead fell against mine as he granted my wish, pounding into me so deep and hard the mattress squeaked and drifted away from the wall. I blinked away the wetness pooling in my eyes and looped my arms around his neck, holding on tight.

Our mouths came together in a sloppy kiss until my legs went rigid again. Tyler's eyes widened, and he pulsed inside me, snaking his arm under my waist and pulling me closer before he collapsed on top of me.

"Did we break the bed?" I asked as he slid out of me and rolled onto his back. The headboard had separated from the mattress, the bed now inches from the wall and on a slant.

"I don't know." He turned to me with a wry grin, sliding a hand through my tangled curls. "And I can honestly say I don't care."

"I'll split the damages with you," I joked, despite already feeling the loss seep in.

He laughed and climbed off the bed. I rolled over, closing my eyes as I focused on the squeak of the bathroom faucet before the bed dipped behind me and Tyler climbed back in. I was surprised when he pulled me back into his chest and kissed my shoulder.

"Already tired, sugar?" he asked, burying his head in my neck.

I turned to face him, wincing at the new ache between my legs and trying like hell to ignore the one pulling at my chest.

"That was a pretty vigorous workout just now, so maybe a little." I pursed my lips and scooted up on the bed, pulling the sheet over me. "Why, you're not?"

A playful glint shimmered in his eyes. Smiles from Tyler were rare. At least, his smiles for me always were. This was a side of him I'd never seen, a long night of firsts for the both of us.

"It was a good workout, I grant you. But," he said, sliding his hand over the nape of my neck, "I don't think we're done yet." He brushed his lips over mine with a soft kiss, then one more. "At least I don't want to be."

He ran a finger along the edge of the sheet barely covering my breasts. "You were amazing tonight, Olivia." The sear of his gaze made my heart pound. "Not just this, but—" He sucked his bottom lip into his mouth before he took in a long breath through his nostrils. "I liked having you with me. I liked it a lot."

I leaned in, cutting him off with a kiss. I liked being with him too, but we were still in character. He may not have realized it yet, but I couldn't help taking more of what I thought I'd never have while I had the chance.

I rolled on top of him, straddling him again as I let the sheet drop from my body.

"I told you it wasn't a bad idea," I whispered before

pressing my lips against his. My mouth was raw and chafed from our desperate kisses, but he tasted too good to stop. I ground against him once, and his erection came back to life under me.

"Not bad at all," he said, his fingers delving into my hair as he slanted his mouth under mine.

No, we weren't done yet. I was a stellar actress, but I had no clue how to not act like I wanted more when there was nothing left.

FOURTEEN
TYLER

The far-away chime of my alarm and distant buzzing jolted me out of a dead sleep. I could barely see as I leaned over, feeling around the floor for my pants, and dug out my phone.

Eli: *I know you said you're coming in late, but just wanted you to know we had a small leak from all the rain. I handled it, and there doesn't seem to be much damage. Crazy storm, right?*

Crazy was one way to look at it.

I turned to Olivia, naked under the sheet next to me, her disheveled hair spilling over the pillow. There was only so much I could reason away from being in the moment. From the time I picked her up until a couple of hours ago, it was as if I'd stepped into another world. The girl who tortured me as a kid, then both tortured and tempted me as an adult drew me under a spell I couldn't explain.

Now we were in the light of day and there would be no excuse. When she opened her eyes, the moment would be over, but I wasn't sure if I wanted it to be.

Tyler: *Thanks. I'll be in in a couple of hours.*

I didn't want to get into how I'd stayed at the hotel overnight or who I was with. We'd put on a pretty good show for my whole family, but at some point, it stopped being an act. Or maybe it wasn't one to begin with. I'd have some explaining to do to my parents about what they saw between us—and what I was sure they heard happened against the wall by the bathrooms last night.

First, I had to figure out what that explanation was, beyond the fact that I'd gone from lusting after my childhood enemy to being infatuated with her and having the best sex of my life last night, even though that was everything in a nutshell.

I raked a hand down my face and groaned. I thought I was screwed before, but this was so next-level fucked I doubted there was even a name for it.

"Is it still raining?"

I turned to Olivia's throaty voice, soft and groggy with sleep. Her hair fell over her forehead in chocolate waves, and I had to fist my hand at my side not to brush it away.

We were different now, but I wasn't sure what to call us. We weren't enemies anymore, but despite last night, we weren't lovers either, even if the image of Olivia's naked body was branded into my brain. My eyes were glued to her while she stirred under the sheet, hoping to catch just one more glimpse.

"No, it's nice and clear." Unlike my head right now as it took a long minute to answer her question.

"I guess we should get going, see what the damage is like at home." She leaned over the side of the bed, keeping the sheet over her as she plucked her dress and underwear from the floor. "No sense in lingering, right?"

"Right," I replied with a husky rasp, imagining what it

would've been like if we'd woken up tangled up in each other instead of looking for the quickest escape. I had the confusing inclination to both leave as quickly as possible and to say the hell with it and fuck Olivia until they made us leave.

When she closed the bathroom door behind her, I stood from the bed, laughing to myself at all the times I couldn't wait to get away from her compared to the pang in my chest now at the thought of taking her home.

I pulled on my boxers and suit pants and was buttoning my shirt when the door creaked open.

"This doesn't look like a walk of shame at all, does it?" Olivia shot me a sleepy grin as she dipped her head, motioning to her dress from last night. "I'll look completely ridiculous in the lobby, but I guess a lot of wedding guests didn't plan on staying." She lifted her gaze to mine, the side of her mouth curving up. "I know we didn't."

She'd washed the makeup off her face and her hair was tied into a messy bun, but she was every bit as breathtaking as she was last night. And as my father had pointed out at our table, I was still drooling over her.

"You still look beautiful. I mean..." I trailed off, rubbing the back of my neck. "You're fine—we're all walking out in our clothes from last night."

She nodded as she scooped her shoes off the floor. The one thing Olivia and I never had was a loss for words for each other, and now the air crackled between us, charged with things unsaid and unfinished.

"Think it's early enough that I can walk barefoot into the lobby?" she asked, dangling her shoes at me. "My feet usually need a day to recover from these."

"I think so. I can call ahead so the car is waiting for us."

Her eyes bored into mine, dark and wide. The pull to her

was so strong, I had to lean against the wall to prevent myself from closing the distance between us. The real light of day wouldn't show until we got out of this room, which I both couldn't wait to do and dreaded at the same time.

The silent walk to the elevator unnerved me even more. We were alone as we descended the three floors down. I tore my eyes away from the graceful slope of her neck and tried like hell not to fixate on what her curves were like under that wrinkled dress or how much I wanted to tear it off her again.

We still said nothing as we waited for the keys to my truck at the front counter, but Amy's voice came across loud and clear behind us.

"Thirty minutes? You can't get our car faster than that?"

Jayden tried to shush her in a loud whisper, but she groaned in response. I didn't turn around and didn't need to. I no longer cared if they were miserable or what they'd done. If not for them, I would have come to this wedding alone and probably gone back to the same miserable life today. I had the weird urge to thank them. So many things felt clearer, lighter, other than what to do about the beautiful woman I felt more than saw standing next to me.

"Hey, sorry about that." I recognized Donnie's voice. "Thanks to the wedding and the storm, they were at capacity last night. The garage is across the street."

"It's fine," Amy replied with a loud huff.

Was she always this petulant? I honestly couldn't remember. I turned to nod good morning at my cousin.

"Oh, hey, guys. I guess you're waiting a long time too. Sorry about that," he sighed, shaking his head. "Last night was supposed to be an easy wedding."

"No apologies needed," Olivia said next to me. "We had a great time."

"I know," Amy scowled at the both of us, looking Olivia

over with a laughable level of disdain. “We were in room three twenty-four.”

The valet handed Jayden a key, and he held it up to Amy, giving us all a quick wave as he pressed his hand against her lower back to guide her toward the entrance.

Olivia’s eyes danced when I cut her a look. Sex between us last night was loud, destructive, and unforgettable. We had been too into each other to notice the room damage or think of who could hear us. I was sure we gave our neighbors on the other side of us a good show too.

“Sorry,” Olivia said in a loud whisper, sliding her arm into the crook of my elbow and cuddling into my side. “And after you guys were so quiet too.”

Amy leveled us with one last glare and headed out the glass entrance doors.

I gazed down at Olivia, both of us stifling a smile. “Couldn’t resist?”

“What do the kids call that? Next level achievement unlocked?”

Her lip curled into a smirk, and the effort it took to hold myself back from kissing her was exhausting.

Donnie looked between us, laughing as he approached. “Well, thanks for the cake and for coming.”

I took Donnie’s extended hand. “My pleasure. And,” I leaned closer to whisper, “let me know if there are any additional charges to our room.”

He waved me off with a chuckle.

“It’s fine. Safe drive back. I heard there are some trees down, so be careful.”

When I retrieved the keys from the valet, I held out my hand for Olivia to walk ahead, allowing myself one more chance to ogle her from behind. The more I tried to figure out what to say or do next, the more clear it became that I didn’t have a fucking clue. The only thing I could say with certainty as I stole another glance at her profile when she fastened her seat belt next to me was that every second of last night was worth it and I didn't regret any of it.

Now if I could only figure out what the hell to do about it.

FIFTEEN
OLIVIA

The ride home was quiet and painful. There was a better rapport between us, but I almost wished for the old days of nasty little quips back and forth. At least that was easy and familiar. This, as much as I had struggled to name it since waking up, was a weird kind of limbo that had me constantly searching for the right thing to do or say.

We exchanged pleasantries on the way back to my apartment, noting a couple of downed trees or errant branches on the road, but as far as the mind-blowing sex we had until the wee hours of the morning? Not a single word. I smiled, thinking of the way we'd left the hotel room. Even after attempting to straighten out the sheets, it looked like a war zone, and I guessed it sort of was. I should have stepped out of the room victorious because I finally had Tyler's undivided attention, and for one glorious night, he was all mine.

But with every step toward the elevator and then trudging barefoot to Tyler's car, my chest had grown tight, squeezing harder each time I tried to rub away the ache. What did I expect? After years of bickering and hating each other, one night—no matter how amazing it was—would make us fall in love?

Part of me, a pretty large part, wanted to nestle against him when I woke up. Bury my head into the crook of his shoulder and drag kisses down his chest. Slow, sleepy morning sex followed by breakfast in bed was a fantasy, but one that my brain kept playing out over and over again.

"Be careful walking inside," Tyler told me after he cut off the engine. I'd been so buried in my thoughts that I hadn't realized he'd already pulled up in front of the house. "Branches are down everywhere, and since you have no shoes on you may get cut."

"I'll be fine. I've come home barefoot before." I held up my shoes. "After a night of dancing in stilettos, I've learned that walking home barefoot even on the ice is the better alternative."

"I'm sure you have," he said with a tiny lift pulling at the corner of his mouth.

Of course he thought that. I was Olivia the party girl, the spoiled only child who didn't care about anything beyond a good time and herself. Even when that was me, it wasn't all of me. Tears stung my eyes as I released my seat belt. Even if I was the one with the inappropriate romantic aftershocks from spending the night together, I hoped that maybe he saw me just a little differently now. That maybe by helping him last night, I showed him more of me than he'd realized after knowing only the petulant and bitchy version our entire lives.

But he didn't hate me anymore. We'd go back to our lives, minus a little sparring when we had to see each other. I at least had that now, and going forward, I would figure out a way to make it enough.

He grabbed my arm before I could open the door.

"Thank you," he said as he leaned over and brushed my

cheek with a kiss. His lips were still soft and warm, his morning stubble leaving a little more scratch across my skin than last night. "This meant a lot to me. All of it. I always knew that I was carrying around a lot that I didn't need to, but until last night I never could shake it. I feel a little lighter today, as stupid as it sounds. We made a good team." He shot me a crooked grin, and I smiled back, hoping I didn't look like my heart was melting inside my chest.

"I told you I was happy to help. Least I could do, right?" I sputtered out a laugh, darting my eyes away from his heavy stare because it was too much.

A couple of curls slipped out of my bun and fell over my face. Tyler tucked a lock of hair behind my ear before I could brush it away. I pushed my tongue into the roof of my mouth, the only way to stop the tears threatening to cascade down my cheek. He still didn't bring up the sex out loud, but the way he cupped my cheek and let his thumb graze my jaw was enough of an acknowledgment. This wasn't a show or appeasing our mothers in trying to get along. He was touching me, in the privacy of his car, with no one around but us.

With Tyler this close, it was hard to keep my expectations as low as I'd wanted to.

"You're all right, Sanchez."

"Thank you," I replied, breathless. "That game of yours may not be so bad after all."

I climbed out, not looking back as I carefully walked to my apartment. After I unlocked my side door, I noticed Tyler still parked out front, watching me. I nodded another goodbye and pushed my side door open as quickly as possible.

Leaning against it once I locked it, I sank to the floor. I was a puddle of sequins and feelings, and I needed to peel both off me as quickly as possible.

I pulled myself together enough to stand, setting my shoes

on the rack in my bedroom before I moped to the bathroom. Smelling like Tyler and sex all day wouldn't help me get my head screwed on straight.

Morgan was right. Sex with Tyler was epic because it was the payoff after years of buildup. All our fights were foreplay that bled into last night. Our mothers would be thrilled we finally got along once they found out, and I was sure they would. They knew we spent the night at the hotel, and whoever hadn't seen us against the wall had probably heard about it by now.

"Olivia?" And speaking of, my mother's voice drifted from the hall as she knocked on my inside door. I laughed to myself, thinking of when I'd lived upstairs as a teen and in my early twenties, trying to cover up all I'd done with a boy the night before. I hadn't come home from doing anything with anyone in a long time, and my kiss with Tyler was too public to attempt a denial.

I guessed odd news traveled fast.

"Hey, Mom," I breathed out when I opened the door. My mother pursed her lips as she looked me over, her brow almost reaching her hairline while she leaned against the doorjamb.

"Looks like it was some wedding."

"You could say that." I sighed, dragging a hand down my face. "I was about to get into the shower. I'll come upstairs and fill in all the blanks from whatever Helen already told you if you'd like."

"How about coming upstairs for dinner later, and we can talk—or not talk—about anything *you'd* like?"

What was there that my mother didn't know? I spent the night with Tyler, and we were seen *together*—you didn't have to be a genius to figure out the rest. There was more to last night for me, but I wasn't ready to say it out loud. My mother's warm gaze soothed my turbulent soul because she already knew those parts of last night too.

"Sounds good, Mom."

She squeezed my shoulder, and I smiled at her.

When I stepped into the shower, I let the hot water pound on my scalp and thought about my mother's story of falling in love with my father and how rejection could seem more terrifying than simply being hated.

She was spot on because I'd gladly take "antichrist in heels" over just a woman Tyler knew but didn't want.

SIXTEEN
OLIVIA

"Here, take this upstairs." My abuela shoved two tin trays of food into my arms.

I kissed her cheek, then looked at the pounds of food almost burning my hands.

"There are only five of us today, unless you know something I don't," I teased, cracking up at the dirty look she leveled me with.

"Ah." She waved me off, peeling off her peacoat and draping it over the coat rack in the hallway. It was chilly for late September, but both of my grandmothers always dressed as if they'd just gotten a tip about a blizzard at the slightest breeze.

"Go, Livie." She pushed me in between my shoulder blades, which was about eye level for her. The big joke was always how a big man like my father came from a tiny thing like her. "The food will get cold."

I shook my head and rushed up the stairs as fast as I could with two heaping trays of food. Today was my parent's anniversary... or should've been. My grandmothers and Helen came over last year and spent the day reminiscing about their wedding while taking turns laughing and crying. Mom was drained by the end of the day, but they'd left her with a wide smile on her face. I guessed they were making it a tradition, and I was glad, especially since I was here tonight if she needed me after they all left.

I appreciated the sentiment, but reminiscing about my father was still painful for me. I remembered him every day, all the time. I missed how we used to hunt for the best restaurants or how he'd tease me about whatever Yankees player I had a crush on that year while we watched games together. He was probably a big reason I took up this influencer foodie side gig and usually dined alone. Being solo let me remember him quietly. The joy of finding something delicious, chuckling to myself when I learned a popular dish didn't come close to the hype. It was almost as if he was with me, breaking apart what was great or not so great about it.

Everyone would leave sad today but content in sharing their love for all things Javier Sanchez, but I would be just as angry and guilty because he should've been here. I'd head downstairs and relive my last birthday dinner, recalling the inkling that he wasn't feeling well yet letting him blow us off. I'd dissected that night a million times in my head.

There were too many what-ifs for me to accept anything.

"Wow—looks like both of us won't be cooking this week," Mom said before scooping the trays from my arms and bringing them into the kitchen.

"I doubt I'll be eating much this week after today," Helen told me over her shoulder as she scrubbed a dish in the sink. My eyes fell to the drainboard and my parents' wedding china.

"We're using the good dishes today?" I asked, the sting at the sight of the dishes taking away the heart drop of seeing Helen for the first time since Donnie's wedding. None of us had talked about what happened, including Tyler and me. We hadn't spoken in two weeks, even though I'd started and deleted about ten texts.

Stirring the pot with Tyler was easy. Reaching out to him as a friend, or at least someone who he didn't despise anymore, just to see how he was—that seemed complicated as hell. I'd never had this issue with other men. Shyness was not me, and I was annoying myself at how immature I was by trying to appear aloof. Maybe he thought I was the same brat as always and that night didn't mean anything to me. But it did. And silly me wanted to know that it meant something to him too.

I'd half hoped having sex with Tyler would get him out of my system, but I was smart enough to know that never worked. A taste of something you knew you'd never get again only made you want more of it.

"Helen and I stumbled upon them in the closet just now, and I thought, what are we saving them for? I didn't want fancy dishes, but your grandmother and aunts thought they were some kind of a necessity when you got married. In over thirty years, we used them three times." She chuckled to herself, shaking her head. "Today is a celebration, sort of."

"Absolutely," Helen chirped as she dried her hands. "Good to see you, Olivia."

"You too, Helen." I went over to the sink and gave her a hello hug. She squeezed tighter for a moment before pulling back. I was sure my grandmothers would be all over me today too. No one acknowledged how I was struggling out loud, but the looks and the long hugs were both a comfort and a torment. I appreciated the extra love but had a hard time truly believing that I deserved it.

"Still trying to one-up me, Carmen?" Nana hugged Abuela with a long sigh.

"Keeps me going, Maria." She hugged her with a quick pat

on her back. "Now, are we going to chat about dishes or are we going to eat?"

"I'll get the plates," I said, a smile pulling at my lips. They always had a friendly competition, but there was never any true animosity between them. Nana was short too, although Abuela was the smaller of the two. Both still had their hair and nails done every week, and I aspired to be that beautiful in my eighties.

My grandfathers passed away when I was young, but I had all the grandparent love I could ever want. Uncle Frankie and his wife lived out west, and we'd see them for the occasional holiday, and my father was an only child like me, so I was the queen of the grandchildren, as my dad liked to say while I was growing up.

I had to take both pernil and chicken parmesan with a side of rice and pasta once we sat down to avoid an argument. I'd put on my loosest leggings earlier, knowing I could eat my grief to my heart's content.

I didn't say much as everyone chatted about nothing, eyeing my mother to see if she was eating or crying or both. She'd smile extra wide, but that didn't hide her glassy eyes. At least from me. I noticed and felt every ounce of pain etched in her features, wishing I could make it better and hating myself for not preventing it in the first place.

"How is it two years already?" Mom finally said, flicking a lone string bean back and forth with her fork on her plate. "Do you know what the first thought in my head was this morning?" Her watery gaze swept across the table. "That I didn't get a card for him. Javier always got the cards first. A couple of times I forgot and he'd swear it didn't matter, but there was always a card waiting by the coffeemaker for me on every birthday or anniversary."

I set my fork down, wishing I'd known that so I could have

set out my own card for her today. My parents had that epic kind of love even after all the years they were together. They had their private jokes and other little intimacies only they shared.

Now all Mom had were the memories.

"Javier was always like that," Abuela said. "Even as a little boy and later a rotten teenager, he never forgot the important things. Although before you, he tried to be cool about it." She muttered some Spanish under her breath as she dabbed her blue-shadowed eye with a napkin. "You made him *loco*."

Mom draped her hand around her eyes, her shoulders shaking with a laugh even as I spotted tears snaking down her face.

Helen looped her arm around Mom's shoulder. "I remember those days. How about we clear this off and have some dessert? Thanks to my baker son, we have a good variety today."

"That wedding cake was so beautiful," I blurted. Where the hell had that come from? I'd been careful not to talk or ask about Tyler all afternoon. I missed him, which was ridiculous since I'd hardly seen him in recent years, but the entire night we spent together was that damn unforgettable.

"It was," Helen agreed. "He's talented and a hard worker. I didn't give him the credit he deserved when he first opened his bakery, so I'm trying to make up for it. I was so glad to see both of you having such a good time together at Donnie's wedding a couple of weeks ago."

"Together?" Nana's brows pinched while Abuela's shot up.

"Didn't you used to pick on him when you were small?" Abuela tsked and turned to Nana. "She was so mean."

I exhaled a long breath when Nana responded with a slow nod.

"That poor kid. Livie never gave him any peace."

"*Sí,*" Abuela agreed as Mom and Helen snickered beside me.

They didn't even know how I'd continued the torture in our teenage years. A shiver rolled up my spine as Tyler's face flashed in my head, jaw clenched, eyes narrowed to slits, when he'd said he'd known I flirted with his friends to get a rise out of him. I'd gotten a different rise out of him later, but there were too many mothers and grandmothers in this room to fantasize about that memory.

"I wasn't very nice to Tyler, no. I came along as a favor, let's just leave it at that." The chair screeched beneath me as I popped up. I gathered the empty plates and carried them to the sink, not lifting my head to the four pairs of eyes I felt zeroed in on me.

I reached up on the high shelf of my mother's cabinet for the large tray she always used for desserts when slow footsteps came up behind me.

"You still like that boy." Abuela sighed. "I knew you did. *Qué pasa?*"

"Nothing is going on, Abuela." I set the tray down harder than I'd meant to. "We're friends, maybe. At least not enemies. Like you said, I was mean."

"I think that's pie." She motioned to the smaller box. "Bring it here and sit down."

I knew better than to argue with her, so I found dessert plates, the large cake knife, and two forks for us.

"Now," Abuela started as she slid the string off the box. "What happened at the wedding?"

"We put on an act for his family and his ex-fiancée. It was fun, and it didn't feel like too much of an act by the end of the night."

Or to begin with.

She cut a piece of the chocolate cream pie and slid it to me on a plate.

"Did you tell him that?"

"No," I said, holding in a moan at the first bite. Tyler was talented with his hands, that wasn't a question.

"Because you're like your father. Feelings scare you. They scared the shit out of him too. But once he gave in..." She motioned behind her to the dining room. "That marriage was one for the ages. All that love, a beautiful child." She reached over to squeeze my hand. "But he had to stop being *estúpido* first." She pushed off the chair and leaned in to plant a kiss on the top of my head. "Finish the pie. I'll take the cookies inside. Think about it."

"Abuela," I called out to her. "You were right. I was mean, and you don't even know how mean, but how can I make up for all of that? What if it's too late?"

She turned on her orthopedic shoe, lifting her tiny shoulder.

"It's only too late when you don't do anything at all."

SEVENTEEN
TYLER

"She's cute." Eli pushed my phone at me, tapping on the screen. "DM her and see what happens."

I took it back with a groan. A root canal was more exciting and promising than searching for someone to date on an app. After the wedding, assured I was totally over Amy and her dick of a husband but confused as hell over Olivia, in a weak moment I let him download the stupid dating app he'd been pushing on me for months.

I scrolled along her profile. She was cute and seemed normal. While I appreciated the boldness of some of the women on this app, actually noting that they were looking to get pregnant in a year was extra pressure I couldn't handle.

But her hair was blonde and short, without any thick, dark chocolate waves. Since the night of Donnie's wedding, I'd become obsessed with Olivia's hair—or allowed myself to call it an obsession after all these years of fixating on it. Every time I pictured sifting my fingers in the silky strands and pulling her in for a kiss, my dick twitched in my pants.

"Why are you making this so difficult?" Eli sighed. "For fuck's sake, just pick one. Maybe have a little dinner or a drink if you don't want to overextend yourself or even get laid. Just get back in the game. You aren't proposing marriage. You've been less tense lately, but maybe this will finally get rid of that perpetual scowl you always have."

I doubled it since now my game only mattered with one person.

After spending the night with Olivia, none of these girls compared. There were some beautiful women on this app, but as I browsed through, none of them caught my eye because none of them were Olivia.

A sigh of relief ran through me when I didn't find her as I swiped through all the eligible women that matched my profile. But why would she be on this app anyway? Men had flocked to Olivia for as long as I could remember. She could date a hundred guys with the crook of her finger if she wanted to.

The thought made me sick enough to throw my phone down onto the counter.

"Tyler," Tegan called with a panicked voice as she rushed to the back. "We need some help at the counter. There's a big line."

"A big line is good. Why do you look so freaked out about it?" Eli asked, snickering as he looked over at me.

"It is, but it's out the door."

My jaw dropped when I jogged to the front, and sure enough, the line was so long I couldn't tell where it ended. We had a healthy stream of customers throughout the day, but this was something I'd never seen and wasn't in the least bit prepared for.

"They're all ordering the same thing—chocolate cream pie," Tegan whispered over my shoulder. "Most of them are getting extra cookies or pastries, but we sold out of the four you had in the display and already have orders for twenty more. I don't even know what kind of timing to give any of them."

"It's okay, T. Weird but okay." Chocolate cream pie becoming such a hot item was strange. Sometimes we'd get increased demand on certain seasonal things during the year, but I couldn't explain this.

"Do you think I could pick it up by the weekend?" An excited customer asked Staci, one of my cashiers. "I've been dreaming about it ever since I saw it on Instagram."

No. It couldn't be.

I ran to the back to grab my phone off the counter and headed straight to Olivia's Instagram page. I'd been looking—or stalking—on and off but hadn't checked in a couple of days. Her last post was a slice of chocolate cream pie on a fancy dish with the bakery tagged as the location.

Today, foodies, I decided to do something different. I've taken you with me to a ton of restaurants, but what is better than dessert from the local bakery? I've always thought of chocolate cream pie as the unsung hero of desserts, and from Hey, Batter on Sunrise Highway, it's a delicacy. With its flaky crust and rich chocolate slathered with whipped cream, this baker knows exactly what he's doing—making his customers beg for more.

A smile tugged at my mouth as I heard it all in Olivia's voice. The post was dated yesterday evening and already had over ten thousand likes. I'd have to make a giant restock order and was looking at a long night of baking, but this was an amazing opportunity I never thought I'd ever get and couldn't pass up. We earned the occasional social media recommendation when someone posted a birthday cake or pie on a holiday that would attract a few extra customers, but never had a demand this high or this quick.

Still, I'd make it work. And if they were buying additional items, I could keep them coming back.

Olivia Sanchez was full of surprises.

Before I did anything though, I finally found the balls I'd been missing for weeks and dialed her number.

"Hey, Tyler, what's up?"

My heart leapt in my chest at the sultry voice floating in my ear. I was an eternal fool for this girl and had to do something about it, but I was too busy right now to figure out what.

"Hello, your majesty. The line is around the block and all the customers seem to be ordering the same thing. Any idea why?"

"I may have a little idea." She chuckled. "Helen brought your chocolate cream pie over to my mom's yesterday, and it was so damn good. That picture was of the second slice I had. I'm glad it's bringing people in. I told you I had a little power."

If she only knew the power she had—especially over me. Not just pissing me off as we grew up, but how she'd invaded my almost every thought for weeks.

"Little power?" I scoffed. "I have to go get enough ingredients to make pies all night and probably all day tomorrow. I don't know how to thank you."

"You don't have to thank me. I'm very happy you're getting new customers, but if I didn't think this pie was so good, I wouldn't have recommended it. It's a big reason I keep this quiet, so family and friends don't ask me for promo when I don't feel comfortable doing it. I would have made that post whether I knew you like I do or not. So enjoy it—you deserve it."

The idea of Olivia *knowing me like she did* brought back all the memories I'd been trying to forget. Despite being adversaries for our entire lives, sex was never that incredible with anyone else.

"Know of anyone I could put to work tonight? Help me

navigate through all this good fortune they dropped into my lap?"

I smiled at her chuckle.

"The last time I baked anything was with you and my Easy-Bake Oven. But I could stop at the store if you tell me what to get and how much of it?"

"A few of my bakers are coming back in at eleven, and I have enough stuff to keep things going before then, but I could text you a list and then help you bring it in."

A long pause lingered between us. Why couldn't I just ask to see her again? Not just to thank her, not just for fucking groceries, because I wanted to. Because the one night we shared wasn't enough.

"Sure," she finally said. "I can do that. And even if I have no baking skills, I can at least clean up. Can't have you make my recommendation lose its validity, right?"

"Exactly. Can't let that happen, now, can we?" My cheeks ached from my wide grin as I leaned against the counter.

"All right, I'll be there. Now stop wasting time. Hang up and text me what you need. I can be there around five."

"Okay," I said, already anxious from the anticipation of seeing her again. As a child, I'd just felt dread when my mother would warn me that Olivia was coming by. How times had changed but, once again, Amy was right. Olivia had captured my focus and thoughts for longer than I'd wanted to admit.

"It may be a late night. Half the cookies in the display are gone and most of the cakes in the window," Eli said, leaning against the wall. "We're gonna need a bigger place."

"Don't get cocky—it's a rush for the moment. Let's give them what they asked for and hope they come back." I shrugged, trying to act like a thousand butterflies weren't ricocheting around my stomach from all the possibilities swirling around in my head.

I exhaled a long gust of air, squaring my shoulders before stepping back outside. My eyes fell on my cousin Ross, chatting with a confused Staci as he held his wallet open.

"Oh, hey, Tyler," he said when he noticed me. "I was just letting your cashier know about the family discount you always give me."

"Hmm, about that," I started, crossing my arms over my torso as I made my way over. "It's too busy to give discounts right now. As you can see, the line is out the door so I can't bother my staff with who does or doesn't get a special price. You being a numbers guy and all, I'm sure you understand. I hope the kids enjoy the cookies."

I turned, hiding my smile until I pushed through the swinging door into the back.

EIGHTEEN
OLIVIA

"So what can I do?" I asked Tyler after we'd brought everything in. "As I said, I have no baking skills, but I can clean up after you or something."

"Just making the trip for me was plenty." He lifted the bags onto one of his counters and started unpacking. My eyes fell to the flex of his biceps as he pulled out each item. Other than the unfortunate cake batter incident from our childhood, I'd never seen him in action before. As he set everything up, it reminded me of his baseball days. I was always captivated by his focus and effortless skill. He had a masculine grace that was mesmerizing and sexy as fuck.

When he turned his head to smile at me, my knees wobbled. As usual, I soaked up attention from Tyler like a needy sponge. I honestly gave him a recommendation because he deserved it. I never thought I'd see him again other than some kind of function our mothers planned. I wanted to do this for him not because I wanted to connive a way back into his life but because that pie and his bakery earned it.

Although when he'd asked for help tonight, I'd reached for my car keys before we even hung up. Morgan and my family had always noticed how I felt about Tyler, but did he? I'd spent years torturing him because I couldn't say the words. If he ever truly paid attention, even in my bitchiest of moments, I wouldn't have had to. I was never sure if I should be relieved or sad that he never saw through my act.

"If you're going to stay back here," Tyler said as he pulled an apron off the wall, "it gets messy." He held it up and draped it over my head. We locked eyes for a moment, the brush of his touch against my chin as he set it on my shoulders sending a path of goose bumps down my back. His golden eyes were dark as they searched mine. Something about the way he was looking at me, as if what he was seeing was too much for him to take, reminded me of the moment he asked where the zipper was on my dress.

But we didn't talk about that. Or at least we hadn't yet. As ballsy as I was, I couldn't find it in me to bring it up.

"Thanks," I squawked out as I tied the apron around my waist.

"My goal is to bake as many crusts as I can and set most of the filling in the fridge. When the guys come back in later tonight, they can put it all together. I never thought I'd have trouble finding enough room to keep up with customer demand."

I shrugged, trying to be cool despite the flutters in my belly just from being this close to him. "You should have. Maybe you should think about expanding."

"You aren't the first one to say that today. I'll ride this out and see if it sticks." He lifted a shoulder. "I'm a low-expectations kind of guy. That way I'm not as disappointed later if something happens."

"I get that." I crossed my arms and leaned against the wall. "But when you're as talented as you are, you need to dream a little big sometimes."

"Well, thanks for the vote of confidence," he said as a bashful smile tilted his mouth. "You know, giving my mother the chocolate cream pie was an accident. She asked for apple, but I was out."

"Some things are meant to be, I guess. But I'd bet the apple is just as amazing."

He lifted a shoulder. "It did okay around Thanksgiving time last year. If this keeps up over the next couple of months, I may need to double staff over the holidays since it was busy enough around then."

"See, it's good to plan." I jabbed his shoulder, making him laugh.

"Mom said it was your parents' anniversary, so she left with pounds of cookies and pastries, plus the pie and a cake."

"It was. Mom's second one without my dad."

Tyler stopped setting up the mixer, placing his hands on the counter as he turned to face me. "How is Carla? Mom always says she's holding her own. She's always so upbeat when I see her, but—"

"But she's still heartbroken. They were best friends and did everything together." I shifted against the wall. "I worry about her all the time. Dad looked out for her, and now she's all alone."

It was the main reason that I'd come back. She always sounded so lost over the phone, and when I was staying with her more often than at my apartment, the move made sense.

"Mom said she hasn't been sick in a long time. She watches her too, if that makes you feel any better."

"It does. She yells at me if I ask about her meds or how she's feeling. I just... I can't spare her." My voice was scratchy as one of my biggest fears slipped out.

"I get that," he nodded, peering up at me with a sad smile. "I think your dad would love seeing us like this."

"Like what?" I asked, my eyes narrowed.

"Getting along, working together. I told you, he was the only one on my side back then."

A laugh fell from my lips. "Yes, I was punished by him many times for not being nice to you. The poor man had to deal with his brat of a daughter for so long."

Tyler shut the mixer off and shook his head. "He'd always tell me that you didn't mean it. That you actually liked having me around, but you didn't know the right way to show it. And if we could only learn how to get along, we'd be great friends."

Dad knew. Of course he did.

I gulped, trying to get rid of the lump cutting off the air in my throat.

"Your father worshipped you," Tyler went on. "Whereas my parents tolerated me most days."

"That's not true. Your mom just told us how proud she is of you and how she feels terrible not showing it more. Your dad"—I shrugged— "I think he just tolerates people in general."

"That's a good point." He poured the mixture into a bowl and slid it toward me. "If you'd like a job, grab the roll of clear wrap on the side and set a piece right down on the chocolate. You can put it into the fridge as we go. Sound good?"

"I think I can manage that." I gave him a wink and pulled out a long piece, pressing it down just as he said and taking it over to his large refrigerator. I never knew he had so much equipment back here. The one time he brought me in the back to talk a few weeks ago, the shock of him not running away from me for once had made everything else fade into the background.

We worked in comfortable silence. I fluttered back and forth, doing whatever Tyler asked as he mixed and baked. Things were easy between us for once. He wasn't eyeing me as if he was trying to figure out my next move, and I worked hard to be a more amiable version of myself while fighting the intrusive fantasy of Tyler in an apron and nothing else.

I had issues, but I'd managed to keep them at bay for a couple of hours.

"You aren't bad at all." He grinned as I carefully took a tray of crusts out of the oven and set them down to cool. "I'd hire you."

"I'm moving things back and forth, not really touching any of it." I cocked a brow as I pulled off the protective gloves. "But it's good to know if both my jobs fall through, I have something to fall back on." I pointed to the smaller bowl of chocolate on the counter. "Is that for a mini pie?"

"No." He smirked at me and dropped a small spoon inside the bowl. "For you."

I gasped and scooped it up.

"If this is my payment for tonight, I'm totally into it." I moaned around a spoonful. "My God, you're amazing."

The smile faded from his face, new tension running through his shoulders. The last time he'd heard me cry out how amazing he was, I was sitting on his face.

"You earned it." He said, his voice raspy as he ambled over to me. "The third night of us getting along. We keep setting records."

"I guess we do," I mumbled through a mouthful of chocolate. We still weren't talking about the sex, but the memory crackled between us.

That's what I had to accept it as—a memory. A great memory, but as bittersweet as the chocolate he'd given me.

A dollop fell onto my apron thanks to my shaky hand.

"Ugh, I guess I needed an apron after all." I reached for a paper towel to wipe it off and felt Tyler's eyes on me. "What? I can't help it if your chocolate is that good."

He inched over to me, tapping his knuckle under my chin for me to look up. I stopped breathing when his thumb slid across my bottom lip.

"You're a messy eater." He slid that thumb into his own mouth and sucked the chocolate off.

I clenched my thighs together under my apron to get rid of the sudden throb. I wanted to flirt back and say, *So are you,* but I was too entranced by his hooded eyes to say a word.

"All right, let's make some pies."

We jumped apart when three guys came in through the back door.

"Wow, boss, you brought in extra help and didn't tell us." A man with a crew cut and tight beard made his way over to me. "I'm Eli, one of the bakers. This is Kevin and Aiden."

I took his extended hand. "I'm Olivia. I just came to help out, I'm a… friend of Tyler's."

"Nice to meet you, Olivia." He shot Tyler a glance. "I guess we could use all the help we could get, right?" Eli slapped Tyler on the back and headed to the rack to pull on an apron.

Tyler briefed the guys on what we'd done so far and his plan for tonight, flicking his gaze to me a couple of times.

"You're welcome to stay," he said when he came back over to me.

"I don't want to be in the way. I'll head home." I pulled the apron over my head, and Tyler grabbed it from my hands.

"I'll put this in the laundry." He threw it into the bin next to the counter. "Let me walk you to your car. It's late."

He said something to Eli that I couldn't hear before he led me out the door.

"Thank you. Again." Tyler laughed when we got to my car. "This was a big help. All of it."

"I told you, you deserve it. What are *friends* for, right?"

He didn't reply, only nodded and pressed a quick kiss to my cheek, lingering a moment.

"You're all right, Sanchez." The side of his mouth curved up.

"So you've said." The memory of him telling me that after Donnie's wedding squeezing my chest. "I guess you are too, Bennett." I shot him a quick smile before I climbed into my car and drove off, trying not to stare at Tyler in my rearview mirror, still watching me.

My father was right. Once we learned to get along, we made a great team.

I'd made us enemies because I couldn't be his friend. Even as a kid, I'd known having only a piece of him would never be enough.

NINETEEN
TYLER

"Sam, Tyler is here!" my mother called over her shoulder as she pulled me inside her front door.

"You don't have to bother Dad. I can't stay that long anyway."

She took the boxes and bread from my arms, exhaling in a huff as she looked behind her.

"Since he retired, he hangs out in the basement all day long. He can unearth himself for just a little while to say hello to his only son."

"I just saw you a few weeks ago. Dad had a tough job." I followed her into the kitchen. "After all those years of fighting fires, he could use the rest."

"He rests enough, trust me." She pointed to the kitchen table. "Sit. Can I get you something to eat? I know you've been working late." Mom looked me over, her brow furrowed. "I hope you stop to eat sometimes."

"I do. You don't need to worry. Busy is good. I don't mind the grunt work when it's my own place."

She slid into the seat next to me, her eyes glassy. "I'm very proud of you. And I don't think I ever really told you. Not just for what's happening recently, but in general." She squeezed my hand. "Please know that."

"I know," I replied with a crack in my voice. Truth was, up until Donnie's wedding, I *didn't* know. I knew my parents loved me, but it never seemed like they took a genuine interest in what I did or was trying to do by opening up my own bakery. Both of them warned me of the pitfalls of starting a business, which I took as their disapproval. The bakery was a dream and a goal I assumed only I cared about, but the pride radiating off my mother from across the table was an unexpected thrill and a relief.

"I know you love me for more than free baked goods." I smirked, trying to lighten the mood as I draped my hand over hers.

"I love you more than anything." She leaned back, narrowing her eyes. "You sliced the bread for me, right?"

I cocked my head to the side. "Don't I always?"

She smiled and patted my hand. "Perfect. I'll make you a sandwich before Carla and Olivia get here." She stood and headed to the refrigerator.

"Oh, I didn't know they were coming by today."

She craned her head at me, lifting a brow as she pulled out a platter of cold cuts. "Why the face? I thought you and Olivia got along now? Or you did at Donnie's wedding." Her gaze slid to mine, a recognition flickering in her eyes I wanted to ignore. I wasn't sure if she was referring to how well Olivia and I got along that night at the table or later on against the wall.

It had been almost a month, and no one had brought up what else happened between Olivia and me. Every time I'd seen Olivia since then, the air was charged with it, but neither of us mentioned a word.

"That was a nice thing she did for you too," Mom noted.

"We do, and it was. I was just surprised, that's all."

I asked Olivia if I could tell my mother about the post, but of course, she already knew about Olivia's secret job. There wasn't much our mothers didn't share.

"Olivia's actually helped me out over the past couple of weeks."

Mom cut me a look, scrutinizing me for a long minute before she pulled the plastic wrap off the platter.

"When her post went viral and we had all these pie orders coming in, she went to buy ingredients for me so that I could keep working and stayed to help me set up before the night shift guys came in."

Mom shot me a look as she reached for a plate in the cabinet. "Turkey and Swiss? I have some honey mustard."

"Yes, and please." I leaned back in the chair, anticipating what she was about to say. "She's gone to the store for me a few times since it's been so busy I couldn't send anyone out. I'm going to have to staff up soon."

Usually, whenever I came to my parents' house, Mom did all the talking and I'd respond with a grumble, not wanting to get into anything. It was like that for a while after Amy and I broke up and a couple of years ago when I'd first told them my plan for leasing an old bakery space and making it mine.

Now, I was running my mouth in a neurotic effort to fill the silence and stop my mother from asking the questions I knew she had but that I didn't want to answer.

"Hey."

We turned to my dad's shuffle behind us. He reached into the bag of bread and pulled out a slice, stuffing two pieces of roast beef inside before folding it and taking a bite.

"My God, can you at least get a plate?" Mom groaned as

she placed a sandwich in front of me. "I didn't know when my husband retired he'd revert to a frat boy."

I chuckled around my first bite.

"I was watching the game when you told me to come up and say hi to Tyler." He turned to me as he chewed. "You're a busy guy now, huh?" He slapped me on the back.

That was the most recognition I'd received from my father about anything since my baseball days.

"I am. I told Mom I can't stay long."

"Of course you can't. When I drove by yesterday, the line was out the door. Nice of you to stop by now that you're a big shot. Now if you'll excuse me," he said as he grabbed a napkin, holding it up to Mom before heading back downstairs.

Mom glared at his departure but sucked in her cheeks as if she was holding a laugh. Whatever they had between them all these years, it seemed to work.

"Anyway," she started, turning back to me, "there are a lot of teenagers looking for a job around here if you need help with customers. I can ask around."

"Thanks. I have a couple of interviews this week for assistant bakers. There may be more night shifts in my future, but it's all good."

"Just promise me you'll find time to sleep."

"I do," I lied and headed for the refrigerator to pull out a bottle of water. I tried, but true sleep was hard to come by these days. The anxiety over how I'd handle the new crowds combined with constant thoughts of Olivia flashing through my brain made it difficult to unwind.

Why was it so hard to talk about what happened between us? Or what was happening now? If Eli hadn't come in when he did on that first night, I would have kissed her. Hell, I would have done anything she let me. That night fucked with my head more than the wedding. There she was again, doing another favor for me after this huge break she'd given me, showing me all the ways I might have misjudged her our entire lives. We were so busy being at each other's throats we never took the time to really get to know each other. The friendship we'd found these past few months, after all these years of exhausting strife, seemed a little too natural. The conversation was easy with no stupid pretense about why we were together or attempting to get along—we just did.

When she devoured the bowl of chocolate I'd given her, I was thankful for the apron hiding the bulge in my jeans. Olivia was full of passion, and I wanted more than just the taste of it we had that night.

But I had no idea how to tell her.

I stiffened in the seat when the doorbell rang. The rush of anticipation at seeing Olivia almost made me forget the dread I'd feel whenever she'd come here with her family. The more time we spent together, the harder it became to remember a time when I hated seeing her.

But if I was honest with myself, it was because there wasn't one. Even when she was at her worst, Olivia made me feel alive. Maybe I'd written her off as an enemy for so long to prevent the fixation that she was becoming now.

"Tyler! I didn't expect to see you here." Carla greeted me with a hug when I stood. "What a nice surprise."

I smiled at Olivia over her shoulder, but her lips pulled into a deep frown as she stood behind her mother with her arms crossed.

"Good to see you too, Carla. Mom asked for a few things, and I thought I'd take a break while I could."

"I'm glad." She squeezed my shoulder and jerked her chin behind her. "My daughter thinks I need an escort to my friend's house, so she drove me here in the middle of a workday."

"You were dizzy this morning," Olivia said, her shoulders rigid. "You can't drive like that."

Carla turned to her with an eye roll. "That happens sometimes when I change the insulin dose. I had a glass of juice to level off, and I was fine. You didn't have to stop what you were doing and drive me."

"Yes, I did. I wish you'd take your health a little more seriously."

"You don't think I do?"

I'd never heard Carla almost yell. I shouldn't have been staring, but something in Olivia's stance unnerved me. She worried about her mother and was still grieving for her dad, but I hated seeing her upset like this.

Carla shook her head and breathed out an exasperated sigh. "My daughter decided to take her father's place and micromanage how I take care of myself. She's finding it hard to relax since she's been back."

"Fine. I'll pick you up later if Helen can't drive you home." She sucked in a breath and forced a weak smile. "I need to get back to work before I *micromanage* my mother any more. Good to see you guys," she said as her gaze slid to mine for a second. My stomach sank when I glimpsed the lost look in her eyes.

"Do you want something to eat, Olivia?" my mother asked.

"No, thank you, Helen."

"Take a sandwich, Olivia. The only time you eat lately is when you have an appointment at night," Carla said, a gleam of regret in her expression.

"I eat. I'm just not hungry now." She told Carla and rushed out.

Before I knew what I was doing, I followed her out the front door.

"What's going on?" I asked as I jogged to her car.

She sighed, throwing her purse into the back seat before

she leaned against the passenger side door. "I know my mother is right. But when I stopped upstairs and saw her holding on to the counter and almost falling over, it scared the shit out of me." She scrubbed a hand down her face, the zipper from her moto jacket sleeve dangling as she rubbed her eyes.

I fought to keep my eyes on her face and not let my eyes roam down her body. The way her legs were poured into those tight jeans made it a struggle.

"All I could think was, *Not again.*" She dropped her head back, exhaling a long gust of air. "I need to get over this. Other people lose parents and find a way to handle it. They don't panic like this."

"First of all, yes, other people lose parents, but not as sudden as you lost your father. Carla may be used to adjusting to dosages of insulin, but you're not used to being there to see it. You'll get over it in your own time, so stop being so hard on yourself."

"You of all people know how extra I can be. Too much." She shook her head, her wistful gaze landing on my mother's front door. "I need to dial it back."

"No, you don't," I whispered, easing closer. Her dark hair was wild and curly, and before I could stop myself, I tucked a loose lock behind her ear. "Extra is the best thing about you." I let my thumb graze the delicate curve of her jaw. "Your mom is lucky to have you looking out for her."

She reached up to grab my wrist as a slow smile spread across her mouth, the mouth that haunted my dreams and invaded almost every thought when I was awake. "You're all right, Bennett."

I laughed, bunching my shoulders in a shrug. "I have my moments. We both better get back to work."

And one of us needed to make a move before I completely lost it.

"Getting my mind off things with work would help." She nodded and walked around her car to get in.

"If you want me to put you to work, just say the word."

"I will," she said, opening her mouth as if she was about to say something else before she waved and drove off.

I waited until she turned at the end of the block, and I headed back inside.

"Is she okay?" Carla asked, a deep frown pulling at her mouth. "I shouldn't snap at her like that."

"No, you shouldn't."

I flinched when both Mom and Carla leveled me with a glare.

"I'm sorry, Carla. I meant no disrespect, but she's struggling. I know you both are, but she worries about you. Maybe if you took her with you to the doctor sometimes so she doesn't panic when she sees something you think of as normal, it may help."

The anger running through me on her behalf almost cracked me up. The conversations I'd had about Olivia with our mothers usually involved them pleading with me to try to get along. The need to fight for her like she'd fought for me lately was as strange to me as it probably was to them.

"That's a good point, Tyler. I'll do that. And I know she's struggling." Carla's chin dropped to her chest as she played with a napkin on the table. "Javier and Olivia were inseparable, you know that. I'm glad she has a... friend like you. One who knows her mother well enough to not be afraid to say when she's being a jerk to her daughter."

I met her gaze and laughed.

"I better get back." I scooped up my sandwich with a napkin and bent to kiss my mother's cheek. "Talk to you later."

Mom stopped me, draping a hand over my cheek with a tiny smile, a smile that told me she knew everything I couldn't admit.

Right after I started getting used to the idea that Olivia and I were friends, confirmation popped up everywhere that we weren't—then or now.

TWENTY
OLIVIA

"Just like the old days, isn't it?" Morgan asked as she nudged my side.

Strolling through the mall did feel like we were back in a time warp. Before either of us had a driver's license, our parents would drop us off here and we'd gorge ourselves in the food court and people watch. We'd meet up with other friends, but as most of the people we knew turned their backs on us at the beginning of junior year, it was usually just us.

"It is," I said. "That's the one thing I miss about my apartment. I liked the hipster coffee shops and cobblestone streets when I'd shop."

"You're not throwing shade at Cinnabon are you?" Morgan tipped her chin toward the source of that heavenly sweet scent that hit you the second you stepped inside the main doors, although today it made my stomach roll.

"Of course not," I said with an exaggerated gasp. "I told you, I'm glad to be back. It was nice, but as I said, it became lonely after a while."

I tossed my empty iced-coffee cup into the trash. Even

before my father passed away, I missed being around family and friends. They were a short train ride away, but after being so excited to be on my own, the single party life wore on me quicker than I'd expected.

My phone buzzed on my hip. I dug it out of my purse and spotted the photo on the screen of rows of chocolate cream pies in Tyler's bakery's front window.

Tyler: *That was this morning, and it's already half gone.*

Olivia: *Why you need extra staff, like I keep telling you. A man your age can't do all these all-nighters.*

Tyler: *We're the same age, in case you forgot.*

Tyler: *And I may not have a choice. Guess who just came in to do a story on us for next Sunday?*

Olivia: *Moved on with another blogger? Figures.*

Tyler: *The New York Times*

I gasped and hit the Call button.

"You're going to be in the Sunday *New York Times*? Tyler, this is fucking huge!" I blurted into the phone before he even said hello.

When an older couple looked back at me with faces twisted in disgust, I realized how loud I was but didn't care.

"I know, or it could be." His deep chuckle in my ear did things to me, but my excitement for him outweighed my infatuation—for the moment. "It's a small feature about local bakeries in the suburbs."

"The cautious optimism is cute, but please get over it already." I sighed.

"Did you just call me cute?"

"Don't change the subject!" I was too hyped up for him to flirt back, even though my belly dipped along with the husky tone of his voice. "Do you need any help?"

"I might, if you're up for it."

"Of course," I answered too quickly. "Just... tell me when

you need me. You know my limited skills, but if I can help you, I can be there after my meetings this week."

Over the past couple of weeks, I was still navigating this new friendship of ours that came with a side of blinding and exhausting sexual tension. I was fully aware that the novelty and thrill of him wanting me around was a strong motivator but, not-so-secret lusting aside, I wanted to help him if he needed it.

"Helen is going to flip! Have you told her yet?"

"No, the reporter just left. She was here for a while and was a fan of the chocolate cream pie—and apparently of yours too, your highness. You're the gift that keeps on giving, Sanchez."

"That may be one of the nicest things you've ever said to me," I teased. "Was I the first one you told?"

"Well… I…" he stammered into the phone. "Everyone here already knows, but I wouldn't get the reaction I was looking for if I called anyone else."

"Aw, Tyler, I'm touched," I croaked out, trying to sound playful. Warmth flooded my chest at the notion he cared about me that much to tell me a huge piece of good news first.

But we were friends now, so yes, he cared about me as a *friend*. It was wise not to read into anything, no matter how strong the temptation was—but wise was never my thing.

"If we get a jump, it won't be until next week. Just the usual insanity, but I'll text you if I need any help."

"Sure," I said, ignoring Morgan's tapping foot as I pulled at the back of my hair. If he was anyone else, I'd ask to see him simply because I wanted to. But something kept holding me back.

"So Tyler's bakery is going to be in *The New York Times*," Morgan said as I stuffed my phone back into my purse.

"Yes, could be a big deal. I told him I'd help him if he needed it."

"Hmm," was all she said.

"What?" I stepped in front of her.

"I think..." she started and exhaled a long breath. "I think the two of you are too old to play this game. You can't come out and just say you want to see each other so it has to be under the pretense that he needs your help. Have you said one word to him about what happened after Donnie's wedding?"

I shook my head, and I trudged ahead of her. "No. It's all a little weird, you know that."

"Olivia." She pulled my arm back. "It's not that weird. If this were anyone else but Tyler, your patience would have run out a long time ago. I know how you feel about him." I turned away when her face softened with sympathy. "I knew years ago, even if you never said it out loud. And I know what you're afraid of."

"I'm not afraid of anything. We had sex." I shrugged. "It happens. And now we're friends. Sort of." I trailed off. "It's not a big deal."

"But it is. Just say it."

"Say what?" I spat out through gritted teeth. "That it was easier being the girl he hated than the girl he doesn't want? That I'm taking scraps of Tyler like I'm some pathetic little puppy but I can't seem to stop?"

"Oh my god, seriously?" Morgan narrowed her eyes at me. "You were *never* the girl he didn't want. Stop doing this to yourself, and talk to him."

"I don't want to ruin it." My voice was small, the bravado that always came easy now gone and pointless with Morgan since she always saw right through it.

"Liv, come on—"

"Look, let's change the subject." I clenched my eyes shut

when she flinched. "Sorry, I just don't feel like talking about my screwed-up life anymore. Let's talk about you for a change. What's going on with you? Aside from having a perfect marriage to brag about?"

"It's not perfect, but there is something," she said, a slow smile curving her mouth. "We're going to have a baby."

"What?" I grabbed her arm. "And you're just telling me now?"

"Not *now*." She patted my hand, still white-knuckled on her bicep. "We both decided it was time to try. We talked to a fertility doctor, and when my next period starts, we start. Which, as you know, is soon."

"As I know?" I squinted at her.

"You know we always get our periods around the same time. I finished almost a month ago and I'm due to get mine soon, like you probably are."

I stilled. Morgan didn't notice I wasn't keeping pace beside her for a few steps.

"What?" She asked when she realized I was lagging behind.

We did tend to get our periods at the same time, even after I'd moved. I'd always blown it off as coincidental, but Morgan insisted it was that weird phenomenon where women's cycles synced with those close to them. Synching or not, the blood ran ice cold in my veins when I realized I had no period at all since... before Donnie's wedding.

"I didn't get my period last month."

Morgan's brow jumped and her jaw went slack. "You're about to miss two periods and you just realized it now?"

"I've been distracted." I couldn't handle looking her in the eye for a few minutes. "Getting used to working from home and around town, watching Mom, the wedding." I covered my mouth with a shaky hand. *And Tyler.* "I can't be pregnant. We used a condom. A few of them. I didn't see any holes when he rolled them off."

She grimaced. "Not to make you panic, but they aren't foolproof. I once heard my mother refer to my little brother as the condom that could."

"Shit," I hissed as I stalked over to a bench and plopped down, dropping my head into my hands.

"Hey," Morgan crooned as she rubbed my back. "It's okay. Whatever it is, it will all be okay." She dipped her chin to meet my gaze. "I promise."

"I'm smarter than this, Morgan. One man shouldn't distract me to the point I miss my own late period." I pinched the bridge of my nose. "What a fucking cliché. I'm a thirty-five-year-old woman pregnant from a one-night stand."

"You don't know that. If you are, it's not the end of the world. Tyler is a standup guy. You have friends and family to help you. I'll give you a pregnancy test in the car."

My head shot up. "You keep them in the car?"

She shrugged. "I was shopping at Costco. They had them in bulk, and I figured why not pick up a package since the doctor said it may take a few tries."

"Pregnancy tests aren't like paper towels. How many did you think you'd need?" A hysterical laugh slipped out of me.

She cocked a brow. "Are you going to give me crap, or do you want one?"

I nodded, and she grabbed my hand, yanking me off the bench.

The entire ride to my apartment, poor Morgan exhausted herself trying to make small talk in a failed effort to distract me. All I could do was offer her a quick nod. How was I going to tell him or make any of this work?

This one favor I offered Tyler caused an unexpected rippling effect that wouldn't stop.

I raced for the bathroom the minute I unlocked my apartment door, Morgan on my heels. I placed the test on the sink as if I were setting down a grenade. I stared at the results screen, waiting for it to go off and blow everything up.

"This could be a fluke," she tried to reassure me. "All the adjustment from moving, worrying about your mom. It may not be positive."

I didn't answer as I watched the unmistakable plus sign float up to the surface. The example on the box showed the results as faint lines, but this was bold and almost glowing as I plucked the test off the sink for a closer look, as if a different angle would change what it was telling me.

"Okay, so," Morgan began, scrambling for something to say while I was consumed by the little stick that upended my afternoon and was about to change my life. "They aren't always accurate. Go to the doctor and see what they say."

I nodded, even though I had all the confirmation I needed. It all made too much sense. The emotions that were all over the place, even for dramatic me. Weird smells and foods were turning me off for no reason. And now that I was paying attention to it, my stomach and breasts felt heavy.

I'd go to make sure everything seemed okay, but not for an answer because I already had one.

And then, finally, I would talk to Tyler.

TWENTY-ONE
TYLER

"You know, word on the street is that the deli next door is closing and putting the space up for sale," Eli said as he lined up the trays in the back. "Might be worth looking into. Isn't it the same landlord for the block?"

"You're expanding?" Tegan squealed, the hoop in her eyebrow jiggling as her eyes widened. "I totally think you should."

"And I think you're both getting ahead of yourselves." I turned to adjust the ovens. "The buzz or whatever this is could very well be temporary, just like when I first opened, so I'm just enjoying the ride and saving the profits."

"Dude, it's been almost a month and it has not stopped. If it was just from that random post, it would have faded by now, but we still have a line all day long, sometimes even before we open. And even without *The New York Times* doing a feature on this place, you've been popping up on Instagram more and more."

"How do you know?" I smirked at Eli, ignoring the twinge at his reference to Olivia as a random post. I told everyone that it was luck, not a connection I had, that a popular food blogger recommended us. She'd done so much for me, and I had no idea how to thank her. Or how to ask to see her again.

Instead, I just accepted her offer to come by with groceries or do busy work in the back. Despite the palpable attraction between us every time, we hadn't acted on it—or said one word about the glorious night that we did.

"I may or may not search *Hey, Batter* to see if we get any more hits—as you should be too. And I've seen posts about the chocolate cream pie, the vegan and sugar-free items, and a few other things. I get keeping your hopes low, but I think instead of expecting it to end you should bank on it continuing and how to handle it. Just a thought." He shrugged and pushed the door open.

I followed him, trying to think like a businessman and not a lovesick moron. The line wound outside past the display window, and several people stood next to the counter. We needed someone to handle crowd control, and that was first on the list of new hires I needed.

A smile pulled at my lips as I thought of what my uncle would say now about my "noble profession."

"I'm sorry, the line starts outside." Gabby, a new cashier that Staci was training, said in a timid voice. She seemed to work the register okay from what I could tell, but like me, she probably wasn't expecting a crowd this large at a bakery.

"I actually need to speak to Tyler. Is he around?"

My head whipped toward the familiar voice, and sure enough, my eyes locked with Olivia's.

"It's okay, Gabby," I said while I watched Olivia. Shit, she was gorgeous. Even in just leggings and a hoodie, everything clung to her in all my favorite places. Her hair was curly and wild, cascading over her shoulders. My fingertips tingled, wanting to sift through it, and I had to stuff my hands in my pockets.

She gave me a timid smile while her chest heaved, as if she were bracing herself. An ominous feeling grew in my gut, overpowering my excitement at seeing her again.

"Everything okay?" I asked.

"Can we talk?" Her tone was clipped, and her avoidance of my question ignited a little panic.

"Sure, come in the back." I motioned to the double doors behind the counter.

Olivia nodded, rushing over and pushing the door open without looking back at me.

"What's wrong? Is it your mom? Or mine?"

"No, no. Nothing like that." She shook her head. After knowing her all my life, it was unnerving to see Olivia this rattled.

"But it's something. Do you want to sit?" I grabbed the folding chair leaning against the steel counter and unfolded it for her.

"No, but you might." She pressed a palm to her forehead, coughing out a laugh that made my blood run cold.

"What is it?" I pressed, now exasperated as hell. "Just spit it out."

"I'm pregnant, Tyler."

The air sucked out of the room as I fell back onto the chair.

"You're..." My brain and my heart halted at the same time while I slowly absorbed what Olivia had just said.

"And it's yours." She folded her arms and leaned against the counter.

"I know. I mean..." I trailed off, dropping my chin to my chest and trying to collect my frazzled thoughts enough to make words. "I know that you wouldn't have come to me if it wasn't, and you wouldn't have... been with me like that if you were with someone else."

I didn't *know* for a fact that Olivia wasn't seeing anyone else that night, but she'd offered herself to me in a way she wouldn't have if she was. I didn't need proof when my instinct was that strong.

This felt like a month-long dream or altered reality I'd stumbled into. Olivia Sanchez was having my baby after one explosive night neither of us could talk about.

"I'm sorry to do this to you at work. It's a big shock—one I'm still not even over yet." She wrapped her arms around her torso as she inched closer. "I took a test at home and had it confirmed at the doctor today. My first thought was telling you, so I came straight here. But I should have waited until tonight."

"No, I'm glad you did." Her urge to tell me right away gave me a weird type of comfort.

A long silence washed over us. I'd already known sex with Olivia was life changing, but I hadn't known the half of it.

"We keep surprising people, don't we?"

Her shoulders jerked with a chuckle. "Yes, I suppose we do." She dropped her gaze to the floor and nodded.

"I need to get back out there, but can I come to your apartment tonight? So we can really talk about this?" I rose from the chair and stepped toward her. We were overdue to finally talk about a lot of things, and now our hands were forced.

I'd have been relieved if I wasn't so terrified.

"Sure. Text me when you're on your way. Judging by the crowd, it looks like you may be late, and that's okay. Whatever time you can come is good for me."

"Okay," I replied, not knowing what the hell else I should say. "Why don't you take some stuff home? I'll tell Staci in the front to let you pick whatever you want. You should eat, right?"

A tiny, almost sad smile curved her lips. "That's very thoughtful, thank you. I guess I'll see you later."

A timid and lost Olivia was too much for me to take. All I wanted to do was pull her into my arms and tell her it was all going to be okay, even if I was clueless as to how. But other than the random touches that teetered on the borderline of friendly, we didn't show any affection. At least, not since that night. My feet were speared to the floor. Not knowing my place around Olivia was its own kind of torture.

"See you later." I held the door open for her to walk through and told Staci to give Olivia whatever she wanted at no charge.

The rest of the afternoon, I baked, prepared, greeted customers, but I couldn't actively remember any of it. I was a scared-shitless zombie for the rest of the day.

Amy and I had talked about kids as a *maybe someday* type of thing. Having children was something I figured I'd do eventually but never gave much thought to it beyond that. Other than my cousin's kids, I hadn't been around any in a long time. Since Ross's offspring were as annoying as he was, I didn't have experience taking care of kids or even hanging out with them.

My father was a good man, but he wasn't one for encouragement or deep conversations. I'd always looked at us as the same kind of person, but I didn't want to grunt at my kid when he or she was having a problem. Mom was always the caregiver and fixer.

With a mother like Olivia, I was sure our child would have nothing to worry about. Olivia would be like one of those lionesses in those memes with the blood dripping down her chin after fighting whatever idiot tried to mess with her baby. My mouth split into a grin at the thought.

What could I really offer my kid?

I felt the wary eyes of my staff as I helped them clean up the counter at the end of the night. We still had a small line, but it was contained inside at this point, and we were ready to lock the door for the night.

A little girl's giggle broke me out of my afternoon-long trance.

"You can't have it all, Amara. Mommy will kill me."

My gaze landed on a broad-shouldered man with full sleeves of tattoos drifting up to his neck, crooning at the child in his arms. He whispered something that made her laugh again. She reminded me of Olivia with her olive skin and her long, dark hair pulled back with an oversized bow. She probably didn't make little boys cry for sport like Olivia had at that age, but the beauty that radiated from this little girl was the same.

The man laughed when he caught my eyes.

"I keep telling her to pick one thing, but her finger points everywhere." She folded in laughter when he tickled her side. He let out a sigh and groaned. "Pretty girls get me every time. Can I get a cake pop, please?" He pointed to the red-and-blue chocolate pop next to the counter. Before Gabby could get it, I popped it off the stand and handed it to him.

"Daddy! A Wonder Woman pop!" she gasped and took a bite, chocolate crumbs dropping to what I now noticed was a Wonder Woman sweatshirt.

"See, Amara, it was meant to be! What do you say?"

"*Gracias*," she told me with a mouthful of cake.

"Very good! *Titi* will be so happy when I tell her how nice you said thank you." He kissed her cheek as she ignored him to take another bite. "I've seen this place on Instagram, and since I was in the neighborhood, I thought we'd stop in," he told me as he tried to wipe the icing off her chin with a napkin. "My daughter is right—everything looks awesome."

"We've had some new customers lately, thanks to Instagram," I said, still focused on the little girl as she finished off the cake pop and regarded her father as if he was her entire world. I probably wouldn't have noticed them if they came on any other day, but watching them now got me right in the chest. "We were used to just locals before then."

"My wife is a writer and had a signing at the library a few blocks away. This one got antsy, so I thought some sweets would tide her over."

She rested her head on his chest when she was finished, holding up the empty stick for her father to discard.

"You finished that in three bites, *mija*!" He kissed her forehead as she cuddled into his neck.

As Staci rang him up for the cake pop, I plucked the stick from her little hand. "I'll take that, sweetheart. Glad you liked it."

She turned toward me, still burrowing into her father's chest, and gave me a big smile. Pretty girls got me every time too.

"Thanks," the man said. "I'll have to find an excuse to drive out here and come back." He adjusted her on his hip and waved. "Have a good day."

I watched them go, an odd yearning blossoming in my chest.

I still didn't know what kind of father I would be or what I could give my kid.

All I did know was that they'd get the best of whatever I had.

TWENTY-TWO
OLIVIA

I lounged on my couch, mindlessly scrolling through my phone. Over the past couple of years, when I was feeling things I didn't want to acknowledge, the best way to get my turbulent mind off anything was to cue up a true crime documentary—the more disturbing the better.

Morgan constantly got on me for my "abnormal way of self-soothing," but getting lost in the mystery while creeping myself out seemed to do the trick if my intention was to forget, at least for a little while. I'd lost a night or two of sleep as what I'd watch sometimes got to me a little too much, especially when I lived alone in Manhattan and heard every single noise in and around my apartment after the gruesome episodes.

I'd spent the last two birthdays in solitude with my phone off, watching serial killers. Morgan had a point, but I'd ponder that later.

The creepy narrator noted all the gory details of whatever twisted true story I'd found on Netflix, but I wasn't tuned in. There was no way to ignore or forget this. The surprise baby I was having with Tyler took all of my focus, so distractions of any kind weren't possible.

My phone vibrated in my hand, a jolt of anxiety running through me when a text message popped up.

Tyler: *I'll be there in fifteen minutes.*

What was I looking for when I headed for the bakery after the doctor's office?

Since I'd been pregnant for so long without a clue, my very kind doctor got me in for an early ultrasound right after my appointment so we could estimate the due date. The sonogram they'd given me was still on my coffee table, the corners already frayed from where I'd been thumbing it on and off all day. I'd planned on being a mother someday, but over the past few years, I figured surrogate aunt was a more certain future. For the brief moment I'd thought my best friend was pregnant, I was thrilled. Minutes later when I realized that I was, dread and bone-deep fear filtered through me.

All I could see was a tiny, blurry circle in a sea of gray, but I kept gravitating toward it.

My baby.

That little dot terrified me, but I loved it anyway.

I was always relentless in demanding Tyler's attention, good or bad. Now I guessed I'd found a way to capture it forever. Part of me loved that idea, to be tethered to him for the rest of our lives beyond our mothers' friendship. A bigger —and louder—part hated that, however unintentionally, I'd forced the connection. Six-year-old me and nineteen-year-old me would've reveled at closing in on him with no escape, but a much older and wiser me felt nothing but guilt over doing it like this.

I was pulled out of my thoughts when my doorbell rang. In only a day, I felt every textbook symptom of pregnancy, almost as if I'd brought them on myself. The nausea might have been partly caused by the power of suggestion, but the sore and swollen boobs couldn't be faked. Putting on a bra almost brought me to tears thanks to my oversensitive nipples.

"Hey," I said to a weary-looking Tyler as he leaned against the doorjamb at my side entrance. Even after a long day of baking for all those customers I had to weed through earlier, he was still so gorgeous. The full lips brought out by the scruff dusting his cheeks, his light eyes beautiful even with the hint of dark circles underneath, the sparkle of gray I'd just noticed near his temple. Our baby had an awesome pool of DNA to pull from.

"I'm sorry. I'm here later than I wanted to be," he told me before stepping inside. My nose burned as the weird and sudden influx of emotion washed over me once again when he passed me.

Having a baby together was as close as two people could probably get, but we were still feeling our way around this new friendship between us. I wished things between us were as easy as the night of the wedding, when I didn't hesitate to kiss him or let my eyes shut as I rested my cheek on his bare chest.

It wasn't just the physical proximity I yearned for from Tyler. We had moments at the wedding and recently when I'd come to his bakery to help him late at night that we felt like true friends, like a team. I wanted—or more, needed—that now. I'd always been fine on my own, but the loneliness I'd felt since the walk home from his bakery earlier scratched at my throat.

"Are you feeling okay?" Tyler asked, settling onto my couch as his eyes fell to the black-and-white photo on the coffee table. "Is that..." He looked up at me.

"It is," I said and lifted it off the table to show him. "It's right there." I pointed to the dot in the center. "It's too early to tell anything, but the doctor told me all looks good and healthy."

"Good," he said, still staring at the picture.

"And I'm feeling okay. I haven't felt much like eating, but not sure if that's pregnancy or shock. Thanks for the cookies. I've been picking at them all day."

"You're welcome," he whispered. "I'm probably not saying any of the right things, but since Donnie's wedding I don't know how to act around you."

"I know what you mean." I set the picture on my thigh but couldn't tear my eyes away. "We should have talked about... what happened between us sooner."

"And I should have reached out to you before you doubled my profits for the year." He smiled, tilting his head. "I was so used to thinking about you in a certain way. We were supposed to only *pretend* to be into each other. I guess I freaked out when I realized I didn't have to try that hard. Or at all."

"Same." I sighed. This was so fucking complicated already, now I was really clueless as to how to handle things between us. "Listen, I don't want to make you feel obligated."

"What are you talking about? Obligated?" His shoulders went rigid as he shifted to face me.

"Well, you just started to not hate me, and I sprung a baby on you—"

"Sprung a baby on me? Jesus, Olivia. You didn't spike my drink and take advantage of me. I was right there with you. The condoms that didn't fucking work came out of *my* wallet. I'm not obligated. I'm here because that is my baby too." He pointed a finger at the sonogram picture in my shaking hand. "And because it's finally time to be adults and talk about what happened between us and what to do about it."

"I'm...I'm sorry, Tyler," I stammered, still unnerved by the clench of his jaw as his eyes narrowed at me. "I didn't mean to judge you or assume anything. It's just like you said, we don't know how to be around each other and now we're going to be parents. I'm catching up, so I'm also probably not saying the right things."

"I know."

I relaxed when his features softened.

"I'm catching up too, Sanchez. And I should have said this earlier too, but that night, even looking at it from where we are now..." He sank his teeth into his bottom lip, the intensity in his eyes making me squirm. "I don't regret it. Not for one single second."

"Neither do I." I returned the tiny smile spreading across his lips.

"Good," he rasped, scooting closer to me on the couch. "What if we do this, see each other because we want to? Not because of obligations from our mothers or because I need two dozen eggs after closing time. I want more of the Olivia I've gotten to know recently, the one who I can't seem to get out of my head."

"Yeah?" My voice cracked, a sudden but innate relief rushing through me. "I rocked your world, huh?" I darted my eyes away for a moment after I tried to deflect.

"You absolutely did," he replied, his voice was low and husky, sending a chill down my spine. He'd more than rocked mine. One night in his bed had obliterated it.

"But we went from zero to sixty since even before the wedding, and I don't know about you, but I have a little whiplash over it. And now"—he motioned to my still mostly flat stomach— "we owe it to someone else to get our shit together over the next few months."

"Agreed." I put the photo down, making a silent promise to

the dot that I would try my best to do just that, even if my lifelong track record said otherwise.

"Can I get you anything?" he asked, his hands running up and down his legs. "You said you were nauseous. Tegan makes these ginger cookies that she swears help digestion and nausea. Maybe I could bring you some of those."

"Sure. I'll try them." I shrugged, my nose burning again as I tried to swallow the lump in my throat at his concern. The thought of being this much of a sap for my entire pregnancy already exhausted me. "Thank you. Go and get some sleep. I know you have an early morning, and I haven't slept much since yesterday." I reached out and draped my hand over his. "I have an appointment tomorrow night out east. If I'm going to make the hour drive back and forth, I think I need to turn in soon."

"I can go with you. We close earlier on Fridays. What time do you have to be there?"

"Seven thirty. But you don't have to."

A groan erupted from the back of his throat. "I don't have to. I *want* to. Even if you weren't feeling well and were too tired to make the drive. So I'll be here at six thirty to pick you up. Got it?"

A grin split my mouth as I nodded. "Got it."

"An agreeable Olivia." He pushed off the couch. "Another thing I have to get used to."

"Don't get used to it too much," I said, cocking a brow as I followed him to the front door. "I'm still me."

He leaned in and planted a soft kiss on my cheek, close enough to the corner of my mouth to remember how his lips felt on mine. He lingered, resting his forehead against my temple for a second before turning down my side steps.

"Hey, Tyler," I called out. "Do you know why I knocked the cake batter out of your hand that day?"

"Other than you were mean?" He lifted a shoulder, a smirk tipping the side of his mouth. "No."

I smiled and shook my head.

"You just had a haircut, and your cheeks looked bigger. You mixed that tiny bowl *so* slowly." He laughed at my exaggerated eye roll. "But I kept staring at you because you were so damn cute, I wanted to kiss you. I came close, but when I thought you noticed, I knocked the little pan out of your hand so you'd be mad at me and forget." I leaned on the doorjamb, laughing at the pathetic bully I was. "I *was* kind of the antichrist. Maybe if I just kissed you, things would have been different between us. Or I would have grossed you out and you would have hated me for a whole different reason. I guess the world will never know."

A blush crept up on his cheeks.

"I wouldn't have been grossed out. If you tried to kiss me at any point in our lives, I would have let you." His voice dipped to a low rasp that my entire body noticed, especially my tortured nipples. "And I wouldn't have hated you for it, not that I ever really did." He nodded inside. "Go get some sleep. I'll see you tomorrow."

I shut the door, resting my hand on my bloated lower abdomen as I came back inside. Maybe hope and second chances were a real thing, even for me.

TWENTY-THREE
TYLER

"You seem almost in a good mood," Eli noted as we cleaned up the counters for an extra early morning tomorrow. "Did you finally slide into someone's DMs and get a date?" He winked as he hung up his apron.

"Tyler has a date?" Tegan asked—or more, squealed. "I bet it's with that girl who came to see him yesterday." She turned to Eli with a loud whisper. "Staci said the sexual tension was crackling."

"First of all, I'm right here. And second, Staci should pay attention to the customers and not whatever she thinks she sees crackling." I groaned as I scrubbed my hands at the sink. Olivia and I did have electricity between us, enough to destroy a hotel bed headboard, but what Staci thought she picked up on was the overall stifling tension. I was excited to see Olivia but trying not to show it, she was nervous about what she had to tell me, and all our complicated history bubbled to the surface.

Still, Eli was right, although I wasn't going to give him the satisfaction of admitting it. I wanted to see Olivia tonight. Not because she was having my baby, as I was still wrapping my head around that. Tonight, I hoped there would be no games or pretense because, after a lifetime of both, I was exhausted.

"Good night," I said, feeling everyone's stare at my back as I unlocked the door to leave, still not offering any explanations. Whatever was between Olivia and me was something I wanted to keep to myself for the moment. My staff would be thrilled for me, as even the idea of me dating someone had them chattering for days. Only the late-night bakers saw Olivia come in after hours and would give me loaded looks when she'd leave but hadn't called me on anything—yet. I could wait for all the wide eyes and slacked jaws when they found out that we were having a baby together.

This simple dinner was something I never thought I'd want but had anticipated all day long. If I was being honest, I'd anticipated it since I dropped her off the morning after Donnie's wedding, I just didn't know how to ask for it.

After I jogged back to my apartment for a quick shower and change of clothes, I headed to Olivia's. I wasn't sure what kind of place this was tonight, but I pulled out a button-down black shirt and black pants. The pictures I'd glanced at online of the restaurant seemed trendy, at least not a jeans kind of crowd. As I pulled into a spot in front of Carla's house, I ignored the thrill of dressing up for Olivia tonight. The excitement over being close to her and having her to myself without having to pretend I didn't want her was a little bit of a mindfuck.

I was here for it because I wanted to be here for her.

The click of heels drew closer after I rang her outside doorbell.

"Hi! You're early," Olivia breathed out, her grin fading when she met my eyes. I drank in her short-and-snug leather dress and matching jacket and the spike-heeled, knee-high boots. The neckline wasn't low, but I could spy the swells of her breasts. All her curves pulled at the leather as if it was spotlighting it all. I rubbed the side of my mouth, checking to make sure I wasn't drooling.

Olivia's bitchiness as we grew up wasn't the only reason I steered clear of her. I had no idea what to do with the beauty in front of me now, and I definitely hadn't in our younger days.

"You look nice. Black on black suits you. And we match." She waved a hand down her body. "I figured, before everything becomes too tight to wear, may as well flaunt it now. I think any leather in my closet has a very short shelf life as I may need help out of this dress already."

A devious grin curled one side of her mouth.

"I'm here to help you with whatever you need." My wide smile and husky rasp were involuntary. I had to push the thought of getting Olivia out of that dress out of my head as my pants didn't leave much to the imagination.

"That game gets better every time," she whispered and kissed my cheek. Her soft, wet lips sent a current down my body, right down to my soon-to-be obvious dick. I didn't want to push too far ahead, even though spending the night together after the wedding was a big leap. A reckless voice in my head kept saying the damage was already done. She was already pregnant with my baby, so if we ended up in bed together what was the big deal? But it was. The next time we were together, I wanted it to be deliberate, not the sloppy result of blinding lust.

Although when Olivia turned around and I saw what the leather did for her ass, it was almost impossible to focus on anything else.

"Sorry, it's a little bit of a mess. Mom is on an organizing spree, and she brought the old photo albums down here to make room for whatever she's doing to her closets." She shrugged as she stuffed items into her purse. "She gets into these projects lately." A flash of sadness drifted across her face. "I go along with it if it keeps her busy and gets her mind off things."

"Everything okay from the other day?"

She stopped, raising her head with a slow nod. "I need to stop being a pain in the ass." She heaved an audible sigh. "You know how that's a struggle for me."

"I do." I laughed when she shot me a scowl.

"Mom told me earlier about how you stood up for me when I acted like a brat. How the tables have turned for us." She traced the edge of my collar, the side of her mouth curving as she peered up at me.

"You weren't acting like a brat. You were looking out for her. I know she's happy you're back."

Olivia replied with a shrug. "I am too—if only I came back sooner, right?" She met my gaze with a sad smile. "Let me grab my phone from the charger. Give me one second."

I opened one of the albums as she raced toward her bedroom. I recognized her yard and the balloon arch from one of her birthday parties. Olivia and I were ten years old, and she sat underneath the balloons in a big queen-like chair, beaming as she was obviously loving it all. I found myself in the group picture by the cake, as far off to the side as possible, a deep frown on my face. The next picture was the one our mothers always forced. Olivia and me by the cake, her squeezing my shoulders as a wide grin split her mouth, as she knew full well I hated being there, much less posing right next to her. My face was scrunched up like she was hugging me to death.

"Blast from the past, right?" Olivia said, her flowery perfume invading my senses from where she stood behind me. "I always tortured you, huh?"

"I was an ornery kid, or so I was always told." I flashed a

grin over my shoulder. "But if you had a birthday party now, I think I could appreciate it more. Especially those sick, three-tiered themed cakes your dad always found. That inspired me a little, I think. Whenever we have to make fancy cakes like that, I think of your parties."

She snatched the album from my hands and slammed it shut.

"Well, no more birthday parties for me, so you can rest assured in being spared an invitation." She tossed the album onto the other end of the kitchen table. "Ready to go? Hopefully there's no traffic."

What happened to make Olivia hate her birthday? It bothered me, especially when I thought of how she loved every moment of all those parties of hers I'd been forced to attend and the stories I heard of big birthday trips she'd taken when we were older. But after the way she'd shut down at the wedding when I asked her about it and now this reaction, I didn't press and just followed her out her front door.

"Let's see if this place lives up to the hype," she said as she fastened her seat belt next to me. She hadn't been in my truck since I'd dropped her off after Donnie's wedding. As she'd shuffled her bare feet to her door that morning, I'd been unable to tear my eyes off her. The need to get out and call after her was paralyzing. I regretted not walking her to the door, but the urge to kiss her would have been too powerful to overcome.

Like the coward I was, I'd stayed back, watching her. Even with matted hair and a wrinkled dress, she was still a goddess.

"What?" she asked when she caught me staring.

"You're beautiful."

A blush ran up her cheeks.

"I'm bloated, but thank you." She pulled down the hem

and turned back to me. "I'm happy to give this dress one last night out—"

I leaned over and kissed her, soft and quick.

I smiled as she blinked her eyes open.

"What was that for?" she whispered, the tiny curve of her mouth tempting me back for more.

"Because I wanted to. Feels good to stop pretending, right?"

"Yeah, I suppose it does." Her lips pursed as she feathered her hand down my cheek. "I should warn you about a couple of things I've learned about pregnant me so far."

"Okay, what's that?" I asked, still leaning in close. One more kiss and we would be late.

"I'm weepy, which I'm not sure is due to hormones or anticipation of all the huge changes coming our way. I've even been crying over TikTok videos today. It's hurting my antichrist rep."

I burst out laughing and nodded. "All right. What else?"

She sucked in a breath and slid her hand to the back of my neck. "I seem to be very easily... aroused. And my body is over-sensitive. So while I'm happy we're admitting how attracted we are to each other, I'm not built to make good decisions right now. Especially with you in a button-down and the bulge in your pants." Her gaze flicked to my cock, now twitching at her acknowledgment. "Can we try to be careful? Not get swept away in each other tonight?"

Fuck.

Careful with an easily aroused Olivia in a leather dress, now staring at my dick? I'd try, but I didn't have high hopes.

"You are so fucking adorable when you're flustered." She rested her forehead against mine. "You can't blame me for goading you all of our lives when you were such an easy target." She kissed my cheek. "Let's go before we're late."

Nope, no hope at all.

"How many nights do you go out a week?" I asked after we sat down at our table. The whole thing felt like a spy mission. Even though I'd come with her before to one of these dinners, I was too preoccupied with learning to get along with her to appreciate what she was there to do.

"Depends. Two or three. I try to go during the week so I don't look too conspicuous dining alone on a Saturday night." She smirked around her water glass.

"Why do you come alone? I'd think Morgan would be up for going with you or even Carla."

"They offer, but I like coming alone. My dad and I would find these weird restaurants to check out sometimes and go, just the two of us. Mom is a picky eater, so she never minded that it was just us. He used to joke that maybe he could find a job being a professional restaurant customer." She peered at me with a wistful smile. "After he died, I stumbled on an article about social media influencers and how some food and lifestyle bloggers were making a decent living just posting about what they ate and what they did. I started the page as a fluke, and it blew up after I made a couple of posts."

"I didn't know it happened that quickly." I studied her, hating the gloss in her eyes whenever she brought up her dad. "You must have done something very right."

"I've run enough social media accounts to know some things, but getting something to go viral is tricky. There is no real formula to it, just throwing things against the wall to see what sticks. A secret *royal* blogger who went to affordable restaurants and found amazing dishes was catnip." She shrugged. "Who knew? Not sure if I could make a living out of it or if I would even want to but it's fun. And a good distraction sometimes."

She reached over and squeezed my arm. "But that was

backstory you probably weren't looking for. You asked why I did this alone. If I go by myself, this is something my dad and I still do that's just us. I know it sounds dumb, but it's helped."

"It doesn't." I peeled her hand off my arm and laced our fingers together. Of all the things we'd done, this simple gesture seemed the most intimate. "Why did you invite me with you last time?"

She dropped her head, chuckling to herself. "Dad would have liked me trying to get along with you and doing you a favor. So in a way, being with you was still remembering him. I've been thinking about how he'd react to this, but I'd bet he'd say he saw it coming." She groaned, slipping her hand away from mine to drape it over her eyes. "I sound completely out of my mind right now, don't I?"

"No, you don't." I took back her hand and brushed a kiss on her knuckles. "I like having history with you like that. Other than the fights and broken toys."

"And broken beds." Her eyes twinkled as she lifted a brow.

"This is your idea of being careful?" I sighed, wishing I'd just worn black jeans to shelter my exhausted dick. "Bringing that up?"

"Well, we can finally talk about it now, so that's good, right? And I more warned *you* to be careful since I probably wouldn't be, so..." She held up her hands.

I had to laugh. There was no being careful with Olivia. She was a force that had consumed me for most of my life.

Only this time, I'd stopped fighting it.

TWENTY-FOUR
OLIVIA

"So what do you think they'll say?" Tyler asked as we turned down my block.

"Who?" I replied on a yawn. I'd taken a nap this afternoon so I wouldn't be so wiped tonight, but it was of no use. I couldn't fight my hormones or the aftereffects of adrenaline coursing through my veins from thinking about dinner with Tyler all damn day. I'd been so afraid that he would freak out when I told him I was pregnant, but it had a strange opposite effect. It finally got us talking, since a baby together was something impossible to ignore, even though we managed to avoid bringing up the night we'd made it happen.

Opening up to Tyler about my father was easier than trying to explain my endless grief to anyone else. Even Morgan thought it was weird I only went on my foodie dinners alone even after I'd tried to explain why. Not only did Tyler get it, but he was also the only company I wanted. Spending the past few hours with him was both exhilarating and soothing. The night that led us here would always be a favorite memory, but being together tonight simply because we wanted to—with no agenda or pretense—was a different and exciting kind of high.

"Our parents. Our mothers anyway. My dad may pause for a minute, but he'll let my mother react like he usually does."

"Right. Well, they did ask us to get along, right?"

"Right." Tyler snickered. "And my mother keeps commenting on who of her friends has grandchildren with a not-so-subtle side-eye. They've probably waited for this forever. The shock of it all is just our problem." His lips curled into a smirk, and I wanted to climb over the console and devour them, along with the rest of him.

"The shock is real," I agreed. "But as crazy as it sounds, I'm excited. I never planned for this and I'm positive neither did you, but..." I clicked my tongue against my teeth. "I want it. It's been a long time since I've truly looked forward to anything. And"—I dropped my gaze to where my hands were wringing each other in my lap— "I'm glad it's you."

"I am too. Excited and..." He slid his hand along the steering wheel and lifted his head. "I'm glad it's you too."

I looked out the window, blinking away the threat of a sob. Whiplash was right. Three months ago, Tyler and I were adversaries. Not as vicious as we were younger, but not amiable in the least. I'd never imagined we'd be here: Tyler swoony instead of combative, me being honest about feelings instead of just endeavoring to piss him off. Maybe times really had changed from the awful way we'd treated each other in our younger days.

"Enough," my father yelled as he stretched his hands out at his sides, holding Tyler and me at a far enough distance apart from each other to stay out of the other's face. "You upset your mothers when you do this."

"Helen invited me here," I said. "I didn't sneak in. You say I'm rude? Have manners to at least say hello."

"That's because you're everywhere," Tyler sneered, his heaving chest pressing into my father's hand. "Can't you stay home?"

"Aw, do you think I'm going to upset your little girlfriend outside?" I jutted my lip into a pout.

The more Tyler glared at me, the hotter he was. Those bottomless golden eyes narrowed while his chiseled jaw ticked. He could do so much better than that mousy thing he'd brought over today if he had a better personality. Or a personality period.

"Why do you care so much where I am anyway? Obsessed much?" I pressed, feeling him seethe from where he stood.

"Olivia, basta ya!"

I stiffened and stepped back on instinct at my father's tone. Dad only yelled at me in Spanish when he meant business.

"Sorry, Javier. Look, I'm going back outside." Tyler shot me one last scowl before stalking into his yard with the rest of his family.

"Mija," Dad started, glaring at me despite the twitch of his lips. "Are you sure you don't want to major in law instead of marketing? You love to argue."

"I know everyone thinks I start with him all the time." I groaned at his raised brow. "Fine, maybe I do or used to, but he can't even say hello like a person."

"Someday," he began, framing my face with his hands, "not sure when, but you guys will work this out. But until then, we're guests at Helen and Sam's house. Whatever your reasons are, check whatever you have against their son at the door when you're here, got it?"

I nodded and followed Dad back outside.

Someday. Right.

"I know you have to get up early, but you can come in for a bit if you'd like," I told Tyler as he parked in front of the house.

He smiled as he shut the engine off.

"Do you *want* me to come in?" He stretched his arm over the back of my seat.

"Do *you* want to come in?" I fought a smile. Asking him to come inside was dangerous, but I wasn't ready for the night to end yet.

"Yeah, I do." He sucked in his bottom lip, and all those sensitive places on my body I'd mentioned to him earlier flared to life.

"Look at us being direct," I said, a little breathless as I opened the door, not knowing what else to say other than *the zipper is in the back this time.*

"I know. The milestones are piling up." He held out his hand as I climbed out of the passenger seat. It was on the tip of my tongue to tease him about his sudden show of chivalry but, for once in my life, I shut my mouth and enjoyed it.

"I can make you some coffee."

"Sure," he said as his gaze swept up and down my body, the rush of heat searing my skin along its path.

I made my way to my door, hoping Tyler didn't notice my quivering hand as I finally slid the key into the lock. Ridiculous first-time and first-date jitters took hold of me. We'd already had sex and I'd known Tyler my whole life, although never like this. He'd been different since the wedding, but there was an ease to him tonight I'd never seen.

"I'll give them a recommendation, but admittedly I've had better," I rambled as I grabbed two coffee mugs from the cabinet. "But that could be my bias. I'm always harder on Italian and Spanish restaurants because I know how everything is supposed to be made."

"So Cleopatra is a hard-ass."

I wasn't calm enough to look back at Tyler yet, but the heat from his presence behind me was enough to kick up my heart rate.

"Cleopatra needs to be impressed. Tonight was good enough. The pasta was pretty good, but the dessert wasn't worth the calories. Not that I have to worry anymore, right?"

I sputtered out a nervous chuckle, then he snaked an arm around my waist, and I breathed out an embarrassing moan when he brushed my hair off my shoulder. I was keyed up in so many ways. The right thing to do would be to take it slow, ease into this very unexpected situation and get to know each other on a new level the right way.

The right way flew right out the window the second Tyler's lips ran down my neck.

"Relax, sugar," he crooned as he dragged open-mouthed kisses across my nape. I white-knuckled the counter as I slumped against him, rubbing against the hardness poking at my back.

"I told you, I'm like a stick of dynamite right now... Ah, right there," I panted as he dove into the crook of my neck.

"When weren't you a stick of dynamite? Always too hot to handle."

I whimpered when his hands drifted down my hips.

"I... I want to do this the right way. I don't want to rush in and lose you," I confessed, reaching back and gliding my hand up Tyler's leg to press him against me.

He stilled, cupping my chin. "You won't. I'm sorry for being forward, but after all those weeks of fighting to not touch you, I'm about ready to lose it." Our mouths were so close together that our lips brushed. "But I'll stop if you want me to—"

I cut him off with a kiss, keeping my lips on his as I swiveled around and fisted the collar of his shirt to bring him closer.

"I don't," I murmured against his mouth as his hands roamed my body, caressing my stomach with a sensual reverence. It was impetuous and crazy, but at that moment, I didn't know any other way to be.

When it came to Tyler, I never did.

"You said you're quick to arousal. How quickly can you come?" he asked as his palm skated up my bare thigh.

"I'm not sure," I answered between kisses. "As I'm halfway there just by the question, I'd say pretty damn quick."

I gasped when he slid his hand inside my panties, drifting a finger along my soaked skin.

"Holy shit, you weren't kidding." He moved faster, drawing a circle around my clit until it pebbled against his finger. I slipped as my knees gave out, leaning back on the counter to keep steady. "That's it. Get wet for me."

"I'm always wet for you," I admitted in a scratchy whisper. Another long moan escaped me when he slid a finger deep inside.

"Okay?" he asked with a concerned furrow on his brow.

"More," I begged, not caring how desperate I sounded. I covered my mouth with my hand when he slipped a second finger inside, curling them both as his thumb stayed on my clit. An orgasm hit me fast as my hips bucked against him. The kitchen spun as I dropped my head against Tyler's chest, trying to catch my breath.

"'Sugar' again?" I teased in a raspy, breathless whisper.

He smiled and pulled my mouth back to his, kissing me slow and deep. "Problem?"

"Not if you keep doing that to me while you call me that." I pushed against his chest and sank to my wobbly knees.

Tyler's eyes grew wide, peering down at me as if I was about to give him the best present of his life. "Olivia..." he said as I unbuckled his belt and unzipped his pants. "We could move to the living room where there's a carpet."

My heart warmed at his consideration for my kneecaps while his dick pulsed against my hand.

"I've waited too long, and I don't care. Relax, sugar." I dragged his pants down his thighs and took him into my mouth in one gulp. I wanted to be seductive, lick the tip and tease my tongue up and down his length, but I needed to bring him to the edge now, to drive him completely crazy and fill his world with nothing but me.

That was a constant that hadn't changed—and never would.

Tyler's tortured grunts and groans grew louder the harder I sucked. My eyes teared when he poked at the back of my throat, but I didn't care. I eased him out of my mouth, peeking up at him before I took him all in again. He reached over me and grabbed the counter I'd clutched a few moments ago, the back of his legs tightening every time he grew harder in my mouth.

"How could... How is it even better than... Fuck, Olivia, I'm about to..." His hand tightened in my hair as I dug my nails into his ass, holding him in place until he spilled down my throat.

I dropped a kiss to his thigh and fell against him. I was a satisfied and blissful kind of spent but lifted myself to stand despite the temptation to lie back on the floor and sleep.

"Come here," he whispered and gathered me into his arms. "Please tell me I didn't push you."

"Are you kidding? Tyler, I think you have scratches on your ass." I peeked over his hip. "I wanted it all as much as you did."

He exhaled, his shoulders relaxing as he cradled my face. "I can't stay much longer. I want to, but Saturday is our busy morning, why we close early on Fridays. I don't want you to think—"

"I don't." I pressed a finger to his lips. "I promise. Give me a minute to change. We can hang out on my couch for a little while until you have to go. Never too soon to talk baby names, I guess." I kissed his chin. "Okay?"

His mouth spread into a slow smile. "Okay, sugar."

I rolled my eyes, pretending the silly pet name didn't send goose bumps down my neck. "Let me get out of this dress, and I'll be right back."

"Hey, I said I'd help you." He grabbed my arm, pulling my back flush to his front. "Side or back?"

"Back," I said, sweeping my hair off my neck.

The whir of the zipper in the silence shouldn't have turned me on again so soon. He pressed a kiss to the small of my back and trailed a few more up to my shoulder.

"So gorgeous," he whispered into my hair. "So unfairly fucking gorgeous."

I grinned as I rushed back to my bedroom, peeling off the dress before stepping out of it.

"Bye, old friend." I sighed and hung it back in my closet. I had a while until maternity clothes would be a necessity, but I was already done with skin-tight leather for a long time.

A breath of relief whooshed out of my lungs when I unhooked my bra and slipped on my silk robe, my boobs even more swollen and sore. I wasn't leaving much to the imagination, but Tyler wasn't leaving right that second. I wouldn't be me if I didn't try to poke at his resolve, although this way at least he'd enjoy it too.

I came into the living room, cracking up when Tyler gave me a double take.

"You're never *not* going to make me crazy, are you?"

He laughed at my slow shrug as I cuddled next to him.

I'd forgotten about my seduction mission as I started to nod off on his chest, his scent bringing back memories of the best night of my life, the one I couldn't acknowledge until now.

A knock at my door jolted me up right as I was about to drift off.

Worried enough to forget I was half-naked, I raced to my door and opened it. "Mom, what's wrong?"

"Nothing. I didn't mean to wake you. They're cleaning the curbs in the morning, and you have to move your car behind mine in the driveway. I forgot to remind you—"

She stopped, bunching up the collar of her robe as her gaze drifted over my shoulder.

"Tyler, this is a surprise," she said, cutting me a look.

"Hi, Carla. I imagine it is." He coughed out a nervous laugh. "I didn't realize what time it was. Give me your keys, and I'll move your car before I go." He held out his hand.

"Oh, right." I reached over to grab them from the hook. "Thank you."

"No problem. I'll be right back. Um, good night, Carla, if I don't see you when I come back in."

"You won't. Good night, Tyler."

My gaze followed Tyler out the front door as I ignored my mother for as long as possible.

"So, um, yeah," I stammered as Tyler did a second ago. Getting caught with a guy in your thirties didn't feel all that different than when I was in my teens, although my mother wasn't looking me over and stifling a laugh back then. "I guess it is a surprise."

"A surprise thirty years in the making, sweetheart. Get some sleep after Tyler leaves—you look exhausted." She turned, her shoulders shaking, and headed back upstairs.

TWENTY-FIVE
TYLER

"Ready for the fame?" Eli teased as we set up for another busy Sunday morning.

"It's one article, one time. We probably got a paragraph." I shrugged, hoping to mask the nerves that had kept me up half of last night. "Make yourself useful." I slid the tray of freshly iced donuts toward him. "Staci and Gabby can set these up before the line gets too long."

"The reporter was here the entire afternoon. I'm sure you got more than one paragraph. I never met anyone so afraid of success." He snickered, grabbing the tray and pushing through the double doors to the front.

I wasn't afraid of success. What gnawed at me lately was the fear of setting my expectations too high only to see them plummet—or, even worse, getting the success I wanted and then finding out that I was unable to keep up with it. The thought of failing when it was just me was terrifying enough. Now that I was going to be someone's father, it was almost crippling.

A knock at the back door broke me out of my panic spiral. When I clicked the lock open, I found Olivia, stunning at seven o'clock in the morning in sweats. I loved seeing this side of her. Before we forged this friendship that had turned into something neither of us had the guts to label yet, she was always so put together. I never saw her without a flashy outfit or perfect makeup, even at parties in my parents' backyard. Getting to know her on this level meant seeing her let loose. She was always beautiful, but an Olivia without a stitch of makeup in a Yankees sweatshirt was my favorite. On some level, the pieces of her I'd only recently gotten to know after all these years of her poking her way into my life made her feel different, made her feel like mine.

"Happy *New York Times* day!" She looped one arm around my neck and pulled me in for a kiss. I stole another one when she pulled away and held her flush to my body, burying my head in her neck.

It was funny how the woman who had grated on my nerves my entire life was the only one able to soothe me.

"Hey, what's wrong?" She pulled back and cupped my neck. "Overthinking, or trying to talk yourself into this not being a big deal?"

"Little of both. Why are you up so early? You should sleep."

She shrugged, plopping a bag onto the stool next to the counter. "I was too excited for you to sleep. And I wanted to head to the deli next to the train station since I know they have all the Sunday papers early. I scored five copies. One for both of my grandmothers and my mother, and one for both of us." She pulled one of the papers out of the bag, her brow furrowed as she sifted through the pages. "Here it is," she sang as she held up the article.

I was happy no one else was here to see me try to keep cool while my heart lurched into my throat.

"Eeep, here you are! First mention too and... Oh my God."

My stomach dropped when she trailed off. "And what?"

A hysterical laugh bubbled out of her. "Tyler, you're a thirst trap."

"What?" I snatched the paper from her hand. The reporter asked if she could take a picture of me in front of the bakery. After a long night and half day of baking by the time she came in, my apron was covered in flour, but she'd insisted I'd leave it on. I hated pictures to begin with, so I'd folded my arms and tried not to feel like a total dick as I smiled for the camera.

"The messy hair, the baker muscles bulging out of your T-shirt. My baby daddy is *hot*." She looked up and swatted my ass, coaxing an unexpected laugh out of me.

"What does it say?"

"It goes into how you bought the old bakery space and built it up over the past year, the cute name you chose, why your customers love coming here, and how you were a mostly undiscovered gem until a popular food blogger called attention to one of your desserts." The pride in her eyes made my chest pinch. "It's a great article, and they got your name and address right, which is the most important. A lot of businesses would kill for a *New York Times* mention." She slid her palm against mine and entwined our fingers. "I'm so damn happy for you."

"This is all because of you. That one post led—"

She waved me off. "I gave you a push maybe, but this is all you and how hard you've worked. Enjoy something for once." She elbowed my side and kept reading.

I rested my chin on her shoulder, winding my arm around her waist and bringing her back against my front. I'd enjoy this because she was here to share it with me. I needed her more than I wanted her lately. Olivia Sanchez had gone from my childhood enemy to my person.

So why couldn't I tell her?

"And..." she started, her eyes sparkling when she turned her head, "this reporter just hit on you a little." She pointed to the next to last paragraph. "*Tyler Bennett, thirty-five, was not who some pictured as the owner of a bakery on a quiet patch of highway on Long Island. His boyish good looks and quiet intensity are said to make him a hot local bachelor commodity.*"

"You're kidding me. *Ugh.*" My mind went to that stupid dating app that Eli made me download. I needed to delete it as soon as possible. The last thing I needed was for anyone to Google my name now and find me there.

Even if we hadn't discussed it, as far as I was concerned, I was more than spoken for—I was owned.

"You do have a quiet intensity." She turned toward me, chewing on her bottom lip. "Why I always loved pushing you. It's sexy as *fuck*." She looped her arm around my neck from behind and brushed her lips against mine. "I'm proud of you. And since you said you're keeping your day off for once and closing tomorrow, how about a celebration dinner at my apartment tonight? You could even maybe"—she cleared her throat and stuffed the paper back into the bag— "maybe even stay over. If you'd like."

There wasn't an inch of Olivia I hadn't touched or tasted in the past week, but we always stopped right before we had sex, and I hadn't spent the entire night with her since the hotel room. Tearing myself away from her every time was killing me, but even if one night of amazing sex led us to where we were, I wanted to do things the right way. We didn't need any more complications between us than we already had, but it seemed pointless to step so lightly now.

"I'd like." I kissed the back of her neck, running my finger down the path of goose bumps prickling down her shoulder. "I'd like that a lot."

"Good," she replied with a gravelly whisper as she

slumped against me. "It's mean to turn on a pregnant woman and leave her hanging."

I laughed and turned her around, cupping her face. "I have no intentions of leaving you hanging, sugar. Just warming you up for later," I whispered as I inched closer.

"You better get back to work." Her hands skated down my back, stopping at my waist. "I know I just said it, but I am proud of you." She brushed her lips over mine. "Go kick some ass today, and I'll see you later."

"See you later," I said, taking her mouth in a kiss too deep and wet for the middle of a busy morning, but I didn't care. Her lips against mine, her body pressed up against me was all I could think about and all I wanted. *She* was all I wanted. When she whimpered into my mouth, I hooked her leg over my hip and rubbed my cock against the sweet heat between her legs. She smiled into the kiss when I squeezed her legging-covered ass.

"Hey, we got copies— Oh shit, sorry."

We broke apart, swiveling to where Eli stood, holding up a paper.

"Didn't mean to interrupt. I'll find the article myself." He laughed, looking between us as he headed back outside.

"I think you just ruined your hot eligible bachelor reputation." Olivia coasted her hand down my chest, peering up at me with a wicked grin that made me want her lips all over again. "I'll be waiting for you and your boyish good looks tonight." She gave me a quick peck and headed out the back door.

I smiled at her departure and the exaggerated sway of her hips that I knew was purely for my benefit. She'd started doing that when we were teenagers, and although she aggravated me on the daily back then, I was just as hypnotized watching her walk away.

I'd been under her spell for longer than I cared to think about, only now I enjoyed the shit out of it.

Sundays always went by fast, but this one seemed to slip by in the blink of an eye. Tegan had already framed the article and hung it right by the front entrance, at Eli's suggestion, insisting it was good for business. I wasn't thrilled at the notion of seeing my awkward mug every single day after I opened but couldn't stop the pride flooding my chest whenever I'd glance at it.

"What a day," Staci sighed as she locked the door behind the last customer.

"The best day," Tegan said, nudging my side as she cleaned up the front register. "We work with a celebrity now."

"Right," I said although my cheeks ached with a wide grin. It *was* the best day, and I couldn't wait to close up the bakery and have the best night.

"Did you guys notice all the... women in here today? I didn't realize that many people still get a newspaper." Staci crinkled her nose as she swept the floor near the entrance.

"It was an online piece too, according to the reporter anyway. I haven't checked, but a few customers keep up with it on Sundays I suppose." I shrugged, trying to sound flippant and not think of the customers who slid their phone numbers to me while I was covering the register. The article and its popularity could only help us, but I hoped whatever attention I'd personally get from the article would fade quickly.

"Get out of here," Eli said, slapping me on the back. "We have this handled, and I think you have somewhere to be, no?" He raised a brow and jutted his chin toward the door.

"Thanks. I just need to grab the pie that I set aside. And thanks for being the pain in the ass I need around here."

"Well, boss. I'm touched." He clutched his chest. "Judging by how this place keeps blowing up, we can chat about an increase in my pay for such services. Until then, have a good night."

I waved a quick goodbye, and I headed out and to Olivia's. Tomorrow was the first time I didn't need to be up before God to start baking and setting up, but I had the feeling my hours would be even longer starting this week. And even when I brought in new staff, we'd run out of room for all the extra items and bodies.

I wasn't ready to think about expanding yet. I'd celebrate my little place doing well for the moment—and the woman who kept changing my life in unexpected but amazing ways.

TWENTY-SIX
TYLER

"Hey." Olivia greeted me in what looked like a sweatshirt dress after I knocked on her door. She met my gaze through the locks of hair that had fallen from the bun on top of her head. "I was hoping you'd bring dessert." She kissed my lips and plucked the box from my hands.

"I saved the last one for you."

She stilled, sucking in a gasp. "If this is chocolate cream pie, you can do anything you want to me tonight."

She set it on her counter and came back to me, wrapping her arms around my waist.

"Does that mean I couldn't before?" I coasted the back of my hand down her cheek. "That's disappointing."

"Was it a good day?" She framed my face, but I had to look away for a minute. Olivia always frightened me a little, but the pure adoration in her eyes combined with all I felt for her now terrified me.

"It is now." I cupped her neck and pulled her in for another kiss.

"Have a seat. I had planned on baked ziti, but there was no

more sauce in Mom's freezer, so I pulled together spaghetti carbonara. I used to make it for Morgan all the time in college and she loved it, but I wanted a little better for you tonight."

Was this what it was like to have a woman who supported what I did instead of resenting it? I'd come home wanting to tell Amy all about the progress we'd made at the bakery, and she'd roll her eyes and ask me if it was all worth it.

It was, and now I had someone who made everything else worth it.

"I'm sure it's great, and as long as I have you tonight, I'm happy."

Olivia froze, almost scaring me that I might've said something wrong. We'd grown up barely giving each other pleasantries, so I guessed nice words from me were still a bit of a novelty.

"You have me tonight," she whispered, a rare shy smile pulling at her mouth. "Go sit and relax. I'm sure you didn't get a second to rest today."

"No, but that's how Sundays are." I sat at her kitchen table and noticed what looked like a bottle of champagne.

"It's sparkling cider," she told me as she set a plate of pasta in front of me. "It's boring, just like decaf coffee, but rules are rules."

I never forgot that she was pregnant. Hell, I thought about it all damn day. But sometimes, the gravity of our situation barreled over me when I was reminded of it. A baby wasn't why we were spending more time together, it was just what made me stop denying how much I wanted to be with Olivia all along.

Maybe my kid could somehow help me take it the rest of the way so I could make her mine for good, but that was a worry I'd push away for another time.

It was good to finally unwind, not have to be on all day

long when old and new customers came in to chat about the article. I finally started to relax when I caught Olivia's smirk.

"What's with the staring, Sanchez?" I asked as I swirled my fork around more spaghetti.

"You still slurp your spaghetti."

I set my fork down to glare back at her. "I don't slurp my spaghetti."

She crinkled her nose and nodded. "You do. I'm not giving you a hard time—it's cute. Whenever I'd come back from your house when we were kids, I'd slurp it too. Until I got into trouble for making a mess. I never said anything because I knew if I did, you'd stop doing it."

"So haircuts and slurping spaghetti are what does it for you?" I lifted a brow.

"When it's you, I guess it does." A tiny blush stained her cheeks. Olivia's focus on me always exhausted me as a kid, but I had to hide a wide grin whenever we reminisced about it now.

I almost married a woman who couldn't care less about me, a total contrast from the one who could never stay away, no matter how many times I'd told her to leave me alone.

"Did you get a chance to see the comments on the online piece?" Olivia asked, clearing her throat as she emptied the rest of the cider into her glass.

"No, not yet. Why?" I asked when she smiled around the rim of her glass.

"I told you that you were a thirst trap. The comments were *amazing*. My favorite so far is the one offering *you* pie."

"Ugh," I groaned, scrubbing my hand down my face.

"It's so adorable how uncomfortable this makes you." She reached over to squeeze the back of my neck. "How many women tried to slip you their number today?" She raised a brow.

"A few," I admitted. "Couple of guys too. I guess if it brings in business it's fine. Attention was never my thing. That was all you."

She narrowed her eyes at me as she tore off a piece of bread. "You never knew how good you looked in a baseball uniform? Please. So you just had to peel your shirt off at practice?"

"Baseball uniforms look the same on every— Wait. Practice? When were you at practice?"

Her cheeks blushed red for a moment. "Once. Not at the field, but a bunch of us hung out outside. I found it so unfair that someone with such a miserable personality had muscles and abs to spare. And before you get on me, yes, I looked. And so did everyone else."

"But only *you* were there for me, right?"

"Whatever," she said, rolling her eyes. "Go sit in the living room while I clean up."

"I can help you clean up."

"You worked all day, and I'm just loading this into the dishwasher."

"I'm not letting my pregnant girlfriend clean up alone after she cooked me dinner. Go."

I took the plate from her hand and pointed to the living room. Judging by how her jaw went slack, I'd broken the unspoken rule of not labeling whatever this was between us. She stared at me, eyes wide, but didn't fight. Only nodded and padded back inside.

Once I loaded the dishwasher and cleaned up the kitchen, I found Olivia folded into a ball on her couch, completely passed out with her hair cascading over the arm.

I sat beside her, easing down slowly on the cushion so I wouldn't wake her. Unable to help myself, I brushed the hair off her forehead. Watching her sleep reminded me of that morning after the wedding. I woke up completely clueless as to what to do next and unable to take my eyes off her. She was so beautiful, it hurt not to touch her.

"Did I do it again?" Her voice was groggy as she stirred. "I sit for more than five minutes and I'm out. Your kid is already slowing me down." She shot me a crooked smile as she rubbed her stomach.

"Well," I said, draping my hand over hers. "Then he's—or she's—already a step ahead of me. I could never keep up with you."

She laughed through a yawn. "I've always been too much."

"No," I said, my clipped tone surprising both of us. "You're everything, Olivia."

"You're sweet when you want to be, Bennett," she told me as she squirmed on the couch, fisting the collar of my T-shirt to pull me on top of her. "I wanted to make tonight special for you. I didn't mean to pass out in the middle of it."

"You did," I whispered as I settled between her legs. We'd been in this position most of the week, but knowing I was here for the night made it hit a little different. "Nothing would have been special today without you. I still don't know how I can thank you."

"I keep telling you, you don't. Although I would like to apply to take over your social media accounts." I melted into her as she ran her nails up and down my back. "It's cute that you guys throw up a holiday meme or random cake, but now that you have eyes on you, you need to make the most of it."

"Can I afford you?" I asked as I ran my thumb along her bottom lip.

She squinted at me, tapping her chin. "We can work out a good rate. Considering you knocked me up and everything, I'm sure that qualifies for a discount."

"All right. We can give it a try..." I stilled after I hooked her leg around my hip and drifted my hand up her bare thigh. "What's this?" I asked as my fingers trailed what felt like lace.

"That's the other little present I have for you today. I just drifted off before I could show you." She shifted under me and tapped my shoulder. I sat up as she stood from the couch and pulled her dress over her head.

"Fuck, Olivia," I growled. She was in a red lace bra and panties—*panties* being a relative term as they were only a scrap of material draped over her hips. The swells of her breasts strained against the cups, already spilling out. My eyes roamed her body as she turned around, and I almost swallowed my tongue as I drank in the rest of her.

"I'm not showing yet, but my boobs are going to need their own zip code soon." She grinned as her hand slid across the slight swell of her abdomen.

This fantasy brought to life was mine. *She* was mine, and maybe she always had been. I'd resisted her for the very reason she said—she was always too much for me in all the best ways.

"I think you're trying to kill me," I rasped and closed the distance between us, crushing my lips to hers. Her back arched as I ran my tongue down her neck and across her chest. All I needed was one small tug on the cups until she came right out of that bra. She screamed when I took a nipple into my mouth and rolled it between my teeth. Her body was still soft and sensitive—and always gorgeous.

My head spun, dizzy from the loss of blood from my brain to my cock. Seeing her like this, wrapped up like a red lace present just for me, I couldn't open it fast enough. I devoured her mouth as I reached behind her to unbuckle her bra. The package was nice, but nothing beat Olivia naked. And I needed her naked *now*.

"Tyler, I... oh God, yes..." She moaned as I found more

sensitive skin—wet, swollen skin dripping all over my fingers. I trailed kisses down her body, resting my cheek against the tiny bump for a moment before I licked a path up the side of her thigh.

"Please," she begged on a moan as I pressed soft kisses between her legs, taking a peek at her hooded eyes and swollen lips, and moved the lace aside and sucked her clit into my mouth. Her thigh trembled against my cheek as I lost all mercy and self-control, sucking and biting, letting it slip between my teeth when I eased off only to dive in harder.

She pushed against my shoulders, shaking her head when I glanced up at her.

"What's wrong?" I asked, standing and cupping her neck. Her face was flushed, and she winced when she met my gaze as if she were in pain.

"Take your clothes off and fuck me." She dug her nails into my biceps, then searched for the hem of my T-shirt. "I can't take it anymore."

I peeled my shirt off and brought her mouth back to mine. Taking it slow was pointless and stupid. Olivia and I were explosive, all-consuming, and inevitable.

I framed her face, my chest heaving along with hers. "Can I make love to you instead?"

She blinked, her face crumpling for a moment. *Love* was not a word we ever used between us, although it scratched at the back of my throat more often than I could face just yet. What we had together was new and confusing sometimes, but the one thing I knew was there would be no going back from this.

There was never any going back from Olivia period.

"Can we do both?" Her voice quivered as her nails scraped down my chest.

I backed her into her bedroom, both of us stumbling onto the mattress with our lips still fused together.

"I'll give you whatever you want."

My eyes held hers as she fumbled with my belt. When it didn't open fast enough and she bit her lip in frustration, I couldn't help but laugh.

"Always so impatient," I teased, even though I was hard to the point of pain and certain I wouldn't last ten minutes the first time I was inside her again.

"That kiss this morning and that picture riled me up all damn day. Lose the pants, Bennett."

I kicked my pants off and dropped my boxers before I climbed back on the bed, hovering over Olivia for a minute.

"What?" she asked, breathless as she cupped my cheek.

"This, us... it's a little surreal."

A devious grin pulled at the corner of her mouth. "Getting naked with the girl you never wanted around?"

"No," I whispered, lifting her leg over my hip as I settled on top of her. "I always wanted you. I just never thought I'd ever get you."

"Same," she whispered, pressing her forehead against mine. "I haven't been with anyone since you or for a while before you. And the damage is already done," she said with a nervous chuckle.

"I haven't been with anyone else either, for a long time. If you're asking me what I think you're asking—"

She nodded, and I didn't waste any time. Her eyes bulged when I filled her with one thrust. Between being inside her bare and the confessions that slipped out, the shock and the need made us even more ravenous than the first time. She leaned forward, moving against me as I inched in and out of her, both of us wrestling to get as close as possible.

I love you, Olivia.

It was right there, as close to the edge as I was, but I sank my teeth into my bottom lip to hold it in. Not because of our weird transition from enemies to lovers. We didn't even label what was between us until tonight, but losing it was something I couldn't bring myself to think about.

When the bed started to creak, she wrapped her arms around my neck in a tight hold, lifting her hips to meet mine as I plowed into her. Control was never in my grasp when it came to Olivia.

"Come for me, sugar." I snaked my hand around her waist and brought her closer, ready to spill everything I had into her. Despite the effort I'd always put in to run away from her, I'd been chasing Olivia my entire life.

Her legs went rigid as she clenched around me, quivering in my arms as her nails scraped down my back. I pulsed inside her, then lowered us both to the mattress, fisting the sheets as I buried my head in her neck.

"Holy shit," she breathed out. "So, good day?" Her giggle shook against my cheek.

A sleepy smile pulled at my lips.

"The best day." I brushed kisses across her cheek to her mouth, lingering when I got to her lips.

The woman carrying my baby was the love of my life.

It was the second part of that thought that knocked the air out of my lungs.

TWENTY-SEVEN
OLIVIA

"Thank you for coming with me," I told Tyler as I slid into the passenger seat of his SUV. "I know midmornings can be busy..." I trailed off when I noticed the tilt of his head.

"Stop thanking me. It's my baby too, and I told you I'm here for all of it." He leaned over the console and pressed his lips to mine, moving his palm across my disappearing waistline with a quick caress. I melted whenever he gave my stomach any attention. It was an unspoken reassurance I never knew I needed, especially today.

Although I'd had an ultrasound when I had my pregnancy confirmed, this was a more official picture now that I was at twelve weeks. I'd never expected a baby with Tyler—or at all in recent years—but I wanted it so badly the notion of finding something wrong today triggered a full-body panic.

And, if I was being honest with myself, I was afraid that a baby was the main reason Tyler and I had leveled up from the awkward friendship we'd begun after his cousin's wedding. Consciously, I knew it wasn't. Tyler could never be pushed into anything he didn't want to do, even when we were kids.

But my subconscious, the main source responsible for picking fights with him to both mask my feelings and suck all the attention from him that I could, was a nagging bitch always in my ear.

"Can they tell if it's a boy or girl today?" Tyler asked when we pulled into the parking lot next to the doctor's office.

"That's more the next ultrasound. Sometimes they can, but it's not one hundred percent." I stilled for a moment when he slid his palm against mine and laced our fingers together as we headed into the office. My heart, as always, did a flip-flop at simple gestures like that. It was ridiculous to get that excited over small things like holding my hand or daydreaming about the moment in my kitchen when he'd called me his pregnant girlfriend.

I never swooned over other guys like this. But other guys weren't Tyler.

After I checked in at the front desk, I slid into the seat next to him in the waiting room and kissed his cheek.

"I know you said I don't have to thank you, but I'm glad you're here."

His cheeks lifted with a grin wide enough for his dimple to dent the corner of his mouth. "I'm glad I am too." He kissed my temple and draped his arm around my shoulders.

I sighed and dropped my head to his shoulder, my swooning amplified by hormones.

"Not that we could do anything about it, but any preference for a boy or girl?" I asked as I cuddled into his side.

His brows pulled together. "Not really. This little girl came into the bakery the day you told me you were pregnant. She reminded me of you a little bit. Maybe not as evil."

I elbowed his side, and he chuckled.

"I've thought about her a couple of times since then, but I'm honestly good either way." He brushed the hair off my shoulder as a smirk tipped the side of his mouth. "I'm not sure how I'd handle another one of you, but I'd do it."

I darted my eyes away to stare at the floor. A picture of Tyler holding a little girl who looked like me squeezed at my chest so hard, I wrapped my arms around my torso. The joy and sorrow at the thought almost cut me in half as I imagined all the fun she'd have on her father's arm and how those days for me would always be both my most treasured and most painful memory.

"How about you?" His question knocked me back into the present.

"I don't know. A mini me who would drive you crazy is fun to think about, but a little Tyler would be nice. I'd make sure that no mean girls would stop him if he ever wanted to bake."

"With you as his mother, I'm sure no one would be able to stop him from doing anything," he teased with a small, proud smile drifting across his lips.

"Olivia Sanchez."

The nurse at the front desk waved me in. I headed inside the room with Tyler behind me.

"Take everything off from the waist down and put this over your legs." She handed me a paper sheet. "The tech will be in shortly."

An odd sense of embarrassment washed over me.

"Really, Sanchez?" he said, folding his arms as he leaned against the wall when he noticed my hesitation. "I've seen you naked. A lot. I have it all memorized by now."

I looked away, trying not to focus on the sudden heat in his eyes. "Yes, but this is different. Turn around."

He grumbled as he turned to face the wall. I made quick work of peeling off my leggings and flats and climbed onto the table, grabbing the sheet and lying down.

"Okay, I'm done."

"You know I peeked, right?" He quirked a brow as he took a seat next to the bed.

"In a doctor's office?" I sucked in an exaggerated breath. "You're an animal."

He leaned forward to kiss my lips, soft but lingering long enough to sigh against his mouth. "You're beautiful. Couldn't help it."

I bit back a smile, the warmth flooding my chest relaxing me if for only the moment.

"Ready?" My back straightened at the knock on the door.

"Yes, come in," I cleared my throat, trying to get rid of the rasp thanks to the ping pong rush of emotions all morning.

"Okay, let's get this started." A female technician who looked like a college senior at most poked at a computer screen before rolling her stool over to me. "You're about twelve weeks, correct?"

"Yes," I replied, annoyed at how breathless I sounded.

I jumped when she squirted warm gel over my stomach.

"We should be able to see everything this way, but if the fetus is being difficult, I may have to go in transvaginally." She darkened the lights and scanned across my stomach. As she adjusted the sound on the computer, a loud whooshing filled the room.

"Wow, that's a nice strong heartbeat. I usually have to dig to find it." She smiled as she glanced between us. Tyler's features were frozen in a shock and awe that thickened my throat.

"Just got real, didn't it?" I whispered and squeezed his hand.

"You got that right," he replied in a soft voice. I sniffed away the burning in my nose as I refused to cry during an ultrasound like I had during everything else lately.

"Length looks good, your doctor will give you details, but all looks good to me."

At my first ultrasound, I only saw a dot—a dot that I kept losing track of on the fuzzy black-and-white image. What filled the screen before us was the shape of a real baby. Very tiny, but there was a definable head and a body.

"Do you want to know the sex?"

I leaned forward on my elbows and glanced at Tyler.

"Yes," I replied when he nodded.

"I'd say it's likely a boy." She took a few more pictures and handed me a towel to wipe my stomach. "But they can tell you with more certainty at the next ultrasound."

"Dodged a bullet on that one." I winked at Tyler as I sat up.

"Here are some pictures. Let me quickly show the scans to the doctor and you can be on your way."

"Looks like a real baby," Tyler whispered, still staring at the picture after the technician left the room.

"It does." I gathered the paper sheet around me, mesmerized by the little person I saw now instead of a fuzzy shape. "We should tell our parents. I wanted to wait for this ultrasound to make sure everything was okay, but I can't hide it with hoodies anymore."

"I agree. And my mother mentioned stopping at Carla's today for lunch."

"It will be kind of fun seeing them both react at the same time." I chuckled. "What about your dad?"

He shrugged, handing me my leggings and panties. "Mom can tell him later when he comes out of the basement."

After we left, Tyler and I headed to the car in silence as I kept fighting more tears.

"What's wrong?" He squinted at me before he turned the engine on.

"If it is a boy, can we name him Javier?" My voice cracked as I swallowed the perpetual lump in my throat. "I know it doesn't exactly go with Bennett, but—"

"Javier Bennett is a great name." He slid his hand to the nape of my neck and squeezed. "No one else will have it. Probably. And after playing referee to us for most of our lives, it's the least we could do for your dad."

I roped my arms around his neck and cried into his shoulder.

"Hey," he crooned, kissing the top of my head. "It's okay. I got you, sugar."

A laugh bubbled out through my sobs. I grabbed his face to kiss him with all I had. He brushed his lips over the damp trails of my tears before coming back to my mouth. I loved that silly pet name he'd originally given me as a joke.

I loved him. I loved him when I thought I hated him. I loved him when he let me be his friend. I loved him because he *always* had me. There wasn't a time Tyler Bennett wasn't the center of my world, it just took me a years-long minute to realize why.

"I'm sorry. I'm just a mess." I rubbed at my swollen eyes. "I hate anyone seeing me like this."

"You're not a mess. This is a lot. And I know you miss your dad and can't really talk about it. I like when you let go in front of me. It's like..." He peered out the front window with a wistful gaze a moment and brought his eyes back to me. "It's like a piece of you only I get. I can't explain it." He pressed a kiss to my forehead and put his truck into drive. "Ready to shock our mothers?"

"Sure." I flashed a quick smile as we pulled out of the parking lot.

He had every piece of me. Someday, I'd be able to tell him,

even though if he paid attention, I'd been showing him my entire life.

"Oh, hey, you two," Mom said, her brow pinching after I knocked and opened her door. "Funny to see the two of you out in the middle of a workday."

"Not *funny to see the two of us together*?" I asked as I slid onto a chair at her dining room table next to Helen.

"Nope. We've been waiting for you both to just come out and say it. I know you're here almost every night." Helen's eyes twinkled as she glanced at her son.

"Of course you know that. No secrets, I suppose." Tyler slid his gaze to mine.

"Well, maybe one." I bunched my shoulders into a shrug, holding in a laugh when both my mother and Helen froze in their seats.

I glanced at Tyler and slid one of the pictures across the table. Helen's chair screeched back on the kitchen tile as Mom let out a sound that was a mix of a gasp and a scream.

"Surprise!" I held my hands up, but neither one of them noticed as their eyes were glued to the picture.

"Twelve weeks? Why am I only finding out now?"

My stomach sank when Mom glowered at me.

"I wanted to make sure all was okay before we told anyone."

Tyler draped his arm around me, lifting a shoulder when my gaze stumbled on his. We were studying our parents for a reaction, and so far we had shock from his mother and hurt from mine.

"Wait," Helen said, holding up a finger. "Twelve weeks—that's right around Donnie's wedding? Or maybe the night of." Helen's brow jumped.

"I...I hope that's not a question you're waiting for me to

answer, Mom," Tyler stammered. I held in a laugh when his cheeks flushed.

"Well, it's not like I didn't know what happened. Or any of us—"

"Mom, please," he begged, draping his hand over his eyes.

I laughed until I noticed Mom's rigid stance by the sink. Pushing off the chair, I eased in her direction, but she still wouldn't lift her head.

"I know it's not exactly traditional, but—"

"That's not it. You couldn't tell me? Is this what I am to you now? A fragile piece of glass?" Her voice cracked as she rubbed at her temple.

"No, Mom." I grabbed her hand. "The only ones who know are Tyler and Morgan, and that's only because I was with her when I realized I was. I didn't want to upset anyone if something happened."

"That's what I'm there for, Olivia. To be there when something happens." She waved a hand at me and turned around.

"Don't be like this, Mom. The technician said that it's a boy. Maybe."

She glanced back for a moment but took her gaze back to the kitchen window.

"I didn't keep it from you because I didn't think you could handle it, I didn't want you to be disappointed or hurt...again."

"I am hurt and disappointed." She sniffled and wiped her cheek with the back of her hand. "After all the fights he broke up between the two of you, your father should be here for this." Relief rushed through me when a smile broke out on her lips. I crashed into her the second she opened her arms.

"This also explains why you wear hoodies and sweaters all the time now." She lifted the bottom of my shirt when she backed away.

"It's not a real bump yet. Just looks like I had too many tacos."

"I think she's glowing." Helen smiled at me from over Mom's shoulder. "Pregnancy agrees with you."

"I don't know about that. I'm a hot mess who cries too much, but thank you."

"You can make the cake for her shower!" Helen's eyes widened as she turned back to Tyler. "I think it could be on the small side. Only about fifty."

I shook my head when Mom nodded.

"Fifty is too much," I said but might as well have been silent.

"We need to get a registry going," Mom told Helen, ignoring what I'd said.

"We do. I think I have a printout still somewhere from Ross's son."

"My kid is not going to be like Ross's son," Tyler spat out, that adorable, miserable way of his I'd always found inexplicably hot slipping out.

"Of course not. His kid is a little jerk, I agree, but he's little enough that Ross's wife had all the newest things. So much has changed from thirty-five years ago. And we need those new bottles too."

Mom dug out a pen and pad from the junk drawer, nodding as she sat next to Helen.

"Well," Tyler started as he stood. "I don't think we need to be here for this. Olivia and I should get back to work."

"Yeah, I'd agree." I took his extended hand and made my way to the front door. "A congratulations would have been nice," I said in a loud whisper that wasn't acknowledged by either of them.

"I say let them do what they need to and we just show up."

He shrugged before opening the door and following me out into the hallway.

"That went...weirdly," I said, still staring at my mother's door.

"It did. We keep stealing all of Donnie's wedding thunder."

"I guess we do," I said. "We put on a good show against the wall."

"No regrets," he said, pulling me close and tracing my jaw with the tip of his finger.

"Same here," I choked out. "See you later?"

He slanted his mouth over mine, licking long strokes inside my mouth until I slumped against him, needy and drenched. Pregnancy had given me three speeds: horny, weepy, and hungry. Sometimes all at once.

"I'll be waiting."

It was an exhilarating yet scary thing to be this close to everything I'd never known I always wanted.

TWENTY-EIGHT
TYLER

Olivia was in a dead sleep, her arm gripped tightly around my waist as she cuddled into my side. I smiled at her contented sigh while my hand skimmed up and down her naked back. The quiet moments with her were the only things that calmed me from all the upheaval in my life. It was a good upheaval between the bakery taking off, the baby, and the amazing but still mostly unlabeled thing we had between us. Rent at my apartment was becoming a wasted expense as I was here most nights.

I always intended to leave in enough time to get a couple of hours of sleep before I had to set up for the morning, but every night it became harder and harder to go. My heart soared as I watched the swell of her stomach grow with my baby, satisfying the caveman in me. I loved the widened curve of her hips and her now even fuller breasts that pushed against every top she owned. Olivia was always the most gorgeous woman in the world, but pregnant she was a fucking work of art. A sexy, insatiable work of art that I couldn't stop touching or tasting.

I peeked over her shoulder at the clock, then dropped my

head back with a groan. I had a couple of hours until I had to go back to my apartment and get ready for the day. Too keyed up to attempt sleep, I gingerly inched away from Olivia and slid out of bed.

I poured myself a glass of juice and plopped down on one of her dining room chairs, scrubbing a hand down my face as I tried to decipher where the sudden rush of anxiety came from. There were too many options, but a big one was that I was running out of space at the bakery and needed to do something about it.

Even with a couple of new bakers, it was hard to keep up with demand and find room to store all the items we needed each day. Knocking down a wall and extending the space would be the perfect solution, but as Eli had said, I was dragging my feet and someone else would snatch it up if I didn't make a move soon.

"Still thinking about the new space, aren't you?" Soft hands massaged my shoulders and slid down my arms.

"You always think you're so smart." I leaned back and kissed her cheek.

"Because I'm usually right." She slid into the seat next to me, that almost-sheer robe of hers leaving even less to the imagination the tighter it became. "So what's stopping you from telling your landlord that you're interested?"

"That all this will stop and then I'll have a double rent?"

"As your social media manager," she began, crossing her legs. The knowledge of her naked under her robe combined with that business tone had me hard as a rock despite my frustration. "I've told you there are other things we can do when you're ready. I've just been keeping it mostly at a minimum because you don't have a high budget. If you get the space, I can help you get more customers through the doors in a lot of different ways as long as you keep up the quality, which I know you'll do."

I chuckled to myself.

"What?" she asked.

I picked up her hand, lacing my fingers with hers. "Since I decided to open the bakery, no one has cared about it until you."

She reared back, crinkling her nose at me. "That's not true. Helen talks about it all the time."

I shrugged. "Now, maybe a little, but back then, both her and my father thought I was crazy. Only recently do I see her getting a little excited for me. If I told either of them about expanding, they'd tell me it was too soon and I shouldn't get ahead of myself."

"Well..." She rose from the chair and planted herself on my lap, skating her hand down my bare chest. "Replace their nagging voices in your head with mine. The one that keeps telling you how talented you are and this is only the beginning." She wrapped her arms around my neck and pressed her lips to mine.

I laughed, dropping my head to her shoulder. "You're something else, Sanchez."

She was everything. The girl I couldn't stand had become the woman I couldn't live without in what seemed like the blink of an eye.

I could tell Olivia anything, except how in love I was with her. Words were always hard to come by for me—the right ones anyway. All I felt for her was too important to blurt out, but keeping it inside was another reason I was wide awake at two o'clock in the morning.

"How about you try to get at least an hour of sleep before you have to get ready for work?" She climbed off my lap and extended her hand. I was about to take it when I noticed a radio and a pile of CDs scattered across her end table.

"I didn't notice those," I said when I stood, motioning behind her.

"Mom dropped them off yesterday on another cleaning binge. She found my dad's old radio and CDs and brought them down here in case I'd want them. I don't have the room for them or the player I need to listen, but I haven't brought myself to look through it all yet." She trudged over to the pile, smiling at whatever she plucked off the top.

"Olivia Newton-John's greatest hits." She flipped it over to the back. "My namesake."

"Is it?" I made my way over to join her. "I don't think I knew that." Which wasn't surprising. After spending my life knowing Olivia, I only actually *knew* her over the last five months.

"He had a huge crush on her and was such a dork about it." She chuckled, shaking her head. "When I'd agree to go jogging with him, he'd sing *'Let's Get Physical!'* to me on the rare times I'd manage to catch up to him."

When Olivia talked about Javier, I didn't say anything. I wouldn't press for more or ask questions. I just let her get out what she needed to at the moment.

She opened the case and inserted the CD into the top. "Wow, the batteries still work. That's amazing."

"What song is this?"

"'Magic.' From *Xanadu*." She flipped the CD cover over. "My big, deep baritone, former-high-school-wrestler father played this soundtrack on a loop in his car, and we were the only ones who knew. The reason I say that is that my uncle would have given him serious shit about it."

"To me, that makes your dad even cooler."

She nodded without looking up. "It's not a bad soundtrack

though. I haven't heard this song in years." Her hand lingered on top of the CD player. "I guess I'll give this away. I'll keep the CD though."

I caught her hand before she pressed Stop and twirled her arm over her head.

"What are you doing?"

"Dance with me." I yanked her flush to my body, her confused gaze searching mine.

"In the middle of the night? Why?"

I shrugged. "Why not?"

The Olivia I thought I always knew was a big, bold pain in the ass. And while she was still all those things at times, the part of her that I'd gotten to know recently was someone who thrived on love instead of attention. I had all the love in the world for her, and I wanted to make her feel it even if I couldn't say it.

"That's the second time you've shocked me by wanting to dance with me. Usually at parties, you'd hide from me." She laughed, running her hands through my hair as we swayed back and forth.

"I did," I agreed, sweeping her hair off her shoulder where her robe began to droop. "But I always saw you. You may not believe that, but I did." I drifted my hand down her chest, letting it drop to the silk belt, and untied it. "I remember your sweet sixteen."

"Me too. You grunted a happy birthday at me and sat in the corner with a couple of guys from your baseball team. Not that I looked for you or anything." She batted her eyelashes at me and flashed me a wry grin.

"You wore this blue dress with silver rhinestones across the top that went with the crown on your head."

"Tiara," she corrected me with a raised brow. "You still remember that?"

"It was hard not to look at you for the whole night, so the image is kind of burned into my brain. Mom, of course, didn't give me the option to stay home, so I watched every guy, including my friends, fall all over themselves to dance with you."

"Not every guy." She quirked a brow at me. "Whenever I'd glance your way, you had a permanent scowl on your face. It was hot, but I was told to behave myself and not antagonize you for the night."

"At first, I was annoyed I had to go," I confessed, "but then I was annoyed that I couldn't ask you to dance. Or I didn't know how. I forgot for a bit that I couldn't stand you. You were just this goddess I couldn't take my eyes off. It confused the shit out of me, so I acted like I usually did in those situations. I sat back and watched other people take what I wanted."

I never told anyone about that night or how my friends noticed the way I was gawking at her and had called me on it. How long had this been brewing between us, and how long would it take to find the guts to claim Olivia as mine? Lifelong habits died hard.

"You could take it now." Her hooded eyes were dark as the robe pooled at her feet.

"Fuck, look at you," I rasped, my eyes sweeping down her naked body before I grabbed the back of her neck and hauled her mouth to mine.

She moaned into the kiss, laughing against my lips. "There's more to look at every day."

I backed her against the table, lifting her by the waist to set her down on the wood.

"You're fucking perfection," I whispered and dragged my lips down her throat and over her breasts, closing my mouth around a rigid nipple and letting it go with a pop. I ran my mouth down her torso, coasting my hand over her stomach as I trailed kisses across her hip.

The CD continued to play as I hooked her leg over my shoulder, sucking on the damp skin on the inside of her thigh, teasing us both.

"Jesus, Tyler." She grasped the back of my head, pulling a fistful of my hair when I finally gave us what we wanted. I grabbed her hips to bring her closer, digging my fingers into her thighs as I lost all control and devoured her. I slipped my tongue inside, my eyes almost rolling back at the sweet taste of her in my mouth. Her legs quivered against my cheeks as her heels dug into the back of my neck.

"Tyler, please," Olivia begged, whimpering as she writhed on the table. I was hypnotized by the sway of her breasts as her chest heaved and how her eyes clenched shut in pleasure —pleasure that I was giving to her.

She opened her mouth to say something else when her head fell back, just as she clenched hard on my tongue. When I lifted my head, I took in the flush on her skin and the way she clutched one of the chairs behind her.

I was a lucky fucking bastard.

I swept my tongue across my lower lip, not wanting to waste a drop of her, and laughed when she peeked at me with one eye open.

"You're lethal, Tyler," she said as she sat up, running a hand down my chest before hooking her finger into the waistband of my boxers.

I pushed them down the rest of the way, letting them drop at my feet and grabbed her hips.

"You're magic, Olivia."

She laughed until I slid inside her. We rocked back and forth, our mouths still moving, trading soft moans as we ignited, the table creaking below us as I slammed into her over and over again. She met me thrust for thrust, hooking her arm around my neck to get us even closer.

Deep enough—or *enough*—didn't exist where Olivia was concerned.

When she pulsed around me again, I finally let go, giving her all I had until we slumped against each other.

"Maybe you can sleep a little now. I know I can," she teased as her mouth opened with a loud yawn.

"I only have an hour, but yeah, maybe I can." I brushed her lips and lifted her off the table.

"I'll get up with you. I should scrub the table anyway." Her lips twitched as she scooped our clothes from the floor and shut off the CD.

Olivia belonged to me. Maybe I couldn't tell her yet, but I'd show her in every other way I could.

I could only hope that was enough.

TWENTY-NINE
OLIVIA

"This is good. Nice response so far. What I think we should try this week... Ah, Tyler, please stop," I half begged, really wanting him to continue as his lips dragged open-mouthed kisses down my neck.

"What? I'm listening." He swept my hair to the side as he continued his torture, diving into that tiny patch of skin above my collarbone that always made me lose any train of thought that wasn't Tyler.

We stood in front of my desk as I showed him the metrics from his Instagram account this month. I had his staff take pictures of their favorite items for a couple of weeks, and while they were happy to do it, the perfectionist in me obsessed over the right angles and lighting. In between other client meetings, I was at his bakery a few times per week taking my own shots and uploading to the Hey, Batter account.

"It's your own fault," he said, swirling his tongue around that spot behind my ear that always liquified my knees. "How can I concentrate on numbers with you in that damn dress?"

I was pleasantly surprised to find awesome maternity clothes that didn't make me look like a rag doll and enjoyed showing off my growing stomach and boobs that were their own planets now.

The bigger I became, the more Tyler lost all control. He was never within five feet of me without having his hands somewhere on my body, either swirling over my belly when we were in public or diving into my pants when we were alone. He'd made me come one night next to the cooling racks in the back of the bakery, and I still blushed hot all over whenever I'd see a scone.

Today, I wore a tight black dress and my favorite knee-high boots since I had an appointment after five o'clock. I should've known that Tyler would be too riled up to talk business. Or maybe I did.

I loved the way he looked at me, and still needed to steal every bit of his focus thanks to a nagging new insecurity that didn't want to go away. I'd reveled in any attention he gave me and soaked it up whenever I could. But other than that one time, we never said what we were to each other.

We'd talk for hours about the baby and how we'd fix up the extra room in my apartment. On weepy nights, I'd open up about my father a little bit, glossing over the one night I still couldn't bring up to anyone, but that was it. Our future together that didn't involve our baby wasn't discussed.

I wasn't the kind of girl who needed an *I love you* from anyone. The guys who told me they loved me over the years were sweet, and although I'd say it back, there was never much feeling behind it. I liked them all well enough but shook it off quickly when I'd walk away.

I had no idea how to walk away from Tyler. I could just tell him that I loved him, but the pettiness in me wanted to hear it first. It was as if I craved final confirmation that I was the woman he loved, not the girl he couldn't stand and spent most of his life running away from. I *needed* to hear it from him, and I hated that.

"My metrics meetings with clients usually don't go like this." I leaned into Tyler, rubbing against his denim-covered cock as I reached back to squeeze his leg.

He swiveled me around and weaved his hand into my hair, pulling at the root to make me look up.

"They better not," he growled and took my mouth in a possessive, hungry kiss.

We only had a half hour before my next call, but I found myself dropping to my knees and opening his belt buckle.

Lust burned hot in his gaze as I licked my lips and pulled down his briefs.

"Livie, are you home?"

I groaned at the sound of my grandmother's voice. I'd forgotten she was visiting my mother today, along with everything else thanks to Tyler's lips and hands. I stood from the floor as I helped Tyler buckle himself back up, chuckling against his lips as he rolled my desk chair in front of him.

"I am," I said when I opened the door. "Come in, Nana."

"I know you're working, and I didn't want to bother you." All five feet of her scooted into my apartment with a large tray. "I made extra eggplant for you so you could eat." Her wrinkled hand patted my belly. "Your mother said that you need to eat more."

"Nana, I eat plenty." I motioned down my body. "I promise. Plus, Tyler gives me all the cookies and cake I want."

Nana turned and spotted Tyler by my desk. His sheepish smile told me that his hard-on wasn't deflated enough to come out of hiding just yet.

"Nice to see you, Mrs. Esposito."

"Oh, Tyler, please." She waved a hand at him. "I've known

you since you were a baby. Besides, you knocked up my granddaughter, so Maria or Nana is fine."

"Nana, oh my God!" I dropped my face to my hands.

"I'm too old to sugarcoat things, sweetheart."

I had to laugh as she shuffled into my kitchen, steadying the tray in one hand as she opened my refrigerator door.

"I better get going. We have orders to catch up on." Tyler finally came back out from behind my chair. "I'm sorry I can't go with you tonight. Especially when you look like that." His voice dropped to a husky whisper as his gaze swept down my body.

"It's okay. I'll call you when I get back." I pressed a kiss to his lips, smiling when he went in for another one after I pulled away.

"Take care, Mrs.—I mean, Nana."

"Take care, Tyler." Nana gave him a wave and bent down to search through my refrigerator. I saw more eggplant and a ton of other stuff in my future judging by the sour look on her face.

I opened the door, giving him a little wave as he headed out.

"So what's going on?" she asked while turning her nose up at something she dug out of the bottom shelf.

"All my food is edible, I promise. And other than the chocolate cake, mostly everything is even healthy. You can get rid of the face."

I leaned against the kitchen wall.

"No. What's going on with the two of you?" She motioned between me and the path Tyler had taken out the door with her finger. "Are you getting married or moving somewhere together after the baby is born?"

"No, we both agreed to stay here was the best option with

Mom upstairs and his mother always here. We haven't talked about living together, but there's time."

My stomach rolled when she squinted up at me.

"Not much. How far along are you now?"

"A little over five months. Tyler said he'd take as much time off as he could when the baby is born."

"But he won't *live* with you. So it's all going to be on you. Your mother will help, but you need to make sure you're ready for that."

"I am, Nana. You know me. We'll be just fine." I forced a smile, a sour sting in my gut at referring to a "we" that didn't include Tyler. He wouldn't leave me in the lurch, but Nana was right. If he didn't officially live here, he'd be back and forth between his apartment by the bakery and here. It was one of those things I'd think about and then put out of my mind right after so I wouldn't upset the happy limbo we floated in.

"I do know you." She patted my cheek. "And I know your mother is itching to come down and get her hands on that baby. You'll be fine either way. Come up and sit with us if you have time."

"I will. I just have a meeting first." I kissed the top of her head. "Give me a little bit."

Either way.

I never wanted to think of *either way* with Tyler, but I was running out of time.

THIRTY
OLIVIA

"Look what I made!" Morgan chirped as I sat down in her dining room, setting a large glass filled with familiar lime-green liquid in front of me. "A completely virgin margarita!"

"God, I miss margaritas." I sighed as I twisted the stem between my fingers. Of all the cocktails I'd sampled at my Cleopatra dinners, this was and always would be my favorite. I'd tried virgin drinks, and they were right up there with decaf coffee, a subpar and empty placeholder.

"I bet you won't even miss the tequila."

"I bet you're wrong." I laughed as I lifted the glass and took a sip. "This isn't bad, Morg." I suspected it had to do with the heavy salt along the rim, but I'd take it. There was a bitter irony to never needing a drink more during the one long period of time I wasn't allowed to have one.

"You look great," Morgan's wife said as she set the steaming tray of lasagna onto the table. "How are you feeling?"

Leah was an adorable little pixie with a small, almost whisper-like voice. She was a vivid contrast to her loud, nearly six-feet-tall wife, but they worked. Watching them flutter around each other, effortless and sweet in their little touches and silent communication, made me yearn for the same thing with Tyler. I loved having him around and missed him when he wasn't, but I didn't know if we'd ever have what Morgan and Leah did. I wanted a life with him, and although I had one, it still felt tentative and, on the nights when I was alone, temporary.

"Thank you. Okay, I suppose. I still get wiped sometimes. No more nausea and so far none of the lethal heartburn that every woman in my family keeps warning me about."

"Just trying to get an idea of what to expect." She shot a look at Morgan before picking up my plate.

"Wait." My drink splashed on my hand as I dropped my glass. "Are you guys..."

"Not yet," Morgan answered as she sat next to me, the disappointment in her reply almost triggering tears of my own. The sappiness hadn't dissipated with the second trimester. If anything, it had gotten worse. I burst into tears over the dumbest things lately. Early on, I was able to recognize it and go with the flow. Now, it was too all-consuming to skate around.

"Liv, it's okay. Don't get all hormonal weepy." She squeezed my knee. "The doctor said it would take a while and I'm not in my twenties, so it's not as easy to just get pregnant. Plenty of time and Costco tests left." Her grin was a half-inch too wide, but I'd let it go.

"I've heard it can be harder at our age, unless you make a stupid deal with a childhood enemy and end up pregnant after a night of drinking and bad decisions," I joked to nudge away the guilt over having a baby by accident while Morgan experienced month after month of heartbreak.

"That's because your uterus probably tackled Tyler's

sperm before it could go anywhere." Morgan smirked around her fork.

"That's me." I lifted my glass in a mock toast, the sudden and all-too-familiar burn of tears running up my nose. "Finally getting Tyler to stay with me because now he has no choice."

Morgan flinched and immediate guilt washed over me. She was only kidding, but the notion of me being with Tyler only because we were having a baby together was too real to find amusing.

"Liv? Did I say something wrong?" Morgan's face crumpled in a contrite wince.

"No." I set down my fork and rubbed my eyes. "I know you meant it as a joke, but I can't help but think that Tyler is with me by default. If I have him at all. I mean, he's been great."

My nostrils flared, frustration running through me at the crack in my voice. I was excited for the baby and loved him so much already, but as the weeks ticked by, *everything* had me on edge. I missed my father so much it was almost as if my grief had reset. I was so damn angry at what he was missing now, which made me watch my mother even more closely. All egged on by the constant turbulent thoughts about what was really going on between Tyler and me.

"But lately, I can't shake the feeling he's around because he feels he has to be. It's nothing he's said or done. I haven't had this much sex in probably my entire life." I met their widened eyes and cringed. "Sorry, that was a little too much." I glanced at Leah, who only laughed and shook her head.

"I've seen you guys together." Morgan rolled her eyes. "There is no question he's very into you from what I've seen."

"Something my grandmother said a couple of weeks ago has been nagging at me. She told me that after the baby is born, it's going to be all on me since Tyler doesn't live there. If we were only dating this long, I guess the future wouldn't be so pressing, but we never even discuss just us. We talk about the baby all the time, his bakery, but never us."

"Do you want Tyler to move in with you?" Leah asked.

"I want him to *want* to...eventually. Or want to talk about it, even if it's a distant future type of a thing. We don't talk about any future."

"Tyler is the first guy she's ever wanted a future with past the next date."

Leah smiled when Morgan snorted out a laugh.

"That's not... totally true."

"Really? Tell Leah about the time you traveled to Paris alone, met a guy there, and broke it off via What's App when he offered to come to visit you."

"Because that was weird," I protested as I shoved a forkful of lasagna in my mouth. "We had a fling. We barely spoke the same language. International travel wasn't something I wanted to do regularly."

"Like you wouldn't run anywhere for Tyler."

"You went to Paris alone?"

Leah's question interrupted the start of our argument.

"Yes. Morgan couldn't come and another friend bailed at the last minute. But it was my thirtieth birthday, and I said screw it and went alone."

"Wow," Leah said, her eyes wide. "I'd never have the guts to do that."

"Well, I had to call my parents every morning and night, and my father told me if I missed one phone call he was taking a red-eye to France to drag me home, thirty or not."

"I have to admit, I'm in awe of you." Leah sighed.

"That's Olivia," Morgan said with her eyes still on me. "No one kept her from her birthday celebrations. Back then."

I glared at Morgan's raised brow and turned back to Leah, not interested in kickstarting a two-year-old argument.

"But your wife is right. Men were a pastime to me. I wasn't mean about it, or I tried not to be, but I could take them or leave them." I shrugged. "This is why I made the man I've loved since I was a kid hate me up until recently. Turns out, I was right to do it. Feelings have made me someone I never wanted to be."

"Holy shit." Morgan's fork dropped to her empty plate with a clank.

"What?"

"You admitted to loving Tyler. It took you thirty years, but you did it."

"I do. I always did. But..." I shrugged, not wanting to think about much less say what came after *but*.

"Have you told him?"

I almost dribbled a mouthful of fake margarita. "I just told you. No. We talk about the baby, his room, plans for the bakery, my two jobs. We go over my ideas for his social media accounts. Sometimes in a weak moment, I'll talk about my father. Literally everything except us. He called me his pregnant girlfriend once, and that's the only time he's labeled me as anything."

"I never knew you to be chicken," Morgan said as she cleared off the table.

"I think you have." My head bobbed in a slow nod. "Like that years-long quest to make Tyler despise me so he wouldn't reject me?" I turned to Leah. "She acts like she hasn't had a front seat to all my issues," I told Leah in a loud whisper.

"Can we still have the cake you brought over from Tyler?" Leah chuckled as she looped her arm around Morgan's shoulder.

"Of course." I stood from the table, my belly now big

enough for it to be awkward rising from a seated position. "I wouldn't begrudge you dessert because of my screwed-up love life."

After I helped them clean up, at least as much as they'd let me, Morgan put on a pot of decaf coffee as we cut into a chocolate layer cake, my second favorite dessert of his after the cream pie. Well third, as my all-time favorite was when Tyler made *me* his dessert, but maybe that was part of our problem. The sex was so incredible, I was willing to overlook any connections that we maybe didn't have. I felt love from Tyler when he was inside me and from all the sweet things he'd say and how he'd patiently listen when I'd open up about the grieving I couldn't seem to stop.

But I needed to know for sure, even if I was afraid to ask.

"So I'm doing a story at work on dating apps," Morgan said before moaning around a mouthful of cake.

"Told you," I said and sliced into my piece.

Morgan was a features writer for a news website and entertained me with details from her stories. They ranged from scary to utterly ridiculous.

"I need access to one and didn't want to go through the process of a fake sign-up if you still had yours."

"Of course." I perked up as I dug my phone out of my purse. At a friend's request last year, I'd catfished her boyfriend to find out if he was cheating. I made a fake name and a vague side profile at a good enough angle to entice someone to write back to me. I never used it for real dating, just for laughing at profiles either alone or with Morgan over drinks. Some of them were so obviously fake I was tempted to write to one just to see what they'd reply.

"Just search for eligible men by area and see what comes up."

"You really want to see how many local weirdos there are,"

I said on a chuckle before my breath caught in my throat when I scrolled to the third name.

"What?" Morgan asked.

"I found Tyler." I threw the phone onto the table as a humorless laugh fell from my lips.

"Stop it." She scooped up the phone and studied the screen. When she had nothing to say for a long minute, my heart sank deeper into my stomach.

"Maybe..." My eyes clenched shut at her usual *maybe this isn't so bad* tone. She'd tried it in my bathroom when I found out I was pregnant, and like always, it had the opposite effect. "Maybe someone made a fake profile after seeing him online and in the paper. They do that. I'm sure."

When I'd called him a thirst trap for his cluelessly gorgeous picture in the newspaper and read the comments from those women online, I wasn't jealous. I'd thought it was amusing, especially seeing how it made Tyler want to crawl out of his skin. I'd never thought for even a minute that it was something I had to worry about.

I picked the phone back up, scanning the screen in the hopes of grasping at something to make this discovery less awful.

"He opened his profile right after the wedding and was last active this week. I'm not sure what's worse. That he wanted to meet someone new right after we spent the night together, or that he's still looking now." I pushed my plate away as bile rose in the back of my throat. I'd managed almost six months of pregnancy without throwing up, and now I had to take deep breaths not to puke all over Morgan and Leah's floor.

"I believe there's an explanation other than Tyler is on the prowl while you're about to have his baby, but seriously. Talk. To. Him."

"You're right." I stood from the table and made my way

over to the front door to grab my coat.

"Olivia, I didn't mean charge over there hot." Morgan rushed over to me and grabbed my arm.

I swiveled around, missing the buttons on my coat as my hands shook. "And how should I go over there?"

"I say this because I love you. You're not thinking clearly right now." She squeezed my hand. "Don't rush in and attack when you're only going to regret it later. Sit back down and take a minute. Please."

She was trying to help me, but the sympathy in her eyes only fueled me more. She was right—I was high on emotion and sick of all the uncertainty I hadn't been able to face. Despite my best friend's plea, no number of minutes would make me feel better.

I needed to know what was between us—right now.

"As you said, I avoided this for too long, and I'm done being afraid when it comes to Tyler." My jaw trembled when I spied the sympathy in her eyes. "I'm so exhausted, Morg. Truly exhausted."

She kissed my temple. "Try to calm down enough so I don't have to worry about you driving at least. And text me tonight, even if you don't feel like talking, so I know you're okay."

I dropped my head to her arm for a second to give myself a chance to inhale the tears back in. "I will," I said when I looked up again. "I'm sorry, Leah. Thank you both for dinner."

"Don't be." Leah came over to us, the same pull of sadness across her features as she met my eyes. "I think Morgan is right. There's an explanation."

I nodded and opened the door, rushing to my car and sucking in a few deep breaths before I drove off.

There was an explanation for it all. I just wasn't sure I wanted to hear it.

THIRTY-ONE
TYLER

I sent the rest of the staff home for the night and took my time setting up for the morning, grateful for the silence. A meeting with my accountant this morning to go over my year-to-date financials had indicated the bakery was showing a strong and steady rise in profitability over the past months. I wasn't sold on it being permanent yet, but all things were moving in the right direction, and with the social media help Olivia gave me, it seemed to be holding on.

Despite my grumbling, I'd finally spoken to the landlord about leasing the space next door. According to my accountant, it was doable. I'd been afraid to spend too much on marketing because I wasn't sure I could handle the influx of traffic, but with a new space, we could spread out and staff up to meet any increased demand. It felt like the right move, just a scary-as-hell one.

Olivia was with Morgan tonight and I didn't want to bother her, but she was the only one I wanted to talk to about this. Since I'd opened, recognizing any type of success had been difficult for me. My parents supported me and had a vague idea of what it took to run a bakery but never knew or understood every detail of my hopes and fears. But Olivia was that perfect mix of a cheerleader, mentor, and love of my life.

I was so in love with her that I could barely see straight lately, but my cowardly ass still couldn't tell her.

A loud tapping on the back door pulled me out of my tortured musings. I jogged over to answer and found Olivia. Her red, swollen eyes narrowed to slits and set off a terrifying panic.

"What's wrong? Are you feeling okay?" I pulled her inside and shut the door. "Is it the baby? Talk to me," I begged as I clutched her shoulders.

She didn't answer as she dug in her bag and pulled out her phone, shoving it in my face.

My jaw dropped when I saw the dopey profile Eli had set up for me on that damn dating app on her screen.

"Explain this to me. And before you ask why I have this, I opened an account for a friend years ago to help spy on her boyfriend and kept it because I like laughing at it. Morgan needed to look at it for a story, and wouldn't you know, you're an *eligible man* who lives in my area. Who was just active last week." Her words were clipped and quick, murder in her eyes as she glowered at me.

"Okay," I started and held my hands up. "First of all, I need you to calm down. I have *never* been active on that app. Eli convinced me to join after I spent the night with you and didn't know what the hell to do with myself since we didn't talk for weeks after. I never messaged anyone or responded when they messaged me. Since the article and all the publicity, I keep getting notifications and every time I try to delete the damn thing, something distracts me."

I rested my hand on the counter, my own rage now surging in my chest. "When exactly would I find the time to date? If

I'm not here, I'm with you. After all this time, you just assumed the worst?"

The white-hot anger in her features faded and her shoulders slumped.

"Haven't I done everything I'm supposed to do?"

She flinched, her eyes wide as if I'd gut-punched her in the stomach. "*Supposed* to do? My God, I was right."

She turned away, her shoulders shaking for a moment before she came back around with fat tears streaming down her cheeks. "I believe you. I've been with you enough that I could safely assume you aren't dating anyone." She stepped up to me, her round stomach pressed up between us. "I love you, Tyler. I've loved you for probably my whole life, even when I was too young to understand it. I tortured you because I wanted your attention so much that even if it was bad, I craved it like some kind of drug. Pathetic, isn't it?"

"Olivia, don't. Come on, let's talk—"

She swatted my hand away when I tried to cup her cheek.

"Then we grew up, and I made you hate me. But you hating me was better than having you reject me." A humorless laugh slipped out of her and made my blood run cold. "And I was fine with it for the most part because I still had your attention regardless. Yes, I always knew you were attracted to me. But you don't have to like who you're attracted to, right? Or like them to have sex with them? Maybe we confused that over the past few months."

"*What?*" I yelled, a different kind of panic rushing through me. Olivia never gave up on me. Even when it was to argue with me, she was never far or out of my reach. All she was saying now sounded too much like a goodbye speech, and I couldn't handle that.

"How could you think that? None of that is true. If you could just listen—"

"Look, we can be parents together. I'd never keep you and the baby apart. Good dads are important, and I know you'll be a great one. But this?" She motioned between us with her finger. "I can't do this anymore. I thought by doing one favor for you, showing you that I wasn't the raging bitch you always thought that I was, maybe it would make up for the awful way I'd always acted toward you, and maybe you'd eventually like me a little or we could be friends. I never expected to have the greatest night of my life, or..." She glanced at her stomach. "I don't want you to think being with me is something that you're supposed to do out of a silly obligation. I have no regrets. I just need all of you, and I'll never have that. It's about time that I acted like a big girl and accepted it."

"Olivia, no!" My voice cracked as I reached for her again. "You have it all wrong. So, so wrong." I dragged a hand down my face. It was the greatest night of my life too, for so many reasons. But I'd waited too long to tell her. "Please just let me—"

I groaned at another knock at the door, not wanting to move an inch as I held Olivia's teary gaze. She nodded with her chin toward the door, and I kept my eyes on her as I trudged over to open it.

"Tyler, sorry if I interrupted. I saw the lights on." Kyle, my landlord, looked me over with wary eyes, probably noting the desperation etched in my features. "I was here to meet with other tenants and wanted to chat with you about the additional space if you had time."

"Um, yeah, sure. Just one minute."

I came back to Olivia, her eyes darting everywhere but mine as she wiped her cheeks with the back of her hand.

"This conversation isn't over. I need to talk to my landlord, but I'll come to your apartment right after."

She inched over to me, running her hand down my chest.

"Goodbye, Tyler." She kissed my cheek and dropped her head to my chest, pulling away when I reached for her. She sniffled, wiping her eyes one more time and not looking back as she passed Kyle on the way out the door.

I managed to hold it together enough to have a decent conversation with Kyle regarding rent and the logistics of taking over the deli space. He already had a lease agreement drafted, which highlighted everything we originally talked about. When he left, I stared at it for what seemed like hours. This was the expansion I never would have had the opportunity to even think about until Olivia. Not only by giving me a big break but by believing in me. This should have been something to celebrate, but without her by my side, what was the point of celebrating anything? I was already lost without her.

I closed up as quickly as I could and rushed to her apartment. The lights were off, but her car sat in the driveway.

I stepped out of my truck, wondering if I should knock on her door. Olivia was too fired up to reason with, but I hated the thought of her falling asleep thinking I didn't love her, that being with her was something I was only doing out of obligation. After months of agonizing over how to tell her how I felt, I let something stupid slip out and fucked it all up.

Tyler: *I'm outside. Talk to me, sugar.*

I laughed at the silly pet name I gave her on the fly during our "act" at Donnie's wedding. She *was* the sugar. Life had been sweet since she offered me that crazy favor and changed everything. I leaned back on the car door and rubbed my eyes.

"Tyler?"

I blinked my eyes open and found Carla regarding me with a furrowed brow as she stepped closer.

"What's wrong?"

Everything.

When she clutched my arm, I realized I'd said that out loud.

"Olivia and I got into an argument. I said something stupid that she took completely out of context, and..." I raked a hand through my hair. "If she would talk to me, we could straighten it out, but I think she's sleeping already and I don't want to wake her up only to upset her again."

She looked me over with a sympathy that only made me feel worse. "Sounds like Olivia. She's passionate and hothead-ed." She sighed, shaking her head as she crossed her arms. "And when it comes to you," she said, cocking a brow, "some-times she doesn't think too clearly. Most times."

"Because we drive each other crazy?"

"Because she loves you more than she ever knew how to handle." Carla squeezed my shoulder. "Let her cool off. If there is one thing my daughter is consistent with, it's that she can't leave you alone for very long."

That was something I could always count on, but what if I pushed her too far this time? When she'd said goodbye in the bakery earlier, it hadn't felt like the old Olivia who lived to set me off so I'd come back at her. She'd sounded like she was letting me go. I couldn't let that happen, but at the same time, I had no clue on how to stop it.

"Can you check on her in the morning? Make sure she's okay?" I asked.

She nodded. "I will, and I'll see if I can help her calm down a little. She'll be fine. You both will. Sometimes a fight is good. Gets you back on track when things become a little... shaky. Javier and I had a few good ones."

I pinched the bridge of my nose, trying to figure out how everything good in my life was slipping right through my fingers.

"Go home and get some sleep. You'll work it out in the morning."

"I will." My reply was hollow, just like the middle of my chest until I got Olivia back.

"And Tyler?"

I turned to look at her before I climbed into the driver's seat.

"It's a blessing when someone loves you like that. Just takes a minute to figure out how to handle it."

A surprised laugh fell from my lips. I was so lucky to have Olivia, and if I had told her that a long time ago, we wouldn't be here.

I took one last glance at her window and drove off.

I'd give her a night to settle down, then it was my turn to be relentless.

THIRTY-TWO
OLIVIA

I'd gone right to bed the minute I came home, scrubbing my face while I was still crying and then climbing under my covers. I drifted off quickly, the surge of emotions zapping all my energy, but I woke up even more exhausted. My slumber was restless, vague dreams of Tyler torturing me all night. The last one was all too vivid. We were kids again, playing in his basement while he focused on some kind of action figure. I'd tried to yank it out of his hands so he'd look at me, but he wouldn't. I woke up with a scratchy throat, unsure if I'd screamed in real life as I'd done in my dream.

When it came down to it, nothing had changed that much from when we were young. I wanted Tyler so much that I lashed out instead of just telling him, although I finally admitted to loving him last night. I almost wished for the old days of Tyler and me. The days of him telling his friends what a bitch I was were a much less painful memory than admitting to the fear I'd held on to all these months.

Being his nemesis beat the hell out of feeling like his obligation.

"Olivia?"

I groaned at the sound of my mother's voice and sank deeper into my pillow, the threat of tears burning my eyes when I inhaled Tyler's scent.

What if I made a mistake? What exactly was I looking for from him? I never needed validation from anyone, but no reassurance seemed to be good enough when it came to Tyler.

But this time, instead of picking a fight with him, for the very first time in our lives, I walked away. Morgan was right. I should have taken a minute before I rushed over there and said things that I didn't know how to take back—or even if I could.

When I shifted to sit up on the bed, a fluttering on the side of my swollen stomach made me pause. It felt like butterfly wings, which I'd read was what baby kicks felt like in the early stages. I lunged for my phone to text Tyler and stopped. There was no reason not to text him updates about the baby since that part of who we were to each other was permanent, but I set my phone down anyway and trudged to the door to greet my mother.

"Good morning," I said with a sandpaper edge to my voice. "Everything okay?"

Her brow pinched when she studied my gaze. "With me, fine. I came home last night and found Tyler parked in front of the house. He told me that you guys had a fight and asked if I could check on you this morning to make sure you were all right. I would have last night, but I wasn't sure if you were asleep. Want to talk about it?"

"Does it make a difference?" I coughed out a laugh. "Come in."

I turned back toward my bedroom as Mom closed the door behind her. I plopped back down on my mattress, settling on my side and willing away the jump in my heart rate at Tyler being upset over me. How did you detox from someone who'd been your lifelong focus? I had no idea, but the notion of it was enough to be painful.

"I love Tyler," I began, my voice already cracking.

"I know." I didn't turn to her soft chuckle. "I've known longer than you have. So what happened?"

"I'm his obligation. I thought maybe he loved me and he doesn't hate me like he used to, but he's only doing what he's supposed to do. We're good friends, I guess, and obviously, the attraction is there." I patted my stomach. "But I need to let him go. I can't make him pay attention to me anymore."

Mom folded her legs under her. "I don't believe that's true, but tell me what happened."

I sighed and turned onto my other side, going through the short version of finding his profile, tearing over to the bakery to confront him, and what he'd said.

Mom stayed silent, only responding with a slow nod when I finally finished.

"Now tell me how I can never leave well enough alone and did this to myself." I propped my head on my hand and lifted my tired gaze to hers.

"I think you took what he said out of context because you love him so much that it scares you. When it comes to him, you lash out to protect yourself."

"I think it's too late to protect myself, don't you?"

"If," she began as she inched closer, "if you paid attention, you'd see that he's watched you just as much over the years. You both are very different." She tucked a tangled lock of hair behind my ear. "You wear your heart on your sleeve and say how you feel. He's never been a wordy guy. Helen always said that Tyler could never tell you how he felt about anything, but if you looked well enough, he'd show you. What has he shown you these past few months? When you were together, did it feel like he was only here because he thought he had to be?"

I looked away, pinching the loose string from my comforter between my fingers.

"No, not at all." I swallowed another lump in my throat, the wonderful memories of the past few months running through my mind. "But what if the crazy way we got together and the way I've always felt about him made me believe things that weren't true?" I straightened and rubbed my belly. "What if I saw only what I wanted to see?"

"The guy I saw last night didn't seem like he was doing anything with you out of obligation. He looked brokenhearted and worried out of his mind. You never gave him a chance to explain. Why don't you today? Talk it out with cooler heads. If I know you, you barged in there last night ready for a fight. You probably didn't give him any time to think when you came at him, and, possibly, he said something that may not have come out the right way. Did he try to stop you?"

I darted my eyes away and replied with a slow nod.

"Then call him today and talk it out. Hear what he has to say. There are more people in this situation than just the two of you, so whether or not the inclination is to just retreat, you need to be sure."

"I just feel like," I croaked out, a guttural sob rolling out of me as another truth floated to the surface, "I'm losing everyone important and I can't stop it. I lost Dad, I worry about you all the time, and I'm so afraid of fucking things up with Tyler, but that's all I've ever done."

Mom brushed my hair off my forehead as I dripped more tears into the pillow.

"I know you still miss your father and think too much about how he died. And as far as me..." She shrugged. "I love that you came back, but you can't worry about me all the time. Preparing for the worst doesn't stop it from happening."

I nodded, looking away until she tapped my chin.

"You love loud, Olivia. You do everything bold and loud." She shook her head. "He's never been either, but that doesn't mean he doesn't love you. Since you were kids, you tend to... overwhelm him."

A laugh slipped out at her cocked eyebrow.

"For once in your lives, how about you give him the opportunity to catch up?"

"That would be a first for me, wouldn't it?" I laughed and exhaled with a groan. "But first I need to figure out how to pull myself together for my video call in an hour."

"I need to go food shopping, but I'll check on you when I get back." She kissed my forehead and climbed off the bed. "Pushing away the one you love the most because you're scared will only give you a lifetime of misery. If your father was here, he'd tell you the same thing since he'd be speaking from experience."

Invoking my father was kind of a low blow, but it usually worked, so I couldn't blame her for it.

I loved loud, but I loved scared. And loving Tyler, even though I'd done it my entire life, was terrifying.

THIRTY-THREE
TYLER

I was thankful to be so busy that I didn't have time to breathe, much less think. Despite the influx of customers and the whirlwind of trying to catch up, I managed to still find time to check my phone a thousand times this morning, hoping for a reply text from Olivia. Although we didn't spend every night together, being away from her last night had been a new type of torture. What we had, the little family we'd already created, was everything to me. I should have told my landlord to go and stopped her from leaving. Now I had to figure out how to make her come back.

"Are you okay?" Tegan asked, eyeing me as she shoved cookie trays into the oven.

"Fine," I replied too quickly. "Busy, like the rest of us."

"True," she said slowly, approaching me in my periphery as if she were tiptoeing around a bomb. "But most of us aren't slamming the pans after we're done with them."

Olivia always had that effect on me. But this time, instead of being pissed that she wouldn't leave me alone, I was frustrated that she wouldn't let me tell her how wrong she was or about how I really felt about her. And if I did get the chance, I was terrified she'd never believe me.

I'd thought I loved Amy at the time, but picturing my life without her never triggered the bone-deep sorrow running through me now at losing Olivia.

I still hadn't signed the lease for the space next door, partially because of my usual chicken-shit approach to big risk but also because I wanted to tell her about it first. Accomplishments without her going nuts over it for me seemed meaningless now.

Needing to cool off and get this chip off my shoulder without my employees watching, I headed out back to the alley. I couldn't tell the woman I loved how I felt about her but had no issues stomping around and showing the world how pissed-off I was about something.

I jumped at the buzzing of my phone in my pocket, the blood running faster in my veins until I spotted my mother's name on the screen.

News traveled fast between her and Carla, so this was probably to find out my side of the story. I was tempted to send it to voice mail but accepted the call to get it over with.

"Hi, Mom. I think I know why—"

"Can you leave now?" The urgency in her voice sent my heart free-falling into my stomach.

"Why? What's wrong? Is it Olivia?" I'd never be able to live with myself if this stupid argument did something to her or the baby.

"No, it's Carla. She passed out in the grocery store today and is in the emergency room. She hit her head and is still unconscious. The EMTs called Olivia, and she asked me to take her to the hospital since she didn't think she could drive. I'm not sure what's going on between you since she didn't call you, but I'm worried about her too. The poor thing is shaking, and it's not good to be in this much distress while she's pregnant. How fast can you get here?"

I held the phone in the crook of my shoulder as I rushed inside to tear my apron off and grab my keys. "I can be there in fifteen minutes. I'll tell Eli there's an emergency, and he can cover for the rest of the day."

"Okay, good. I'm going to see if I can get an update from the nurses' station. Carla was brought in right away since she came in by ambulance."

Shit.

"Hold on a second," I told my mother when I found Eli stacking pastries on the cooling trays. "I need to leave and don't know when I'll be back. I'm going to leave you in charge for today and call as soon as I can."

His brow furrowed with concern as he nodded. "Sure. Is Olivia okay?"

My head slumped for a second as the air rushed out of my lungs. "I honestly don't know."

"Go." He shoved my shoulder, and I raced out the door.

"Make sure she drinks," I said as I jogged to my car and pressed the key fob. "The doctor said on the last visit she needs to stay over-hydrated, and if she's upset, she won't. Can you find her some water?"

"I can." Mom's voice came through the car speakers as I peeled out of my spot. "Did you guys have a big fight?"

The fight wasn't big, just significant. And then she left me. Or tried to. I wasn't leaving her side once I got to her, no matter how hard she'd try to push me away.

It was my turn to fight for her like she'd always fought for me.

"It was stupid, but we're resolving it now—or I'm resolving it now."

My jaw ticked as I hit every red light.

"I love her, Mom. And I never told her, so she thought I didn't. That's basically it."

"Then tell her today. She needs it." I heard my mother's long exhale echo in my cab as I turned into the hospital parking lot. "I think Carla's blood sugar might've fallen and she ended up hitting her head. I've seen her stumble when that happens. Or I'm praying that's it. The doctor told us they're checking for a stroke."

"Fuck, Mom."

"I know, it's awful to think about, especially after what happened to Javier. I'm scared for Carla and Olivia right now... She needs you."

"She has me. In every way possible. I'm parking the car, and I'll be there in a few minutes."

I was scared for them both too. As tough as Olivia tried to appear to be, she was terrified of being alone, and I was sure she was here thinking that was exactly what she was now. But she'd be wrong—again.

She'd never be alone as long as I was alive. And I was going to get that into her thick-and-stubborn brain once and for all.

THIRTY-FOUR
OLIVIA

"Here, honey," Helen whispered as she crouched in front of me, holding a water bottle. "Drink for me."

I grunted in frustration when I couldn't grab it, my quivering hands so out of control it was like they weren't even mine. Helen held the bottom as I took two long gulps, not realizing until the ice-cold water hit my throat how parched I was.

Running on pure adrenaline when the hospital called me and before Helen picked me up, I had the mind to race upstairs to check the board for Mom's latest dosage of insulin and the name of her blood pressure medicine to tell the doctor. Her blood sugar had almost made her fall a couple of times now, and I'd learned to keep my mouth shut and grab her a glass of juice when it happened. In a few minutes, she was always fine.

I was fine, mostly, until the doctor mentioned stroke. Helen insisted she was knocked out from the blow to her head, but I was already aware that diabetics had an increased risk for heart disease and stroke. Then, exactly like what I did after my father passed away, I went into shock. My breathing was ragged and my words stunted, and no matter how many deep breaths Helen yelled at me to take, I couldn't get it under control.

"That fall was nasty enough to need stitches on her temple, and I'm sure that's what knocked her out. This sometimes happens when the dosage—"

"Changes. I know." I winced, not meaning to cut Helen off, but no matter what she said, she couldn't put me at ease. "But strokes can sneak up on you like that."

Just like aneurysms did. A silent killer took one of my parents, and now one might've grabbed the other.

"They do, but we aren't going to panic yet. Your mother would want you to take care of yourself and the baby, right? So that means trying to calm down. I know this is scary, but please try. Drink more," she told me and lifted the bottle to my lips for another sip.

I pushed off the vinyl of the chair, surprised my legs felt almost sturdy as I straightened. "They said it would be a while, right? I'm going to run to the bathroom, or waddle, I guess."

Her mouth curved up as she patted my stomach. "You're not quite waddling yet, sweetheart. But yes, they said in a half hour someone would update us. Or I'll be up there in ten-minute intervals until they do. Go for a walk."

She squeezed my hand. I attempted a half smile, squeezing her hand back and turning down the hall to search for a restroom sign. Wandering down a long hallway, I halted right next to what looked like the doorway of a chapel. I spotted a couple of stained-glass windows inside, while three people sat scattered from each other, staring into the void.

That was the logical place to go, but I couldn't bring myself to enter, my feet rooted to the shiny sterile floor. It was as if my guilt over losing my father had erected an invisible wall that prevented me from seeking any comfort.

The logical part of my brain knew that whether Dad was here or not, Mom probably still would have passed out, although if someone was with her, the gash on her head might have been avoided. But what if losing her husband made her health deteriorate in ways I couldn't see? What if moving back and being a pain in the ass by hovering over her didn't do a damn thing because I wasn't what or who she needed? She needed her husband. We both did.

I slid down the wall, my legs folding under me. The fear and the loneliness hit me so hard at that moment that my baby was the only thing preventing me from throwing myself down in violent wails. I owed it to the one man left in my life to hold it together enough for his well-being.

Sobs scratched at my throat, but despite how easily the waterworks flowed lately, tears wouldn't come out. My chest heaved as it all came crashing down around me. My father was our nucleus, the puzzle piece that held us together so that we could go about our lives without a thought or care. The gaping hole of his death left us empty. I missed him every day, but his loss combined with possibly losing my mother too constricted my chest to the point I could barely breathe.

I counted back from ten, clenching my eyes shut and hoping I'd feel some relief when something draping across my back made me jerk with a gasp.

"Shh, only me." I blinked my eyes open and found Tyler, his long legs crossed under him as he tried to nestle into the corner with me.

"What... what are you doing here?" I took in his tired eyes and extra day of stubble. He looked almost as much of a mess as I felt.

He grabbed my hand and brought it to his lips. "Mom called me. I drove here as fast as I could."

I wanted to fall into his chest in tears. I didn't care how much of him I had or didn't have anymore—he was here, and I was already able to pull more air into my lungs.

"You didn't have to leave the bakery. I'm sure it's busy." Not squeezing his hand back took all the control I had left.

Tyler slid his hands under my legs and gently placed me on his lap, cocking his head to the side.

"Okay, first of all," I protested, "you're going to break a wrist or a kneecap with me at my size. Second, you can go back to work. I'm fine—"

"Shut up."

My jaw went slack as I narrowed my eyes at him.

"Shut up? Tyler, just let me—" My voice cracked when he pressed a kiss to my forehead and brought me into his chest.

"Shut up and let me love you. Because I do, even though you ran out on me before I could tell you. I love you so damn much. But we'll talk about that later."

I said nothing as the first sob slipped out, and then the tears wouldn't stop. I cried for my father, I cried for my mother, I cried for my son who'd missed out on the greatest grandfather any kid could ever hope for. My mother was thrilled about the baby, and it was all she could talk about lately. What if she never got to see him or couldn't recover enough to even know who he was?

I melted into Tyler, allowing myself to let go if for only a minute. His tight embrace, his lips on the top of my head were a balm to my broken soul. Not a cure, but soothing for the moment.

His strong arms wrapped around my torso, his hand caressing my stomach as he continued to rock. "I got you, sugar. I'm not going anywhere."

"I can't do this again," I hiccupped into his chest. "I feel so alone."

"Look at me." I lifted my head off his soaked T-shirt and met his eyes, now boring into mine. "You are *not* alone. No matter what happens." He motioned to my swollen belly. "You have both of us. Okay?" He swiped a tear off my cheek.

"It's my fault."

Tyler's brow furrowed as he studied me. "This would have happened if you were there or not."

"No, but she wouldn't be alone so much if my Dad was still here." I rested my cheek against his chest, the thump of his heartbeat against my ear soothing me enough to take the quiver out of my words.

"That's not your fault either," he whispered. "How could you even think that?"

I pushed away from his chest and lifted my head. "Because he could have prevented it if it wasn't for me."

"I'd say that was worth the months-long waiting list." Dad smirked as he draped an arm across Mom's shoulder.

"Months?" I gaped at my father. "When did you make the reservations?"

My father went all out on my birthdays, which was probably why I grew up believing they were national holidays. My last big party was my sweet sixteen, but when I got too old for parties, he planned big dinners for the three of us. As their only child, I was spoiled by both of them, but my father put on the bigger show of it, especially on birthdays. He kept me in line more than Mom did, but he never hesitated to shower me with whatever I wanted. As I became older, the private celebration with just the three of us was more important than wherever it was, but I'd never deny him the sport of trying to outdo himself every year.

"Maybe six months ago, when we first saw this place on that travel show." He shrugged.

"It's not a big birthday. I'm thirty-three."

"They're all big to me, mija.*" He winked, pulling my mother closer. Instead of laughing at him like she used to, she frowned when she met his gaze.*

"How's the headache?" she asked as she rubbed his neck.

"Headache?"

He waved a hand at me. "It's probably this crazy weather, and work has been a pain in the ass."

"While that's true," Mom said then narrowed her eyes at him, "the weather doesn't cause neck pain and blurry vision. I told you to call the doctor."

"Your vision is blurry? Dad, I don't like that."

He rolled his eyes and let out a loud sigh. "The two of you worry too much. I did call the doctor, and they could only fit me in today, so I moved it to Monday. It's nothing, but I'll go and confirm to make your mother feel better."

Mom and I shared a look as he took a pull from his beer bottle.

"Stop, really. There was no need to cancel our tradition for a tension headache." He reached over the table to squeeze my hand. "I don't miss my daughter's birthday."

"He never made it to the doctor." I swallowed, trying to continue the story I hadn't repeated since my father died. "He went to sleep Sunday night and never woke up."

Tyler's head fell back against the wall as his eyes held mine. "Is that why you blame yourself and won't let anyone celebrate your birthday?"

"Maybe if I wasn't so spoiled, if he didn't think I expected it—"

"He loved doing that for you every year. Don't forget, I was dragged to every single party. *He* chose to not go to the doctor —you didn't ask him to skip it. You didn't even know he was having headaches."

I shrugged. "I would have if I lived closer or visited more. I also egged him on every year. I loved the attention too much."

"So what? He loved giving it to you. And he would hate that you feel this way now."

I shrugged as I wiped my eyes with the back of my hand. "I always loved attention too much. You more than anyone know how much of a problem that always was."

He tightened his arms around me, shaking his head when I lifted my gaze. "Whether or not you loved it or that you schemed ways to get it, you had it anyway. From your dad, from me." He skated his thumb along my jaw. "You can't be ignored, no matter what you do or don't do. He loved making you happy, and you enjoyed it all. Why is any of that a bad thing?"

"Because if he didn't think my birthday dinner was so damn important, he would have gotten checked out and he'd still be here."

"Or maybe they wouldn't have found it in time, and you would have missed out on a great night with your father and a good last memory, even though you're torturing yourself with it now." He pressed his forehead against mine. "My grandmother always says that what-ifs are worthless because there's only what is."

"There you are!"

Tyler and I both turned to Helen's voice.

"She's up and talking, with no signs of stroke." She sat down on the floor in front of us. "Just a probable concussion. She still needs a few more tests, but the doctor has the same theory as me—she just took a bad fall."

My entire body slumped against Tyler in relief, yet I kept crying.

"Do you need a minute before you see her?"

"Yes, she does," he answered for me as he adjusted me in his lap and tightened his hold around me.

"Take your time, sweetheart." She cupped my jaw and headed back to the emergency room.

I savored one last minute in Tyler's arms and shifted off his lap.

"You're kinda cute when you go all alpha." A laugh slipped out through my sniffles. "Thank you for being here."

He knelt in front of me, clutching the sides of my face.

"I'll always be here, and you never have to thank me. I'm not with you because I have to be. I *need* to be. But let's go see your mother before we get into all you have wrong lately." He stood from the floor, extending a hand to me. I slid my palm against his and let him pull me up, not fighting him when he wouldn't let go of my hand all the way back to the emergency room.

"My poor baby, are you okay?" Mom asked in a barely audible, groggy voice. I held back a cringe at the dried blood visible under the bandage along her hairline.

"I'm fine, Mom. I'm just glad you're okay."

Helen gently pushed her back on the pillow when she tried to sit up on her elbows.

"I wish they'd let me come home tonight. I don't like leaving you alone like this."

"Now who's hovering?"

She clenched her eyes shut and smiled.

"I'll stay with her tonight, Carla. She won't be alone." Tyler raised a brow when my gaze slid to his, challenging me. Too exhausted to argue, I only nodded when she blinked her eyes open.

"Thank you, Tyler. Even though I have a splitting headache, that makes me feel much better."

"Yes. Tyler, take Olivia home so she can get some rest and

maybe eat something. I can stay with Carla until she gets a room."

Helen looked between us with the same smile that played on my mother's weak lips.

"Okay," I agreed and came up to my mother. "I love you. Get some rest," I whispered, pressing a careful kiss to the top of her head.

She grabbed my arm as I pulled away. "I love you too. It's all okay. I promise." She gave my hand a weak squeeze. "I'm sorry I scared you."

"Don't be. I'm just glad you're all right. See you in the morning."

Tyler led me out of the emergency room, still by the hand, until we made it to his truck.

"I won't break, you know," I said while gazing out the passenger side window. "I'm an adult, not a child. Everyone is regarding me like I'm a ticking time bomb."

I didn't turn around as he parked behind me in the driveway, Mom's usual spot.

"You're a pregnant woman who's had a rough couple of days. And the people who love you are trying to take care of you, if you'd only stop being so damn difficult and let them."

I gaped at Tyler as he climbed out of the driver's seat and made his way around the vehicle.

"Let's get inside. I have a lot to say." His eyes seared into mine as he held the passenger door open. "And you're not moving an inch until you've heard it all."

THIRTY-FIVE
TYLER

Olivia and I didn't speak when we first arrived at her apartment, but I watched her every move. I searched her face for any signs of pain, remembering one of the books in the pregnancy stack back at my apartment mentioning cramps in times of stress. She seemed fine. Exhausted and quiet, but fine. When she trudged into the bathroom and shut the door, I rummaged through her kitchen to make her something to eat or drink even if she'd fight me. I settled on a bag of decaffeinated tea and filled up the kettle after I grabbed a mug from her cabinet.

"Making me tea in hopes that I'll calm down?"

I turned and found her at the kitchen table in a T-shirt and yoga pants.

"Maybe. You need to get something in your system besides water. I can make you something, or we could order whatever you want."

She rested her chin on her hand and shook her head. "I have a box of scones leftover from what you gave me the other day. I'm good with one of those." She pushed the chair back to get up, but I grabbed the box and set it in front of her before she could stand.

She exhaled a loud sigh and opened the box, shooting me a tiny glare from behind the lid.

"Something to say, Sanchez?" I sat next to her and crossed my arms.

She didn't reply or look my way as she brought the scone to her mouth. I was relieved when she took a big bite.

"I think these are my new favorite after the chocolate cream pie," she said, still not looking in my direction. "You're talented, that's for sure."

"Why are we like this, Olivia?"

She stopped mid-chew to finally lift her head. "Like what?"

I let her question linger when I heard the whistle of the tea kettle. I got up, filled a mug with water, added milk and sugar along with the tea bag before I handed it to her.

"How did you know I took it like this?"

"Because I pay attention," I said with a harsher tone than I'd meant. "Why can we talk about everything else but how we feel?"

"Because we're both scared of it?" She shrugged and wrapped her hands around the mug. "At least I am."

"We scare you?"

She pinched the string of the tea bag between her fingers, chuckling to herself. "Honestly, we terrify me."

"*You're* afraid of something? Since when?" I narrowed my eyes at her.

"Longer than you think," she said, breathing out a deep sigh. "Guys in my life have been...easy, for lack of a better or nicer word. I never had some kind of quest for their attention like I always had with you. I could have a boyfriend or not have a boyfriend. It wasn't important. But you, you're important. Too important."

"And you think you aren't just as important to me?"

She darted her eyes around the room, her lips pursed as she leaned back. "A year ago, if I'd walk into a room you were in, you'd walk out."

"And you'd just follow me." I snickered. "So what's the point?"

"That's the *exact* point." She dropped her head for a moment and sucked in a breath. "I loved you, whether I realized it or not, and you could barely tolerate me. As I've said, I'm aware that was my fault. All that friction between us created this inferno of sexual tension, and maybe it clouded things."

"We aren't those people anymore. And yes, I've been attracted to you since my dick knew how to get hard."

"Jeez, if the bakery thing doesn't work out, you could always write Valentine cards instead." She sipped her tea, squinting at me over the rim.

"What I'm saying is, yes, chemistry was never a problem. I have no doubt that was the cause of most of our fights. There was too much, and neither of us knew what to do with it. But it's different in so many ways now. You can't see that?"

"I *want* to see it," she said, her voice scratchy and small, almost unrecognizable. "I want it all with you."

"And I want it all with you too." I slammed my hand on the table, frustrated that even though I was ready to tell her, I couldn't get the damn words out.

I shot up out of the chair and crouched in front of her. "We were only supposed to be pretending at Donnie's wedding, but it was real, even if it didn't make sense at the time. And since then, you've been all I thought about and all I wanted. I'm not good with words, but the way I feel about you, why I want you has nothing to do with the fact that you're having my baby." I grabbed her hands from her lap. "Granted, that's an awesome surprise, but it's not why I'm here. Maybe it gave me the push to stop denying how much I felt about you, but I'd want you regardless."

After months of not being able to say anything, I spilled everything out in a matter of minutes. "My landlord gave me a lease agreement for the new space, but I didn't sign it."

"You didn't?" She crinkled her nose at me. "Why?"

"Because," I said, cupping her neck, "what's the point if I can't celebrate it with you? In fact, without you, *everything* seems pretty damn pointless. You're my person, Olivia." I cradled her cheek, running my thumb back and forth along her jaw. "I'm so fucking lucky to have you. Maybe I couldn't say it the right way and maybe I blurted out something stupid that hurt you, but I *love* you." I tightened my grip on the back of her neck. "God, I love you so much. You're everything to me. Please say you believe that."

Her eyes swam with more tears.

"I know what you mean about being scared," I continued even though she didn't reply. "Or about having whiplash from how we used to be, but I don't think we ever really knew each other at all. Or maybe deep down we were afraid to. I don't know about you, but I can't go back now."

Thick tears streamed down her cheeks even though she barely blinked.

"I can't lose you. You're my best friend and the love of my life. It just took the favor you offered me to realize that." I smiled, but she didn't return it. "I should have told you a long time ago, but it was always the truth." I fell back on my heels and heaved a long sigh, panic taking over the adrenaline running through my system. "Christ, Olivia, say something."

She shifted in her chair toward me, cradling my cheek with a shaky hand. "That game has gotten so much better," she whispered, then her mouth split into a wide grin.

My shoulders slumped in relief as I hauled her mouth to mine, tasting her salty tears on her lips. She slid off the chair and joined me on the floor, straddling my hips as she whimpered into my mouth.

"I love you," she murmured. "I'm sorry. All I feel about you makes me do stupid things. Like knock cake batter out of your hand." She sniffled out a chuckle and roped her arms around my neck. "We've known each other our whole lives, but having you like this..." She fidgeted with the collar of my shirt. "I was scared it was all too amazing to be real. I've been in love with you for so long, it's seemed too good to be true that you wanted me back. It's always been you for me. I love you so much, I think it still makes me crazy. *That* much hasn't changed since we were kids."

I painted kisses down her jaw. "And I love that you're crazy over me. I'm just as crazy over you, sugar."

"Right," she said, a laugh bubbling out through her tears. "I doubt that."

"You make me happy on a level I never imagined. And I want to ask you something, even if it seems fast. But at this point, fuck fast."

"Okay," she giggled against my lips. "Go ahead."

"I don't like spending nights away from you. And when the little guy comes, I won't want to leave either of you. My apartment is fine. For me. You've seen how bare it is, but it was by the bakery and easy. But convenience isn't worth being away from my family."

"Do you want to move in with me?" Olivia asked slowly, her brow pulled together.

"Yes, I do. For the same reasons you want to stay here. You have a nice yard, and your mom is here. My mom is usually here too." We shared a laugh. "And I hate not having you next to me at night or to have to leave earlier to get ready for work.

And I know my dad did his best, but I want to do better. I want to be a hands-on father from the beginning. I told you, I'm all in, sugar."

"Well, if you want..." She gulped, lifting a shoulder as her jaw quivered. "I guess you could live with us." She grabbed my face and kissed me so hard I fell back on the kitchen floor. "I think I melted a little when you called us your family."

"That's what you are."

It was always her too. And it felt so goddamn good to—finally—stop fighting it.

"Right back at you," she whispered before we fell into another kiss, igniting with that fire I never had with anyone else along with a lifetime of relief.

All my life, I'd felt incomplete and not good enough. Olivia was the missing piece I'd never realized was there all along.

THIRTY-SIX
OLIVIA

"If you keep doing that, I'll never want to get up."

Tyler trailed kisses over the nape of my neck and down my back. Despite my protests, I arched into him for more, greedy as always.

"Good, we can skip today. Not like we have to be there anyway." He cupped my breast—what he could get into his hand anyway. At seven months pregnant, my body had blossomed everywhere—meaning ballooned to twice its size. None of my shoes fit, and I busted out of every bra I owned. I had to get a whole new wardrobe a couple of weeks ago, and my new clothes were already tight.

"Yes, we do," I grumbled, turning over on a yawn. "It's a baby shower, so we're kind of important guests. And we need stuff, so I think we can suck it up for a day."

Helen came up with the idea of having more of a party than a shower with both men and women invited, meaning my little family plus Tyler's asshole cousins. I was big enough to be uncomfortable, but I didn't mind seeing family today. Tyler still hated seeing most of his, but Donnie and his wife were in town, and my presence still made Alan uncomfortable enough to be fun.

I searched for my nightgown and reached over the bed to grab it off the floor. Sex required a little maneuvering with my big stomach in the way, and my face pressed into the pillow while Tyler pressed into me had recently become my new favorite position. We were delirious on love, but he was still my adorable grump when it came to parties.

"I guess," he conceded, throwing his legs around the side of the bed and pushing off the mattress. I took a peek at the globes of his perfect ass before making my way into the kitchen. We only had a couple of hours to get ready, and even my fast speed lately was in slow motion.

"I got the keys last night for the new space—I forgot to tell you."

"Really?" I stilled as I set up the coffee pot. My doctor had always told me I could have one real cup of coffee per day, and now that I was more exhausted than ever, I decided to take her up on it and savor every last drop of the eight ounces of real stuff allowed. "That's exciting."

"Seemed like it took forever to get it all finalized. Now to figure out what the hell to do with it. Come with me tomorrow—we can celebrate for a day."

I shot him a glare as I grabbed the mugs out of the cabinet. "Babe, we talked about this."

"We did, but you can't even leave the apartment? I promise I won't even say happy birthday."

"The only reason I agreed to have the shower today was that Mom wanted a distraction from my father's third anniversary. It doesn't have to make sense to you, it's how I deal."

"Am I allowed to stay home, or should I sleep at the bakery?"

I wanted to chuckle at the scowl on his face. "You can stay here. I just have my own routine."

"Shutting off your phone and watching creepy documentaries. No matter what day it is, that's not healthy."

"Probably not," I said, holding back a smile at the concern pinching his brow. I'd started to make peace with the guilt I'd always feel around my father's death, even though now I consciously knew it wasn't my fault. It still felt wrong to celebrate a day so close to when I lost him and to have any kind of birthday at all without him there.

The next few days would be a little hard, but knowing I had Tyler and the baby to look forward to would make it a bit easier to come out of the haze this year, or at least I hoped it would.

We didn't discuss it further as we drove to his parents' house. Tyler was mostly quiet as we got closer, and I wasn't sure if it was due to his opposition over my plan to spend tomorrow watching serial killers alone or having to deal with an afternoon of family.

"Everyone is coming, right?"

"Unfortunately." He coughed out a laugh. "But they don't bother me like they used to. Another thing I have you to thank for." My chest pinched at his wide smile. Tyler still didn't give smiles very often, but he always had plenty for me.

"Have you seen them since the wedding?"

He shook his head. "I still see Ross at the bakery sometimes, which surprises me since I stopped his made-up discount a long time ago. Alan, no. I hear he's got a new girlfriend and she's even younger."

"Ah, good for him for sticking to what he knows." I rubbed the back of his neck. "The last time I was at a family party with you, you told me you were okay staying strangers."

He chuckled as he pulled up in front of his parents' house.

"I was full of shit." He leaned over and pressed his lips to mine. "You're killing me in that dress today."

"I didn't think you noticed." I wore a tight, short dress for today in fire-engine red. Instead of hiding my stomach, I'd decided to flaunt it, knowing it would get Tyler revved up enough for an amazing payoff later.

"Now *you're* full of shit." He kissed me again, close-mouthed but lingering long enough to make my heart kick up a couple of beats. "Now let's get this over with." He put the car into Park and unlocked the doors.

Helen and Mom told everyone to wrap the gifts in clear plastic so I wouldn't have to sit and unwrap them, which I was eternally grateful for. I tried to hype it up to Tyler, but I was ready to get it all over with too.

"You're glowing," Leah said as she handed me a glass of virgin punch. "You must be feeling good."

"I don't know about good, but I'm happy. I'm just anxious for him to get here already."

"Leah's right," Morgan said, coming next to me and elbowing my side. "You look amazing. It's nice to finally see you let yourself be happy."

Morgan's smile didn't make it to her eyes. She still wasn't pregnant yet, and as many times as she assured me she was fine despite the extra time it was taking, I knew the last thing she wanted to attend was someone else's baby shower—even if it was mine.

I slid my arm into the crook of her elbow and squeezed.

"I'll be really happy when we can go home and I can put my feet up." I hated wearing flat sandals with this dress, but heels were a definite no-go. The straps were digging into my ankles already.

"Olivia, I forgot to attach the gift receipt." Tyler's aunt Mary approached me with an envelope. "My grandson loved his vibrating seat, but if you don't like it you can pick something else."

"I'm sure our baby will love it too, thank you." I took the envelope from her as I spied Alan behind her. He'd shown up alone but hadn't mentioned where the new younger girlfriend was.

"I don't remember being at a baby shower where I wasn't at the wedding before." She grinned as she cast a judgmental glance at my belly. I nodded with a tight smile. Tyler loved me and we were happy. Did I want to marry him? Of course. But if we stayed in a simple cohabitation bliss for the rest of our lives, I was fine with it. We were together in all the ways that it mattered, so petty relatives wouldn't derail my happiness today.

"Maybe they're keeping their options open, Mom." Alan snickered behind her. "I don't think I said congratulations earlier."

"No, you didn't, but thank you." Not that we wanted it or needed it, but I could manage bare pleasantries for the next hour or two.

Tyler's aunt made her way back into the small crowd, but Alan stayed, grabbing a beer bottle from the beverage table. His gaze traveled to where Morgan and Leah held hands, and a smirk ticked up the side of his mouth.

"So that's where you landed," he said to Morgan, raising his beer bottle. "Congrats to you too."

"Oh my God, I'm so sorry," I said as I spilled my almost-full glass of pink punch onto Alan's gray shirt. "Pregnant women are so klutzy," I clutched my chest for effect when I noticed a few pairs of eyes staring at us. "And my grip isn't the best from this old injury I have." I shook my hand out and caught Tyler's gaze over Alan's shoulder. He came closer and wrapped his arms around me from behind.

"Aren't you too old to be playing games, Olivia?" Alan sneered at me as he patted his chest. Whatever they put into the punch left a wide neon stain over half of his shirt.

Oops.

"Aren't you too old to be such an asshole?"

"If I were you, I'd back off," Tyler said, "before my woman kicks your ass. *Again*."

Alan glowered at me as he threw his napkin into the trash and stalked off.

"I did plan to be nice but then he made a stupid comment to Morgan, and well, I couldn't help myself." I shrugged, rubbing the top of his hand where it rested on my stomach. "I'm sorry."

"No, you're not." He dropped a kiss on my shoulder. "And I love you for it."

Tyler loved me. No matter who was here today or what stupid comments they had about our life, that was and would always be enough.

"Everything okay?" Helen came over to us with a concerned pinch in her brow.

"Oh, all is fine." I cuddled into Tyler's side. "My hand slipped, and I spilled my drink all over your nephew. Sorry."

Helen bit back a smile. "I think you guys can start loading the car if you want. I know you probably want to get going."

"We're only going straight home. It's not a big deal."

"Well," Tyler said, smiling as he tightened his hold around me. "I thought since you don't want to join society tomorrow, we could stop and take a look at the new space."

"Yes, congratulations." My mother came over to us and kissed his cheek. "So much to celebrate."

I darted my eyes around the yard, not wanting to see the unshed tears I knew I'd find and trigger my own. Today was a wonderful yet hard day for her, even though she'd forced a smile for hours. I hoped a grandson would give her enough joy to ease the heartbreak. We hadn't told her about the baby's name yet. The original Javier could never be replaced, but I knew she'd fall in love with this one.

"We can help you load the car." Helen crooked a finger at Tyler's father. "I'm sure you're both ready to relax after all this family. Thanks for being a good sport, sweetheart."

Tyler gave his mother a shy smile when she cupped his cheek.

"Hey, it's a big deal for you both. Not only do your kids not try to kill each other anymore but you also get to share a grandchild."

"Yes, that is a huge double milestone." I wrapped my arms around Tyler's waist as I looked between Mom and Helen, happiness radiating off them both. After the many times he'd scolded us for upsetting our mothers, my father should be here to finally see them like this. I cleared my throat to halt the spiral of emotion that pulled me in so easily these days. "So congrats."

Mom laughed, even with her eyes wet.

"Let's get you both out of here." Her gaze flicked to Tyler's, and they shared an odd look before Mom followed Helen to the pile of presents.

"So can we stop somewhere since you're secluding yourself in the apartment tomorrow?"

I rolled my eyes at Tyler after he started his truck and nodded. "Yes, we can. Do you have any other ideas other than knocking down the wall?"

"Not really. Tegan said we should make it a part café, but I don't have the head to try to figure that out yet. Serving regular coffee is enough for the staff at the counter for now. I'm just looking to spread out."

"I could spread out too, christen the new space." I looped

my arms around his neck and kissed his cheek as he kept his eyes on the road.

"Don't say that while wearing that dress unless you mean it."

"I *always* mean it, babe," I whispered, and I bit his earlobe. Pregnancy still made me a stick of dynamite, just a much thicker one.

"Take a look and tell me what you think. Since you're my social media manager and all, I'd love your opinion." He turned to me, a half smile lifting his mouth as he unlocked the door and pushed it open.

"Well, I'll try..."

The new space was not at all empty as he'd said.

My eyes fell on the two-tiered chocolate cake on a table in the middle of the room with a balloon arch behind it.

"It took me two tries to figure out exactly what kind of cake you had at that birthday party in the photo album, but I think this is close. And look..." He rushed over to the table and grabbed something. "Your mom still had this." He held up a familiar tiara. "You're thirty-six, not sixteen, but I didn't think you'd ever pass up a chance to be queen, your majesty." He handed it to me, bowing with a wide smile.

"Tyler, look, this is..." I rubbed at my eyes, both overwhelmed and infuriated by what he'd created. "It's beautiful and I love you for the effort, but I've told you a million times that I don't celebrate my birthday anymore—"

"Yes, and I think it's bullshit."

I grabbed the tiara from his hand. "It's not a rule that you have to make a big deal out of one stupid day. Other people just let it go by—"

"Not you. Remember, I was at every single birthday of yours growing up, and I watched you eat it up and love every minute of it. You think you're respecting your father's memory by ignoring it, but if he was here, he'd be pissed at you for punishing yourself like this over something you had no way of knowing would happen or had any control over."

I inhaled a long breath through my nose. "I get what you're saying, I do. And I'm trying to deal with the guilt that I'm not supposed to have over losing him. But it's still not the same. Even if I somehow get over that, because of how he died, I'll never think of my birthday in the same way ever again, and there is nothing you can—"

My heart leaped into my throat when Tyler fell to one knee. "Do you love me?"

"What kind of a question is that?" I screeched. "Of course I love you."

"So you wouldn't want to hurt my feelings, right? Like if I asked you to spend the rest of your life with me tonight, you wouldn't celebrate it with me tomorrow? You wouldn't acknowledge the day I told you that I loved you so much that just living with you isn't good enough? I need you to be my wife. I need it in writing that I get to have you forever."

"Yes, I want all of that too."

"I didn't ask you yet."

I flinched as he pulled a ring box out of his back pocket.

"The only way I'll ask is if you let us celebrate it tonight *and* tomorrow. Because the day I finally made you mine isn't something I'd ignore year after year." He popped the velvet top open. "What's it going to be, Sanchez?"

"You're playing dirty," I rasped, unshed tears scratching at my throat.

He shrugged, his eyes still holding mine.

"Sometimes that's the only way to win. Olivia, will you marry me?"

I knelt in front of him and placed the tiara on my head. It still poked my scalp with its heavy weight, but I could still feel an inkling of the thrill I'd had at slipping it on for my party all those years ago. Maybe Tyler was right and ignoring it was disrespecting all my father had done for me. Not just for all thirty-three birthdays but for loving me with all that he had every day, even if he couldn't do it for long.

My heart still wasn't all that into it, but for him and for Tyler, I'd find my way back to some of the joy.

Because Tyler and the family we were about to create was something to celebrate every single day.

I grabbed his face and covered his mouth with mine, feeling his heavy sigh of relief bleed into the kiss.

I held out my ring finger, wiggling it with feigned impatience.

"I'm waiting for my birthday present."

EPILOGUE

ONE YEAR LATER

Tyler

"That's enough, buddy." I laughed, swiping icing off my son's chubby chin. "You can have more cupcakes later."

Javier grunted, furrowing his brow when I shook my head again. At almost a year old, my personality showed through in him more and more each day. He had his mother's golden skin and dark hair, but the brooding stare and quick temper were all me. He lit up a room when he'd laugh and smile, but he didn't give in easy. Both my mother and Olivia reveled in a baby version of me while I hoped that, unlike his father, he'd loosen up a little as he got older.

We'd told Carla his name after we'd laid him in her arms for the first time, and she still couldn't say it without her voice cracking.

Olivia had her one-year postpartum checkup today, and while our mothers could have taken him, I wanted to do it. The perks of owning your own business included not having to worry if you had to bring a carriage to work, and I liked to steal time alone with my son when I could. Olivia had him during the day since she worked from home, but I enjoyed having him with me at the bakery sometimes even if he was a big distraction to the staff.

I bounced Javier in my arms, hoping to take his attention off the cupcake by walking him around and waving to some of the customers seated around us.

By knocking down the wall, we'd expanded the kitchen and display to almost double, having plenty of time and room to prepare for what we knew would be our busiest days. I took my wife's suggestion and put a couple of tables in, but we weren't a café, at least not now. Hey, Batter still got shout-outs on social media from time to time, and thankfully now that I'd staffed up, it wasn't the working-all-night panic it used to be.

"There they are!" Javier's head whipped around to his mother's voice. He let out a squeal as she made her way over to him and scooped him out of my arms. He kicked against her stomach while she dropped kisses over his chubby cheeks. "My favorite boys in the whole world."

"One of your favorite boys is waiting for a kiss. My son stole them all."

She laughed as she leaned in to peck my lips. "I always have kisses for you." She kissed me again until Javier stirred in her arms, probably annoyed at having to share attention.

That came from his mother.

"How did everything go?" I asked. She didn't answer as she cooed into Javier's neck. "Olivia?"

"What? Oh, fine." Her smile was tight and fake as she looked back at our son.

"I heard he was here!" Tegan rushed over to us, peeling her jacket off and holding out her hands. "Can I take him?"

Tegan was familiar enough to Javier for him to lean into her without much hesitation.

"Actually, can you watch him for a minute?" I asked Tegan while still eyeing my wife. "I'll be right out."

"Sure," she chirped as she tickled his side. Javier was too focused on the new ring in her nose to laugh, and I hoped he wouldn't rip it out before I got to the bottom of why Olivia was acting so weird.

I took Olivia's hand and pulled her to the back room.

"Okay, what's going on?" I folded my arms and leaned against the counter.

"I wanted to wait until you got home."

"Well, you can't now. Did they find anything wrong?"

"No, nothing like that." She shook her head. "Not really."

"Start making sense, Sanchez. You're making me nervous."

She inhaled a long breath, letting it out slowly as she met my gaze. "Remember that romantic weekend when our mothers took care of the baby? We booked that suite in the Poconos with the cheesy champagne glass bathtub and had so much sex that I had to sit on a pillow on the drive home?"

I looked around, something I should have done earlier to make sure we were alone, before I nodded.

"And since I'm still weaning Javi off breastfeeding, the chances of me getting pregnant again, combined with my age, were probably slim?"

"Yes. And?"

"And do you not see where I'm going with this?"

It took a few seconds for realization to spread through me and anchor me to the counter. "You're..."

"Pregnant, yes. Our babies will be less than two years apart and will have overlapping diaper time." She inched toward me. "I didn't want to freak you out at work."

"I'm not freaked out."

"You're not blinking either."

"I'm just..." I ran a hand through my hair. "I'm surprised,

that's all. I wouldn't want you to wait to tell me something like this."

"I told you right here the last time." A smile danced across her lips. "You handled it well then too."

I brought her into my arms. "Because it's not bad news. It's a—"

"Surprise, yes. And I'll need more tests since I'm older. But the good news is we'll know the sex with total certainty since I have to take a genetic blood test. And I think it's a girl. Just a hunch."

"So I'll have two of you?" I shut my eyes as my head fell back.

"And what's wrong with that?" She slapped my chest.

"I'm barely man enough for one of you."

"You're plenty for both of us."

She brushed my lips, backing away with a wicked grin. "You're going to have to be the cocktail sampler again."

Olivia still ran her Cleopatra page, and we used those appointments as date nights. She had managed to keep her identity a secret and only mentioned a man in her life once for a Valentine's Day post. With one baby, we weren't able to get out as much, and with a second, she was going to have to start featuring kids' menus.

"I can do that."

"Hey, there's a big line in the front, so I'm going to have to give him back so I can give them a hand." Tegan handed Javier back to me and smoothed his unruly black curls. "See you soon, big guy."

My son scrutinized me with almost sympathetic eyes as if he somehow knew. He dropped his head to my shoulder, and I leaned my cheek against him.

"We're in for it, kiddo," I said while rubbing his back. "Get all the sleep you can."

"You're not funny." Olivia crossed her arms.

I looped my arm around her waist and brought her in for a kiss while my son dozed off on my shoulder.

Life with Olivia would never stop keeping me on my toes. And I'd never stop loving every single second.

BONUS EPILOGUE

SIX YEARS LATER

Olivia

"Tell her she can't do that!" Gavin, a red-faced and frustrated five-year-old, pointed his tiny finger in my daughter's direction.

Gianna pursed her lips, responding with a bored shrug that a kid her age shouldn't have been able to pull off so well. Since we'd enrolled her in prekindergarten, Tyler and I had heard constant tales of her acting up in school, never wanting to share, and pushing the kids to do what she wanted without even a hint of compromise. She craved attention and preferred the company of kids who followed her lead. We'd talked to her over and over again and stupidly thought we were getting through when she had a great second half of the school year —until it all changed in September.

"Mrs. Maxwell said that the blocks belong to everyone. I can play with them whenever I want," Gianna said, crossing her arms with a hint of a smile drifting over her defiant lips. I'd thought parenting was no big deal after we had Javier, but once this one learned how to walk and talk, I regretted waiting until my thirties to have children.

How was I going to muster the energy for a teenage version of my youngest child?

"Yes, Gianna. But you have to wait your turn, dear. Why do you insist on taking toys away from Gavin?" Mrs. Maxwell said in a soft voice as she squinted at Gianna from behind her desk. Tyler and I sat on either side of our daughter while Gavin and his mother judged all three of us from where they sat toward the back of the room. "I tried to talk to you about it, but you kept doing it. I had to call your parents after you threw the blocks at him this morning."

Last year, Gavin and Gianna were inseparable. He was even at our house some weekends, happy to agree to whatever movie Gianna wanted to watch or toy Gianna chose to play with. They even decorated tiny cakes with Tyler in our kitchen. It was wonderful to see my daughter have her first real friend.

But when they moved up to kindergarten and Gavin wasn't the only one of three boys in their class, he shunned my daughter's Barbie plays for action figures and superheroes with his new friends. My brokenhearted little girl dealt with hurt feelings much like her mother did, by lashing out with vengeance.

"I needed the two triangle blocks to make a diamond, and he was taking too long."

Tyler and I snuck a glance at each other before he rubbed his temple. Our daughter had already perfected the eye roll combined with an insolent tilt of her head. She needed someone to fear, and since both her father and grandfather were mostly wrapped around her little finger, I guessed that had to be me.

"Stop taking my blocks, you bitch!"

A collective gasp sucked the air out of the room, and I grabbed Tyler's knee as soon as he leaned forward, afraid he'd leap out of the chair.

"Gavin!" Mrs. Maxwell glared at Gavin, now slumped against his mother. "Gianna may be wrong for taking your blocks and throwing them at you, but you do not use that kind of language to anyone! Apologize."

He mumbled a barely audible "Sorry" into his mother's arm.

"I don't think we heard you." Tyler's voice was soft but cold as he narrowed his eyes at Gavin. Tyler shot me a quick glare after I elbowed his side, obviously forgetting that once upon a time, he was a boy frustrated by a relentless little girl too.

Gavin stared back at us wide-eyed, as if that word falling from his cherub lips had surprised him too.

"Sorry, Gianna." He flicked his gaze to Gianna before dropping it toward the carpet.

Gianna's golden-brown eyes filled with tears as she lost some of her bravado. The sadness etched in her features made me almost relent on the punishment I planned to give her later. But bad guys had to do what they had to do.

"We'll talk to Gianna." I looked between Gavin and Gianna. "You guys were such good friends. It makes me sad to see you fight. Maybe we could have a little sit-down, clear the air a bit?"

Gavin's mother met my gaze with a slow nod.

I took solace in the fact that at least my child wasn't the one who had cursed—this time.

I pictured my father looking down on us, shaking with laughter as I paid the ultimate price for being a rotten kid—having one of my own. But my Gianna wasn't rotten, she was hurt and didn't know how to handle it. I understood her so much it broke my heart a little.

"Is everything okay?" my mother asked as Gianna moped past her into our apartment. We still lived downstairs, but we saw no reason to leave. This was home. Mom loved having all of us here, and there was plenty of room for the four of us. I'd given up my office for Gianna's bedroom, but I didn't mind setting myself up in the living room for work. Plus, Grams was only a short walk upstairs for a sleepover when Tyler and I wanted a night alone.

"Yes," I sighed. "Unfortunately, she's her mother's daughter." I chuckled before heading to the kitchen table to kiss Javier on the cheek. He was so into his tablet, he barely flinched until I poked his shoulder.

"Oh. Hi, Mommy. Is Gianna punished?"

I brushed the black curls off his forehead as I stifled a laugh. Gianna looked like Tyler, but her personality was all me, whereas my son was my twin on the outside, with the adorable broodiness of his father. He was just as exasperated by his sister as anyone else, but his brow furrowed with worry as he searched for her over my shoulder.

"Don't worry about that, baby. Why don't you go upstairs with Grams for a bit, and we'll come to get you when dinner is ready?"

He nodded, rising from the table to follow my mother out the door.

I took Gianna's hand and led her toward the couch. She held on even after she sat, studying my gaze, then her father's. I sucked in a long breath, trying to figure out where to begin.

"Listen, sweetheart," Tyler started before I could speak. "I know you're hurt. Gavin used to be your friend, and now he's with the boys. It's okay to be hurt, but you can't take his toys in school."

"Why not?" Her lips pursed as she looked at both of us.

"Because it's not nice, G." Tyler lifted an eyebrow. "And you know that."

"*He's* not nice." Her lip jutted out in a pout before it quivered. "He doesn't like me anymore." Her chin dropped to her chest as she sniffled.

Tyler winced before he stood from the couch and crouched in front of her. "Some people aren't nice. Some hurt you, and there's not much you can do about it. But making him mad at you to get back at him won't help anything. Leave Gavin alone for now. I bet he's going to be sorry someday for giving up an awesome friend like you, but if he isn't, there are plenty of other people who want to be your friend. Give them your attention instead."

Her chest rose and fell with a long sigh. "Okay, Daddy."

"There's my girl." He smiled and cupped her cheek.

Despite the day we'd had, I was tempted to make an appointment as soon as possible to get my IUD taken out and have five more of Tyler's babies. He was such a great father, and my ovaries never fully recovered from moments like these.

"But we're still going to take away your tablet until the weekend. If Mrs. Maxwell says that you were good the rest of this week, maybe you can bake with me on Saturday."

Her hands flew to her mouth. "At the bakery?"

He nodded. "After we close in the afternoon. But only if you're good, okay?"

Her mouth split into a grin as she leaped in Tyler's arms. Maybe I underestimated my husband. If anyone knew how to deal with an Olivia 2.0, it would've been him.

"You were amazing today," I told him after we'd gotten both kids into bed. "My father would have been proud of you."

He shrugged without looking back at me as he rummaged through the kitchen cabinets. He turned and dropped two muffin trays onto the counter with an angry clatter. I bit back a smile as he set himself up for a night of stress baking. Punishing the kids, especially his little girl, always seemed to weigh on him.

"I know it's tough, but you handled her beautifully. She's lucky to have a father who loves her beyond reason but isn't afraid to punish her when she needs it. And since she's got so much of me in her, we need to be up for the challenge."

I laughed, but Tyler only glowered back after he fished the eggs out of the refrigerator.

"If that little bastard calls my baby a bitch again, that school doesn't want to know what will happen next."

"How many forms of evil did you call me growing up?" I burst out laughing despite the rush of heat pooling between my legs. Nothing was hotter than when Tyler went alpha daddy. "You were a Gavin once too, so you have to stay strong, babe."

"No," he shot back. "We were different."

"A little, but not much." I cocked my head from side to side. "I hate that he hurt her too, but they're too little to know the right way to do things. It's our job to show her. Let Gavin's mother handle her nasty kid and his mouth."

Tyler's biceps bulged as he mixed the muffin batter.

"She's your baby, but you have to teach her the right things. And you are. I was totally ready to be the bad guy before you stepped in." I wrapped my arms around his waist from behind and kissed between his shoulder blades. "You were perfect, but if you need to make angry muffins every time she acts up, I won't stop you."

He set the bowl on the counter, a sexy smirk tilting his lips as he turned toward me. "Did I hurt you like that when we were their age?" Tyler's twitch of a smile faded to a worried frown.

I shook my head and kissed him, lingering long enough to

make him reach for me when I pulled away. "I didn't give you a chance," I whispered against his lips.

He threaded his fingers into my hair, slanting his mouth over mine before lifting me onto the counter.

"I guess it's hard to remember a time when I wasn't hopelessly in love with you." He ran his finger down the slope of my nose.

"Same. I guess because I always kind of was?" I shrugged before looping my arms around his neck. "So what kind of muffins are you making?"

"Haven't decided." He reached behind me for the jar of Nutella we kept out for Javier's usual breakfast of Nutella on toast. "I could do something with this." Tyler held my gaze, a wicked glint in his eye as he opened the jar. "Doesn't that punk have a nut allergy? We could send one in Gianna's lunch."

"Tyler, you can't threaten other people's kids," I told him with a raised brow. "At least not until they're teenagers."

"I guess you're right." He shrugged as he skimmed a finger over the top.

"Since when do you poke your fingers in..." I trailed off when he dragged a path of Nutella down my neck with his finger, swirling it over my collarbone as he tugged at the hem of my tank top.

"What are you doing?" I rasped, my voice husky as his tongue followed the path of Nutella and ventured lower, right across the swells of my breasts. The scratch of his stubble combined with the wet warmth of his mouth liquified my knees.

"Working off the tension another way. Lose the shirt, Sanchez."

He fisted the hem of my top and yanked it over my head.

"Shouldn't we move this somewhere behind a door... *Fuck*,

keep doing that."

Tyler drew a sticky circle around my nipple before he sucked it into his mouth, moaning as he grazed it with his teeth.

"You still taste as sweet as sugar," he murmured against my stomach as his lips trailed lower.

"We can't do this out here— *Jesus*..." My head fell back on the top cabinet with a thump when he pushed my pants and underwear past my knees and nibbled at my clit. His mouth was all over me but denying me the friction I needed. I spied the glint in his eye as he peered up at me, his tongue skimming up and down my slit, teasing me to the point of madness.

He claimed I knew how to push his buttons at a young age, but he could play me all too well.

"I need..." I started, but too many nerve endings were firing below my waist for me to finish.

"What do you need, wife? Tell me." He dragged kisses across the inside of my damp thigh as it quivered against his lips.

"I need my husband to fuck me already." My head fell back again, this time in frustration.

"Did you guys fall?"

We froze at the sound of Javier's voice, thankfully drifting from his bedroom, not the kitchen. I would never be able to explain why my shirt was off, my pants were around my ankles, and Nutella was smeared across my chest.

"Mommy is helping me bake. Go back to sleep, buddy."

"I want to help too!"

"No!" We both told Gianna as I jumped off the counter, pulling up my pants after I scooped my shirt off the floor.

"I think you can throw that jar out." I motioned to the counter.

"Nah," Tyler said as he reached for a marker, writing a *T*

on the lid before he closed it back up. "This one can be for us." He winked before sliding it onto a high shelf.

"I should have known a baker would have a food kink," I teased. "You've hidden it well all this time."

"I have an Olivia kink." He yanked my body flush to his. "Still want your husband to fuck you?"

"Always," I dragged out the word before I kissed him, biting his lip as I pulled away.

"Then we better go to bed. And lock the door."

I laughed when he looked behind him.

"I love you—we all do." I ran my hand down the cotton of his T-shirt, the sudden rush of emotions scratching at the back of my throat.

"I love all of you too. So much, I don't know what to do with myself sometimes." He chuckled, looking away for a second.

I never knew what to do with myself when it came to Tyler either. The feelings were still overwhelming in all the best ways. That would never change.

"I know what you could do with *me*." I hooked my thumbs into the waistband of his sweatpants and pulled him toward me.

"Always so unfairly beautiful," he sighed and cupped my cheek.

My cheeks heated. I still lit up whenever Tyler looked at me like that. It was hard to believe the bossy little girl and a grumpy little boy who used to be at each other's throats ended up here—crazy in love with two crazy kids. Well, one—Javier hadn't tested us like his sister yet.

"Always mine," I brushed his lips, laughing when he smiled into the kiss.

Loving Tyler was a constant in my life ever since I was my daughter's age, and keeping him was still the best surprise.

ACKNOWLEDGMENTS

Writing a book truly takes a village, and I'm so grateful for mine.

First, to my husband and son for being my biggest cheerleaders and for their unending support for every single book, even though they watch me disappear behind the laptop screen some nights. I love you both more than you'll ever know.

To my betas: Jodi, Lauren, Bianca, Rachel, Lisa, Avery, and Korrie. Thank you for being able to see what I can't and for helping me make Tyler and Olivia's story the best it could be.

To my sensitivity readers: Kathryn and Carla, thank you for setting my mind at ease and for your love of this story.

To Elle, thank you for sharing your experiences with me and making sure all the scenes about Olivia's mother showed diabetes in a respectful and accurate way, plus teaching me a couple of things in the process.

Jodi, this wouldn't be nearly as fun without you. Thank you for your friendship and for all you do for me—and for allowing me to think in "we" not "me" in this author life.

Korrie, you're a ray of sunshine in this book world. I'm lucky to have you in my life and in my corner.

To Najla Qamber, the creative genius behind this amazing cover, and Lindee Robinson for the shot that was so perfectly Tyler and Olivia I still can't believe it.

To Jessica and Jodi, for cleaning up my editorial mess to make Tyler and Olivia shine.

To my beloved Rose Garden, who sticks with me every single release and tolerates my mom-life tales each day. Your never-ending support means the world to me.

To Ari and my street team roses, thank you for your tireless efforts to get all my books seen. I appreciate all you do!

To the readers and bloggers who picked up this book and took a chance on me in the midst of so many other authors and stories. I said after I published my first book that if ten people not related to me bought it, I'd consider it a success. To be here at book twelve, with the love and support of so many readers who have become friends along the way, it's more than I could've imagined. *Thank you* can never begin to cover it.

AUTHOR'S NOTE

Back in February 2020, I signed up for my first round of Tell Me a Story (TMAS) in Lucy Score's reader's group, Binge Readers Anonymous. For those who don't know this awesome group or event, the members pick the trope, characters, and setting and throw in some wild cards along the way. The author has twenty-four hours to create a story based on what the readers tell them to do.

It was terrifying yet exciting, as the readers in this group are so into the event and I was pumped to write it. But they had chosen enemies to lovers as the trope for me to work with, which was unchartered waters for me. I was used to the second-chance, slow-burn friends-to-lovers jam, and I tend to hate and fear the black moment in all romances, including my own books. I was also never a fan of bully romance, so how was I going to create a love story based on hate?

Then I got an idea, what if the heroine was the issue? Usually the guy is the one who can't handle his feelings, but what if *she* liked the guy so much from a young age that she couldn't handle it, so her way of dealing with her unrequited love was to pull on her beloved's proverbial pigtails and torture him?

The heroine was a secret food blogger under the false name Cleopatra who was obsessed with gnomes, and the hero was a grumpy baker who had to pretend to be in love with her. But, spoiler alert, he wasn't pretending any more than she was. Readers loved it, and I loved it too but didn't know if I could ever pull off enemies to lovers for real.

Fast forward to 2021, and I had the inkling to try enemies to lovers again for a side character in one of my books. It wasn't working, no matter what angle I'd looked at it from, and I got that author panic that my story well had run dry, along with a gut punch to my self-esteem. Comparisonitis had wormed its way into my head and made me miserable. Writing is an innate part of who I am, but it stopped being fun. And if a writer isn't enjoying what they're writing, you can bet a reader won't either.

One day while complaining to an author friend about this (I actually think it may have been Lucy), I thought, what if I made my TMAS story real? It was such a blast to write, and although it was short it had all kinds of juicy stuff—enemies to lovers, fake relationships, sexually charged arguments, a grumpy hero, and a heroine I wasn't used to writing but who was a lot of fun. My girls are strong but not what I would call bold. The heroine in that story was unreasonable and calculating, but she was unapologetic and went for what she wanted.

My usual routine is to show my alpha reader the first few chapters, but I didn't show anyone for a long time. I wasn't ready to hear what was wrong with it yet because I was too busy having fun.

When I finally showed the first almost half, I braced myself, but even my toughest beta seemed to love it. It made getting up at 5:00 a.m. each day to write the rest of *Just One Favor* a lot easier.

I'm not only thrilled with how their journey turned out but for what this story gave back to me. Starting this tale as a quick short story had taken the usual hesitation out because the trajectory was more or less done from the beginning, I just needed to add the right development and details to make it complete. I had to write on pure instinct when I first penned the shell, so when I continued it, that's what I relied on. Instead of second-guessing everything, I let Tyler and Olivia tell me where they needed to go. When I got rid of the noise that came from my own self-doubt, they were easy to hear.

Through this book, the universe gave me a loud reminder of why I'm here in the first place. The blank page isn't as scary as it seems. In fact, it's the most exciting thing in the world if you can find a way to leave the fear at the door and pick up the joy instead.

I hope you loved *Just One Favor* as much as I loved writing it.

Love,

Steph

ABOUT THE AUTHOR

Stephanie Rose is a badass New Yorker, a wife, a mother, a former blogger and lover of all things chocolate. Most days you'll find her trying to avoid standing on discarded LEGO or deciding which book to read next. Her debut novel, Always You, released in 2015 and since then she's written several more —some of which will never see completion—and has ideas for hundred to come.

Stay in touch!
Join Stephanie's Rose Garden on Facebook and sign up for Stephanie Rose's newsletter at www.authorstephanierose.com

Follow Me on Book+Main @stephanierose

BOOKS BY STEPHANIE

The Second Chances Series

Always You

"Always You is the debut novel for Stephanie Rose and I have to say she knocked it out of the park."- *Jennifer from Book Bitches Blog*

Only You

"Paige and Evan's story was beautiful yet so very sad - stunning in its romance, love and friendship. -*Jenny and Gitte, TotallyBookedBlog*

Always Us, A Second Chances Novella

"Alpha daddy Lucas is a sight to behold...damn, I love that man!" - *Shannon, Amazon reviewer*

After You

Some books make you wanna shout them from the rooftops. After You is that book. - *Paige, A is for Alpha B is for Books*

Second Chances Standalone Spinoffs

Finding Me

"What a gorgeous book. Five whole-hearted stars." - *Emma Scott, author of Forever Right Now and A Five-Minute Life*

Think Twice

"Four people, two love stories, one amazing book." *Melanie Moreland, New York Times and USA Today Bestselling author*

The Ocean Cove Series

No Vacancy

No Vacancy is undoubtedly the feel-good romance of the year. Stephanie Rose has all your needs covered in this delectable love story - *Marley Valentine, USA Today Bestselling author*

No Reservations

"No Reservations is *"second chance" GOLD!* Tragic, heartfelt, sensuous, touching and romantic......This is your next 5 star summer read!" - Chelè, 4 the love of books

The Never Too Late Series

Rewrite

"Rewrite gripped me from the start and never let me go." - *Award-winning and Bestselling author, K.K. Allen*

Simmer

"A slow-burning romance about friendship, family, love and the true meaning of home. I absolutely adored this book." - *Kathryn Nolan, Bestselling author*

Pining

"One of my favorites! Comics, and steam, and redemption. It doesn't get better than that! Five stars!" - *Award-winning author, A.M. Johnson*

Standalone

Safeguard

Safeguard, a standalone novel in the Speakeasy series in Sarina Bowen's World of True North

When bar manager Matteo asks one of his waitresses, Melanie, to babysit his little girl, he swears to keep it strictly professional -- but it might already be too late.

CPSIA information can be obtained
at www.ICGtesting.com
Printed in the USA
BVHW060140030322
630526BV00001B/17

9 781945 631856